1 MONTH OF
FREE
READING

at

www.ForgottenBooks.com

By purchasing this book you are eligible for one month membership to ForgottenBooks.com, giving you unlimited access to our entire collection of over 1,000,000 titles via our web site and mobile apps.

To claim your free month visit:

www.forgottenbooks.com/free62824

ISBN 978-0-483-96008-4
PIBN 10062824

This book is a reproduction of an important historical work. Forgotten Books uses state-of-the-art technology to digitally reconstruct the work, preserving the original format whilst repairing imperfections present in the aged copy. In rare cases, an imperfection in the original, such as a blemish or missing page, may be replicated in our edition. We do, however, repair the vast majority of imperfections successfully; any imperfections that remain are intentionally left to preserve the state of such historical works.

THE DICTATOR

BY

JUSTIN McCARTHY, M.P

AUTHOR OF 'DEAR LADY DISDAIN 'DONNA QUIXOTE' ETC.

IN THREE VOLUMES

VOL. I.

London

CHATTO & WINDUS, PICCADILLY

1893

PRINTED BY
SPOTTISWOODE AND CO., NEW STREET SQUARE
LONDON

CONTENTS

OF

THE FIRST VOLUME

THE DICTATOR

CHAPTER I

AN EXILE IN LONDON

THE May sunlight streamed in through the window, making curious patterns of the curtains upon the carpet. Outside, the tide of life was flowing fast; the green leaves of the Park were already offering agreeable shade to early strollers; the noise of cabs and omnibuses had set in steadily for the day. Outside, Knightsbridge was awake and active; inside, sleep reigned with quiet. The room was one of the best bedrooms in Paulo's Hotel; it was really tastefully furnished, soberly decorated, in the style of the fifteenth

French Louis. A very good copy of Watteau was over the mantel-piece, the only picture in the room. There had been a fire in the hearth overnight, for a grey ash lay there. Outside on the ample balcony stood a laurel in a big blue pot, an emblematic tribute on Paulo's part to honourable defeat which might yet turn to victory.

There were books about the room: a volume of Napoleon's maxims, a French novel, a little volume of Sophocles in its original Greek. A uniform-case and a sword-case stood in a corner. A map of South America lay partially unrolled upon a chair. The dainty gilt clock over the mantel-piece, a genuine heritage from the age of Louis Quinze, struck eight briskly. The Dictator stirred in his sleep.

Presently there was a tapping at the door to the left of the bed, a door communicating with the Dictator's private sitting-room. Still the Dictator slept, undisturbed by the slight sound. The sound was not repeated, but the door was softly opened, and a young man put his head into the room and looked at the slumbering Dictator. The young man was dark, smooth-shaven, with a look of quiet alertness in his face. He seemed to be about thirty years of age. His dark eyes watched the sleeping figure affectionately for a few seconds. 'It seems a pity to wake him,' he muttered, and he was about to draw his head back and close the door, when the Dictator stirred again, and suddenly waking swung himself round in the bed and faced his visitor. The visitor smiled pleasantly. 'Buenos dias, Escelencia,' he said.

The Dictator propped himself up on his left arm and looked at him.

'Good morning, Hamilton,' he answered. 'What's the good of talking Spanish here? Better fall back upon simple Saxon until we can see the sun rise again in Gloria. And as for the Excellency, don't you think we had better drop that too ?'

'Until we see the sun rise in Gloria,' said Hamilton. He had pushed the door open now, and entered the room, leaning carelessly against the door-post. 'Yes; that may not be so far off, please Heaven; and, in the meantime, I think we had better stick to the title and all forms, Excellency.'

The Dictator laughed again. 'Very well, as you please. The world is governed by form and title, and I suppose such dignities lend a decency even to exile in men's eyes. Is it late? I was tired, and slept like a dog.'

'Oh no; it's not late,' Hamilton answered. 'Only just struck eight. You wished to be called, or I shouldn't have disturbed you.'

'Yes, yes; one must get into no bad habits in London. All right; I'll get up now, and be with you in twenty minutes.'

'Very well, Excellency.' Hamilton bowed as he spoke in his most official manner, and withdrew. The Dictator looked after him, laughing softly to himself.

'L'excellence malgré lui,' he thought. 'An excellency in spite of myself. Well, I dare say Hamilton is right; it may serve to fill my sails when I have any sails to fill. In the meantime let us get up and salute London. Thank goodness it isn't raining, at all events.'

He did his dressing unaided. 'The best master is his own man' was an axiom with him. In the most splendid days of Gloria he had always valeted himself; and in Gloria, where assassination was always a possibility, it was certainly safer. His body-servant filled his bath and brought him his brushed clothes; for the rest he waited upon himself.

He did not take long in dressing. All his movements were quick, clean, and decisive; the movements of a man to whom moments

are precious, of a man who has learnt by long
experience how to do everything as shortly
and as well as possible. As soon as he was
finished he stood for an instant before the
long looking-glass and surveyed himself. A
man of rather more than medium height,
strongly built, of soldierly carriage, wearing
his dark frock-coat like a uniform. His left
hand seemed to miss its familiar sword-hilt.
The face was bronzed by Southern suns; the
brown eyes were large, and bright, and keen;
the hair was a fair brown, faintly touched
here and there with grey. His full moustache
and beard were trimmed to a point, almost in
the Elizabethan fashion. Any serious student
of humanity would at once have been attracted
by the face. Habitually it wore an expression
of gentle gravity, and it could smile very
sweetly, but it was the face of a strong man,
nevertheless, of a stubborn man, of a man
ambitious, a man with clear resolve, personal

or otherwise, and prompt to back his resolve with all he had in life, and with life itself.

He put into his buttonhole the green-and-yellow button which represented the order of the Sword and Myrtle, the great Order of La Gloria, which in Gloria was invested with all the splendour of the Golden Fleece ; the order which could only be worn by those who had actually ruled in the republic. That, according to satirists, did not greatly limit the number of persons who had the right to wear it. Then he formally saluted himself in the looking-glass. 'Excellency,' he said again, and laughed again. Then he opened his double windows and stepped out upon the balcony.

London was looking at its best just then, and his spirits stirred in grateful response to the sunlight. How dismal everything would have seemed, he was thinking, if the streets had been soaking under a leaden sky, if the trees had been dripping dismally, if his glance directed to the street below had rested only upon distended umbrellas glistening like the backs of gigantic crabs! Now everything was bright, and London looked as it can look sometimes, positively beautiful. Paulo's Hotel stands, as everybody knows, in the pleasantest part of Knightsbridge, facing Kensington Gardens. The sky was brilliantly blue, the trees were deliciously green; Knightsbridge below him lay steeped in a pure gold of sunlight. The animation of the scene cheered him sensibly. May is seldom summery in England, but this might have been a royal day of June.

Opposite to him he could see the green-grey roofs of Kensington Palace. At his left he could see a public-house which bore the name and stood upon the site of the hostelry where the Pretender's friends gathered on the morning when they expected to see Queen Anne succeeded by the heir to the House of Stuart.

Looking from the one place to the other, he reflected upon the events of that morning when those gentlemen waited in vain for the expected tidings, when Bolingbroke, seated in the council chamber at yonder palace, was so harshly interrupted. It pleased the stranger for a moment to trace a resemblance between the fallen fortunes of the Stuart Prince and his own fallen fortunes, as dethroned Dictator of the South American Republic of Gloria. ' London is my St. Germain's,' he said to himself with a laugh, and he drummed the national hymn of Gloria upon the balcony-rail with his fingers.

His gaze, wandering over the green bravery of the Park, lost itself in the blue sky. He had forgotten London; his thoughts were with another place under a sky of stronger blue, in the White House of a white square in a white town. He seemed to hear the rattle of rifle shots, shrill trumpet calls, angry party cries, the clatter of desperate charges across the open space, the angry despair of repulses, the piteous pageant of civil war. Knightsbridge knew nothing of all that. Danes may have fought there, the chivalry of the White Rose or the Red Rose ridden there, gallant Cavaliers have spurred along it to fight for their king. All that was past; no troops moved there now in hostility to brethren of their blood. But to that one Englishman standing there, moody in spite of the sunlight, the scene which his eyes saw was not the tranquil London street, but the Plaza Nacional of Gloria, red with blood, and 'cut up,' in the painter's sense, with corpses.

'Shall I ever get back? Shall I ever get back?' that was the burden to which his thoughts were dancing. His spirit began to rage within him to think that he was here, in London, helpless, almost alone, when he ought to be out there, sword in hand, dictating

terms to rebels repentant or impotent. He
gave a groan at the contrast, and then he
laughed a little bitterly and called himself a
fool. 'Things might be worse,' he said.
'They might have shot me. Better for them
if they had, and worse for Gloria. Yes, I am
sure of it—worse for Gloria!'

His mind was back in London now, back
in the leafy Park, back in Knightsbridge. He
looked down into the street, and noted that a
man was loitering on the opposite side. The
man in the street saw that the Dictator noted
him. He looked up at the Dictator, looked
up above the Dictator, and, raising his hat,
pointed as if towards the sky. The Dictator,
following the direction of the gesture, turned
slightly and looked upwards, and received a
sudden thrill of pleasure, for just above him,
high in the air, he could see the flutter of a
mass of green and yellow, the colours of the
national flag of Gloria. Mr. Paulo, mindful

of what was due even to exiled sovereignty, had flown the Gloria flag in honour of the illustrious guest beneath his roof. When that guest looked down again the man in the street had disappeared.

'That is a good omen. I accept it,' said the Dictator. 'I wonder who my friend was?' He turned to go back into his room, and in doing so noticed the laurel.

'Another good omen,' he said. 'My fortunes feel more summer-like already. The old flag still flying over me, an unknown friend to cheer me, and a laurel to prophesy victory —what more could an exile wish? His breakfast, I think,' and on this reflection he went back into his bedroom, and, opening the door through which Hamilton had talked to him, entered the sitting-room.

CHAPTER II

A GENTLEMAN ADVENTURER

THE room which the Dictator entered was an attractive room, bright with flowers, which Miss Paulo had been pleased to arrange herself—bright with the persevering sunshine. It was decorated, like his bedroom, with the restrained richness of the mid-eighteenth century. With discretion, Paulo had slightly adapted the accessories of the room to please by suggestion the susceptibilities of its occupant. A marble bust of Cæsar stood upon the dwarf bookcase. A copy of a famous portrait of Napoleon was on one of the walls; on another an engraving of Dr. Francia still more delicately associated great leaders with South America. At a table in one corner of the room—a table honeycombed with drawers and pigeon-holes, and covered with papers, letters, documents of all kinds—Hamilton sat writing rapidly. Another table nearer the window, set apart for the Dictator's own use, had everything ready for business—had, moreover, in a graceful bowl of tinted glass, a large yellow carnation, his favourite flower, the flower which had come to be the badge of those of his inclining. This, again, was a touch of Miss Paulo's sympathetic handiwork.

The Dictator, whose mood had brightened, smiled again at this little proof of personal interest in his welfare. As he entered, Hamilton dropped his pen, sprang to his feet, and advanced respectfully to greet him. The Dictator pointed to the yellow carnation.

'The way of the exiled autocrat is made smooth for him here, at least,' he said.

Hamilton inclined his head gravely. 'Mr. Paulo knows what is due,' he answered, 'to John Ericson, to the victor of San Felipe and the Dictator of Gloria. He knows how to entertain one who is by right, if not in fact, a reigning sovereign.'

'He hangs out our banner on the outer wall,' said Ericson, with an assumed gravity as great as Hamilton's own. Then he burst into a laugh and said, 'My dear Hamilton, it's all very well to talk of the victor of San Felipe and the Dictator of Gloria. But the victor of San Felipe is the victim of the Plaza Nacional, and the Dictator of Gloria is at present but one inconsiderable item added to the exile world of London, one more of the many refugees who hide their heads here, and are unnoted and unknown.'

His voice had fallen a little as his sentences succeeded each other, and the mirth in his voice had a bitter ring in it when he ended.

His eye ranged from the bust to the picture, and from the picture to the engraving contemplatively.

Something in the contemplation appeared to cheer him, for his look was brighter, and his voice had the old joyous ring in it when he spoke again. It was after a few minutes' silence deferentially observed by Hamilton, who seemed to follow and to respect the course of his leader's thoughts.

'Well,' he said, 'how is the old world getting on? Does she roll with unabated energy in her familiar orbit, indifferent to the fall of states and the fate of rulers? Stands Gloria where she did?'

Hamilton laughed. 'The world has certainly not grown honest, but there are honest men in her. Here is a telegram from Gloria which came this morning. It was sent, of course, as usual, to our City friends, who sent it on here immediately.' He handed the despatch to his chief, who seized it and read it eagerly. It seemed a commonplace message enough—the communication of one commercial gentleman in Gloria with another commercial gentleman in Farringdon Street. But to the eyes of Hamilton and of Ericson it meant a great deal. It was a secret communication from one of the most influential of the Dictator's adherents in Gloria. It was full of hope, strenuously encouraging. The Dictator's face lightened.

'Anything else?' he asked.

'These letters,' Hamilton answered, taking up a bundle from the desk at which he had been sitting. 'Five are from money-lenders offering to finance your next attempt. There are thirty-three requests for autographs, twenty-two requests for interviews, one very pressing from "The Catapult," another from "The Moon"—Society papers, I believe; ten invitations to dinner, six to luncheon; an offer from a well-known lecturing agency to run you in the United States ; an application from a publisher for a series of articles entitled " How I Governed Gloria," on your own terms ; a letter from a certain Oisin Stewart Sarrasin, who calls himself Captain, and signs himself a soldier of fortune.'

'What does *he* want ? ' asked Ericson. ' His seems to be the most interesting thing in the lot.'

' He offers to lend you his well-worn sword for the re-establishment of your rule. He hints that he has an infallible plan of victory, that in a word he is your very man.'

The Dictator smiled a little grimly. ' I thought I could do my own fighting,' he said. ' But I suppose everybody will be wanting to help me now, every adventurer in Europe who thinks that I can no longer help myself. I don't think we need trouble Captain Stewart. Is that his name ? '

' Stewart Sarrasin.'

' Sarrasin—all right. Is that all?'

' Practically all,' Hamilton answered. ' A few other letters of no importance. Stay; no, I forgot. These cards were left this morning, a little after nine o'clock, by a young lady who rode up attended by her groom.'

' A young lady,' said Ericson, in some surprise, as he extended his hand for the cards.

' Yes, and a very pretty young lady too,' Hamilton answered, ' for I happened to be in the hall at the time, and saw her.'

Ericson took the cards and looked at them. They were two in number; one was a man's card, one a woman's. The man's card bore the legend ' Sir Rupert Langley,' the woman's was merely inscribed ' Helena Langley.' The address was a house at Prince's Gate.

The Dictator looked up surprised. 'Sir Rupert Langley, the Foreign Secretary?'

'I suppose it must be,' Hamilton said, 'there can't be two men of the same name. I have a dim idea of reading something about his daughter in the papers some time ago, just before our revolution, but I can't remember what it was.'

'Very good of them to honour fallen greatness, in any case,' Ericson said. 'I seem to have more friends than I dreamed of. In the meantime let us have breakfast.'

Hamilton rang the bell, and a man brought in the coffee and rolls, which constituted the Dictator's simple breakfast. While he was eating it he glanced over the letters that had come. 'Better refuse all these invitations, Hamilton.'

Hamilton expostulated. He was Ericson's intimate and adviser, as well as secretary.

'Do you think that is the best thing to

do?' he suggested. 'Isn't it better to show yourself as much as possible, to make as many friends as you can? There's a good deal to be done in that way, and nothing much else to do for the present. Really I think it would be better to accept some of them. Several are from influential political men.'

'Do you think these influential political men would help me?' the Dictator asked, good-humouredly cynical. 'Did they help Kossuth? Did they help Garibaldi? What I want are war-ships, soldiers, a big loan, not the agreeable conversation of amiable politicians.'

'Nevertheless,' Hamilton began to protest.

His chief cut him short. 'Do as you please in the matter, my dear boy,' he said. 'It can't do any harm, anyhow. Accept all you think it best to accept; decline the others. I leave myself confidently in your hands.'

'What are you going to do this morning?' Hamilton inquired. 'There are one or two people we ought to think of seeing at once. We mustn't let the grass grow under our feet for one moment.'

'My dear boy,' said Ericson good-humouredly, 'the grass shall grow under my feet to-day, so far as all that is concerned. I haven't been in London for ten years, and I have something to do before I do anything else. To-morrow you may do as you please with me. But if you insist upon devoting this day to the cause——'

'Of course I do,' said Hamilton.

'Then I graciously permit you to work at it all day, while I go off and amuse myself in a way of my own. You might, if you can spare the time, make a call at the Foreign Office and say I should be glad to wait on

Sir Rupert Langley there, **any** day and hour that suit him—we must smooth down the dignity of these Foreign Secretaries, I suppose?'

'Oh, of course,' Hamilton said, peremptorily. Hamilton took most things gravely; the Dictator usually did not. Hamilton seemed a little put out because his chief should have even indirectly suggested the possibility of his not waiting on Sir Rupert Langley at the Foreign Office.

'All right, boy; it shall be done. And look here, Hamilton; as we are going to do the right thing, why should you not leave cards for me and for yourself at Sir Rupert Langley's house? You might see the daughter.'

'Oh, she never heard of me,' Hamilton said hastily.

'The daughter of a Foreign Secretary?'

'Anyhow, of course I'll call if you wish it, Excellency.'

'Good boy! And do you know I have taken a fancy that I should like to see this soldier of fortune, Captain——'

'Sarrasin?'

'Sarrasin—yes. Will you drop him a line and suggest an interview—pretty soon? You know all about my times and engagements.'

'Certainly, your Excellency,' Hamilton replied, with almost military formality and precision; and the Dictator departed.

CHAPTER III

AT THE GARDEN GATE

LONDONERS are so habituated to hear London abused as an ugly city that they are disposed too often to accept the accusation humbly. Yet the accusation is singularly unjust. If much of London is extremely unlovely, much might fairly be called beautiful. The new Chelsea that has arisen on the ashes of the old might well arouse the admiration even of the most exasperated foreigner. There are recently created regions in that great tract of the earth's surface known as South Kensington which in their quaintness of architectural form and braveness of red brick can defy the gloom of a civic March or November. Old

London is disappearing day by day, but bits of it remain, bits dear to those familiar with them, bits worth the enterprise of the adven‑turons, which call for frank admiration and frank praise even of people who hated London as fully as Heinrich Heine did. But of all parts of the great capital none perhaps deserve so fully the title to be called beauti‑ful as some portions of Hampstead Heath.

Some such reflections floated lightly through the mind of a man who stood, on this May afternoon, on a high point of Hampstead Hill. He had climbed thither from a certain point just beyond the Regent's Park, to which he had driven from Knights‑bridge. From that point out the way was a familiar way to him, and he enjoyed walking along it and noting old spots and the changes that time had wrought. Now, having reached the highest point of the ascent, he paused, standing on the grass of the heath, and turning round, with his back to the country, looked down upon the town.

There is no better place from which to survey London. To impress a stranger with any sense of the charm of London as a whole, let him be taken to that vantage-ground and bidden to gaze. The great city seemed to lie below and around him as in a hollow, tinged and glorified by the luminous haze of the May day. The countless spires which pointed to heaven in all directions gave the vast agglomeration of buildings something of an Italian air ; it reminded the beholder agree-ably of Florence. To right and to left the gigantic city spread, its grey wreath of eternal smoke resting lightly upon its fretted head, the faint roar of its endless activity coming up distinctly there in the clear wind-less air. The beholder surveyed it and sighed slightly, as he traced meaningless symbols on the turf with the point of his stick.

'What did Cæsar say?' he murmured. 'Better be the first man in a village than the second man in Rome! Well, there never was any chance of my being the second man in Rome; but, at least, I have been the first man in my village, and that is something. I suppose I reckon as about the last man there now. Well, we shall see.'

He shrugged his shoulders, nodded a farewell to the city below him, and, turning round, proceeded to walk leisurely across the Heath. The grass was soft and springy, the earth seemed to answer with agreeable elasticity to his tread, the air was exquisitely clear, keen, and exhilarating. He began to move more briskly, feeling quite boyish again. The years seemed to roll away from him as rifts of sea fog roll away before a wind.

Even Gloria seemed as if it had never been—aye, and things before Gloria was, events when he was still really quite a young man.

He cut at the tufted grasses with his stick, swinging it in dexterous circles as if it had been his sword. He found himself humming a tune almost unconsciously, but when he paused to consider what the tune was he found it was the national march of Gloria. Then he stopped humming, and went on for a while silently and less joyously. But the gladness of the fine morning, of the clear air, of the familiar place, took possession of him again. His face once more unclouded and his spirits mounted.

'The place hasn't changed much,' he said to himself, looking around him while he walked. Then he corrected himself, for it had changed a good deal. There were many more red brick houses dotting the landscape than there

had been when he last looked upon it some
seven years earlier.

In all directions these red houses were
springing up, quaintly gabled, much veran-
dahed, pointed, fantastic, brilliant.   They
made the whole neighbourhood of the Heath
look like the Merrie England of a comic opera.
Yet they were pretty in their way ; many were
designed by able architects, and pleased with
a balanced sense of proportion and an impression of beauty and fitness.   Many, of course,
lacked this, were but cheap and clumsy imi-
tations of a prevailing mode, but, taken all
together, the effect was agreeable, the effect of
the varied reds, russet, and scarlet and warm
crimson against the fresh green of the grass
and trees and the pale faint blue of the May
sky.

To the observer they seemed to suit very
well the place, the climate, the conditions of
life. They were infinitely better than suburban

and rural cottages people used to build when he was a boy. His mind drifted away to the kind of houses he had been more familiar with of late years, houses half Spanish, half tropical, with their wide courtyards and gaily striped awnings and white walls glaring under a glaring sun.

'Yes, all this is very restful,' he thought—'restful, peaceful, wholesome.' He found himself repeating softly the lines of Browning, beginning, 'Oh to be in England now that April's here,' and the transitions of thought carried him to that other poem beginning 'It was roses, roses, all the way,' with its satire on fallen ambition. Thinking of it, he first frowned and then laughed.

He walked a little way, cresting the rising ground, till he came to an open space with an unbroken view over the level country to Barnet. Here, the last of the houses that could claim to belong to the great London army

stood alone in its own considerable space of
ground. It was a very old-fashioned house;
it had been half farmhouse, half hall, in the
latter days of the last century, and the dull
red brick of its walls, and the dull red tiles of
its roof showed warm and attractive through
the green of the encircling trees. There was
a small garden in front, planted with pine
trees, through which a winding path led up to
the low porch of the dwelling. Behind the
house a very large garden extended, a great
garden which he knew so well, with its lengths
of undulating russet orchard wall, and its divi-
sions into flower garden and fruit garden and
vegetable garden, and the field beyond, where
successive generations of ponies fed, and where
he had loved to play in boyhood.

He rested his hand on the upper rim of
the garden gate, and looked with curious
affection at the inscription in faded gold letters
that ran along it. The inscription read, 'Bla-

rulfsgarth,' and he remembered ever so far
back asking what that inscription meant, and
being told that it was Icelandic, and that it
meant the Garth, or Farm, of the Blue Wolf.
And he remembered, too, being told the tale
from which the name came, a tale that was
related of an ancestor of his, real or imaginary,
who had lived and died centuries ago in a grey
northern land.   It was curious that, as he
stood there, so many recollections of his childhood should come back to him.   He was a
man, and not a very young man, when he last
laid his hand upon that gate, and yet it seemed
to him now as if he had left it when he was
quite a little child, and was returning now for
the first time with the feelings of a man to the
place where he had passed his infancy.

His hand slipped down to the latch, but he
did not yet lift it.   He still lingered while he
turned for a moment and looked over the wide
extent of level smiling country that stretched

out and away before him. The last time he
had looked on that sweep of earth he was
going off to seek adventure in a far land, in a
new world. He had thought himself a broken
man; he was sick of England; his thoughts
in their desperation had turned to the country
which was only a name to him, the country
where he was born. Now the day came vividly
back to him on which he had said good-bye
to that place, and looked with a melancholy
disdain upon the soft English fields. It was
an earlier season of the year, a day towards
the end of March, when the skies were still
but faintly blue, and there was little green
abroad. Ten years ago: how many things
had passed in those ten years, what struggles
and successes, what struggles again, all ending
in that three days' fight and the last stand in
the Plaza Nacional of Valdorado! He turned
away from the scene and pressed his hand
upon the latch.

As he touched the latch someone appeared in the porch. It was an old lady dressed in black. She had soft grey hair, and on that grey hair she wore an old-fashioned cap that was almost coquettish by very reason of its old fashion. She had a very sweet, kind face, all cockled with wrinkles like a sheet of crumpled tissue paper, but very beautiful in its age. It was a face that a modern French painter would have loved to paint—a face that a sculptor of the Renaissance would have delighted to reproduce in faithful, faultless bronze or marble.

At sight of the sweet old lady the Dictator's heart gave a great leap, and he pressed down the latch hurriedly and swung the gate wide open. The sound of the clicking latch and the swinging gate slightly grinding on the path aroused the old lady's attention. She saw the Dictator, and, with a little cry of joy, running with an almost girlish activity to meet

the bearded man who was coming rapidly
along the pathway, in another moment she
had caught him in her arms and was clasping
him and kissing him enthusiastically. The
Dictator returned her caresses warmly. He
was smiling, but there were tears in his
eyes. It was so odd being welcomed back
like this in the old place after all that had
passed.

'I knew you would come to-day, my
dear,' the old lady said half sobbing, half
laughing. 'You said you would, and I knew
you would. You would come to your old
aunt first of all.'

'Why, of course, of course I would, my
dear,' the Dictator answered, softly touching
the grey hair on the forehead below the
frilled cap.

'But I didn't expect you so early,' the
old lady went on. 'I didn't think you would
get up so soon on your · first morning.

You must be so tired, my dear, so very tired.'

She was holding his left hand in her right now, and they were walking slowly side by side up by the little path through the fir trees to the house.

'Oh, I'm not so very tired as all that comes to,' he said with a laugh. 'A long voyage is a restful thing, and I had time to get over the fatigue of the——' he seemed to pause an instant for a word; then he went on, ' the trouble, while I was on board the " Almirante Cochrane." Do you know they were quite kind to me on board the " Almirante Cochrane " ? '

The old lady's delicate face flushed angrily. ' The wretches, the wicked wretches!' she said quite fiercely, and the thin fingers closed tightly upon his and shook, agitating the lace ruffles at her wrists.

The Dictator laughed again. It seemed too strange to have all those wild adventures quietly discussed in a Hampstead garden with a silver-haired elderly lady in a cap.

'Oh, come,' he said, 'they weren't so bad ; they weren't half bad, really. Why, you know, they might have shot me out of hand. I think if I had been in their place I should have shot out of hand, do you know, aunt?'

'Oh, surely they would never have dared —you an Englishman?'

'I am a citizen of Gloria, aunt.'

'You who were so good to them.'

'Well, as to my being good to them, there are two to tell that tale. The gentlemen of the Congress don't put a high price upon my goodness, I fancy.' He laughed a little bitterly. 'I certainly meant to do them some good, and I even thought I had succeeded. My dear aunt, people don't always like being done good to. I remember that myself when I was a small boy. I used to fret and fume at the things which were done for my good ; that was because I was a child. The crowd is always a child.'

They had come to the porch by this time, and had stopped short at the threshold. The little porch was draped in flowers and foliage, and looked very pretty.

'You were always a good child,' said the old lady affectionately.

Ericson looked down at her rather wistfully.

'Do you think I was?' he asked, and there was a tender irony in his voice which made the playful question almost pathetic. 'If I had been a good child I should have been content and had no roving disposition, and have found my home and my world at Hampstead, instead of straying off into another hemisphere, only to be sent back at last like a bad penny.'

'So you would,' said the old lady, very softly, more as if she were speaking to herself than to him. 'So you would if——'

She did not finish her sentence. But her nephew, who knew and understood, repeated the last word.

'If,' he said, and he, too, sighed.

The old lady caught the sound, and with a pretty little air of determination she called up a smile to her face.

'Shall we go into the house, or shall we sit awhile in the garden? It is almost too fine a day to be indoors.'

'Oh, let us sit out, please,' said Ericson. He had driven the sorrow from his voice, and its tones were almost joyous. 'Is the old garden-seat still there?'

'Why, of course it is. I sit there always in fine weather.'

They wandered round to the back by a path that skirted the house, a path all broidered with rose-bushes. At the back, the garden was very large, beginning with a spacious stretch of lawn that ran right up to the wide French windows. There were several noble old trees which stood sentinel over this part of the garden, and beneath one of these trees, a very ancient elm, was the sturdy garden-seat which the Dictator remembered so well.

'How many pleasant fairy tales you have told me under this tree, aunt,' said the Dictator, as soon as they had sat down. 'I should like to lie on the grass again and listen to your voice, and dream of Njal, and Grettir, and Sigurd, as I used to do.'

'It is your turn to tell me stories now,' said the old lady. 'Not fairy stories, but true ones.'

The Dictator laughed. 'You know all that

there is to tell,' he said. 'What my letters didn't say you must have found from the newspapers.'

'But I want to know more than you wrote, more than the newspapers gave—everything.'

'In fact, you want a full, true, and particular account of the late remarkable revolution in Gloria, which ended in the deposition and exile of the alien tyrant. My dear aunt, it would take a couple of weeks at the least computation to do the theme justice.'

'I am sure that I shouldn't tire of listening,' said Miss Ericson, and there were tears in her bright old eyes and a tremor in her brave old voice as she said so.

The Dictator laughed, but he stooped and kissed the old lady again very affectionately.

'Why, you would be as bad as I used to be,' he said. 'I never was tired of your *sagas*, and when one came to an end I wanted a new one at once, or at least the old one over again.'

He looked away from her and all around the garden as he spoke. The winds and rains and suns of all those years had altered it but little.

' We talk of the shortness of life,' he said ; ' but sometimes life seems quite long. Think of the years and years since I was a little fellow, and sat here where I sit now, then, as now, by your side, and cried at the deeds of my forbears and sighed for the gods of the North. Do you remember ? '

' Oh, yes ; oh, yes. How could I forget ? You, my dear, in your bustling life might forget ; but I, day after day in this great old garden, may be forgiven for an old woman's fancy that time has stood still, and that you are still the little boy I love so well.'

She held out her hand to him, and he clasped it tenderly, full of an affectionate emotion that did not call for speech.

There were somewhat similar thoughts in both their minds. He was asking himself if, after all, it would not have been just as well to remain in that tranquil nook, so sheltered from the storms of life, so consecrated by tender affection. What had he done that was worth rising up to cross the street for, after all? He had dreamed a dream, and had been harshly awakened. What was the good of it all? A melancholy seemed to settle upon him in that place, so filled with the memories of his childhood. As for his companion, she was asking herself if it would not have been better for him to stay at home and live a quiet English life, and be her help and solace.

Both looked up from their reverie, met each other's melancholy glances, and smiled.

'Why,' said Miss Ericson, 'what nonsense

this is ! Here are we who have not met for ages, and we can find nothing better to do than to sit and brood ! We ought to be ashamed of ourselves.'

' We ought,' said the Dictator, ' and for my poor part I am. So you want to hear my adventures ? '

Miss Ericson nodded, but the narrative was interrupted. The wide French windows at the back of the house opened and a man entered the garden. His smooth voice was heard explaining to the maid that he would join Miss Ericson in the garden.

The new-comer made his way along the garden, with extended hand, and blinking amiably. The Dictator, turning at his approach, surveyed him with some surprise. He was a large, loosely made man, with a large white face, and his somewhat ungainly body was clothed in loose light material that was almost white in hue. His large and slightly surprised eyes were of a kindly blue; his hair was a vague yellow; his large mouth was weak; his pointed chin was undecided. He dimly suggested some association to the Dictator; after a few seconds he found that the association was with the Knave of Hearts in an ordinary pack of playing-cards.

'This is a friend of mine, a neighbour who often pays me a visit,' said the old lady hurriedly, as the white figure loomed along towards them. 'He is a most agreeable man, very companionable indeed, and learned, too—extremely learned.'

This was all that she had time to say before the white gentleman came too close to them to permit of further conversation concerning his merits or defects.

The new-comer raised his hat, a huge, white, loose, shapeless felt, in keeping with his ill-defined attire, and made an awkward bow which at once included the old lady and the

Dictator, on whom the blue eyes beamed for a moment in good-natured wonder.

'Good morning, Miss Ericson,' said the new-comer. He spoke to Miss Ericson; but it was evident that his thoughts were distracted. His vague blue eyes were fixed in benign bewilderment upon the Dictator's face.

Miss Ericson rose; so did her nephew. Miss Ericson spoke.

'Good morning, Mr. Sarrasin. Let me present you to my nephew, of whom you have heard so much. Nephew, this is Mr. Gilbert Sarrasin.'

The new-comer extended both hands; they were very large hands, and very soft and very white. He enfolded the Dictator's extended right hand in one of his, and beamed upon him in unaffected joy.

'Not your nephew, Miss Ericson—not the hero of the hour? Is it possible; is it possible? My dear sir, my very dear and honoured sir, I cannot tell you how rejoiced I am, how proud I am, to have the privilege of meeting you.'

The Dictator returned his friendly clasp with a warm pressure. He was somewhat amused by this unexpected enthusiasm.

'You are very good indeed, Mr. Sarrasin.' Then, repeating the name to himself, he added, 'Your name seems to be familiar to me.'

The white gentleman shook his head with something like playful repudiation.

'Not my name, I think; no, not my name, I feel sure.' He accentuated the possessive pronoun strongly, and then proceeded to explain the accentuation, smiling more and more amiably as he did so. 'No, not my name; my brother's—my brother's, I fancy.'

'Your brother's?" the Dictator said inquiringly. There was some association in his mind with the name of Sarrasin, but he could not reduce it to precise knowledge.

'Yes, my brother,' said the white gentleman. 'My brother, Oisin Stewart Sarrasin, whose name, I am proud to think, is familiar in many parts of the world.'

The recollection he was seeking came to the Dictator. It was the name that Hamilton had given to him that morning, the name of the man who had written to him, and who had signed himself 'a soldier of fortune.' He smiled back at the white gentleman.

'Yes,' he said truthfully, 'I have heard your brother's name. It is a striking name.'

The white gentleman was delighted. He rubbed his large white hands together, and almost seemed as if he might purr in the excess of his gratification. He glanced enthusiastically at Miss Ericson.

'Ah!' he went on. 'My brother is a remarkable man. I may even say so in your illustrious presence; he is a remarkable man. There are degrees, of course,' and he bowed apologetically to the Dictator; 'but he is remarkable.'

'I have not the least doubt of that,' said the Dictator politely.

The white gentleman seemed much pleased. At a sign from Miss Ericson he sat down upon a garden-chair, still slowly and contentedly rubbing his white hands together. Miss Ericson and her nephew resumed their seats.

'Captain Sarrasin is a great traveller,' Miss Ericson said explanatorily to the Dictator. The Dictator bowed his head. He did not quite know what to say, and so, for the moment, said nothing. The white gentleman took advantage of the pause.

'Yes,' he said, 'yes, my brother is a great traveller. A wonderful man, sir; all parts of the wide world are as familiar as home to him. The deserts of the nomad Arabs, the

Prairies of the great West, the Steppes of the frozen North, the Pampas of South America; why, he knows them all better than most people know Piccadilly.'

'South America?' questioned the Dictator; 'your brother is acquainted with South America?'

'Intimately acquainted,' replied Mr. Sarrasin. 'I hope you will meet him. You and he might have much to talk about. He knew Gloria in the old days.'

The Dictator expressed courteously his desire to have the pleasure of meeting Captain Sarrasin. 'And you, are you a traveller as well?' he asked.

Mr. Sarrasin shook his head, and when he spoke there was a certain accent of plaintiveness in his reply.

'No,' he said, 'not at all, not at all. My brother and I resemble each other very slightly. He has the wanderer's spirit; I am

a confirmed stay-at-home. While he thinks
nothing of starting off at any moment for the
other ends of the earth, I have never been
outside our island, have never been much
away from London.'

'Isn't that curious?' asked Miss Ericson,
who evidently took much pleasure in the
conversation of the white gentleman. The
Dictator assented. It was very curious.

'Yet I am fond of travel, too, in my way,'
Mr. Sarrasin went on, delighted to have found
an appreciative audience. 'I read about it
largely. I read all the old books of travel,
and all the new ones, too, for the matter of
that. I have quite a little library of voyages,
travels, and explorations in my little home.
I should like you to see it some time if you
should so far honour me.'

The Dictator declared that he should be
delighted. Mr. Sarrasin, much encouraged,
went on again.

'There is nothing I like better than to sit by my fire of a winter's evening, or in my garden of a summer afternoon, and read of the adventures of great travellers. It makes me feel as if I had travelled myself.'

'And Mr. Sarrasin tells me what he has read, and makes me, too, feel travelled,' said Miss Ericson.

'Perhaps you get all the pleasure in that way with none of the fatigue,' the Dictator suggested.

Mr. Sarrasin nodded. 'Very likely we do. I think it was à Kempis who protested against the vanity of wandering. But I fear it was not à Kempis's reasons that deterred me; but an invincible laziness and unconquerable desire to be doing nothing.'

'Travelling is generally uncomfortable,' the Dictator admitted. He was beginning to feel an interest in his curious, whimsical interlocutor.

'Yes,' Mr. Sarrasin went on dreamily. 'But there are times when I regret the absence of experience. I have tramped in fancy through tropical forests with Stanley or Cameron, dwelt in the desert with Burton, battled in Nicaragua with Walker, but all only as it were in dreams.'

'We are such stuff as dreams are made of,' the Dictator observed sententiously.

'And our little lives are rounded by a sleep,' Miss Ericson said softly, completing the quotation.

'Yes, yes,' said Mr. Sarrasin; 'but mine are dreams within a dream.' He was beginning to grow quite communicative as he sat there with his big stick between his knees, and his amorphous felt hat pushed back from his broad white forehead.

'Sometimes my travels seem very real to me. If I have been reading Ford or King-lake, or Warburton or Lane, I have but to

lay the volume down and close my eyes, and
all that I have been reading about seems to
take shape and sound, and colour and life.
I hear the tinkling of the mule-bells and the
guttural cries of the muleteers, and I see the
Spanish market-place, with its arcades and its
ancient cathedral; or the delicate pillars of
the Parthenon, yellow in the clear Athenian
air; or Stamboul, where the East and West
join hands; or Egypt and the desert, and the
Nile and the pyramids; or the Holy Land
and the walls of Jerusalem—ah! it is all very
wonderful, and then I open my eyes and blink
at my dying fire, and look at my slippered
feet, and remember that I am a stout old
gentleman who has never left his native land,
and I yawn and take my candle and go to my
bed.'

There was something so curiously pathetic
and yet comic about the white gentleman's
case, about his odd blend of bookish know-

ledge and personal inexperience, that the Dictator could scarcely forbear smiling. But he did forbear, and he spoke with all gravity.

'I am not sure that you haven't the better part after all,' he said. 'I find that the chief pleasure of travel lies in recollection. *You* seem to get the recollection without the trouble.'

'Perhaps so,' said Mr. Sarrasin; 'perhaps so. But I think I would rather have had the trouble as well. Believe me, my dear sir, believe a dreamer, that action is better than dreams. Ah! how much better it is for you, sir, to sit here, a disappointed man for the moment it may be, but a man with a glowing past behind him, than, like me, to have nothing to look back upon! My adventures are but compounded out of the essences of many books. I have never really lived a day; you have lived every day of your life. Believe me, you are much to be envied.'

There was genuine conviction in the white gentleman's voice as he spoke these words, and the note of genuine conviction troubled the Dictator in his uncertainty whether to laugh or cry. He chose a medium course and smiled slightly.

'I should think, Mr. Sarrasin, that you are the only one in London to-day who looks upon me as a man much to be envied. London, if it thinks of me at all, thinks of me only as a disastrous failure, as an unsuccessful exile—a man of no account, in a word.'

Mr. Sarrasin shook his head vehemently. 'It is not so,' he protested, 'not so at all. Nobody really thinks like that, but if everybody else did, my brother Oisin Stewart Sarrasin certainly does not think like that, and his opinion is better worth having than that of most other men. You have no warmer admirer in the world than my brother, Mr. Ericson.'

The Dictator expressed much satisfaction at having earned the good opinion of Mr. Sarrasin's brother.

'You would like him, I am sure,' said Mr. Sarrasin. 'You would find him a kindred spirit.'

The Dictator graciously expressed his confidence that he should find a kindred spirit in Mr. Sarrasin's brother. Then Mr. Sarrasin, apparently much delighted with his interview, rose to his feet and declared that it was time for him to depart. He shook hands very warmly with Miss Ericson, but he held the Dictator's hands with a grasp that was devoted in its enthusiasm. Then, expressing repeatedly the hope that he might soon meet the Dictator again, and once more assuring him of the kinship between the Dictator and Captain Oisin Stewart Sarrasin, the white gentleman took himself off, a pale bulky figure looming heavily across the grassy lawn and through the French window into the darkness of the sitting-room.

When he was quite out of sight the Dictator, who had followed his retreating figure with his eyes, turned to Miss Ericson with a look of inquiry. Miss Ericson smiled.

'Who is Mr. Sarrasin?' the Dictator asked. 'He has come up since my time.'

'Oh, yes; he first came to live here about six years ago. He is one of the best souls in the world; simple, good-hearted, an eternal child.'

'What *is* he?' the Dictator asked.

'Well, he is nothing in particular now. He was in the City, his father was the head of a very wealthy firm of tea merchants, Sarrasin, Jermyn, & Co. When the father died a few years ago he left all his property to Mr. Gilbert, and then Mr. Gilbert went out of business and came here.'

'He does not look as if he would make a very good business man,' said the Dictator.

'No; but he was very patient and devoted to it for his father's sake. Now, since he has been free to do as he likes, he has devoted himself to folk-lore.'

'To folk-lore?'

'Yes, to the study of fairy tales, of comparative mythology. I am quite learned in it now since I have had Mr. Sarrasin for a neighbour, and know more about "Puss in Boots" and "Jack and the Beanstalk" than I ever did when I was a girl.'

'Really,' said the Dictator, with a kind of sigh. 'Does he devote himself to fairy tales?' It crossed his mind that a few moments before he had been thinking of himself as a small child in that garden, with a taste for fairy tales, and regretting that he had not stayed in that garden. Now, with the dust of battle and the ashes of defeat upon him, he came back to find a man much older than himself, who seemed still to remain a child, and to be entranced with fairy tales. 'I wish I were like that,' the Dictator said to himself, and then the veil seemed to lift, and he saw again the Plaza Nacional of Gloria, and the Government Palace, where he had laboured at laws for a free people. 'No,' he thought, 'no; action, action.'

'What are you thinking of?' asked Miss Ericson softly. 'You seem to be quite lost in thought.'

'I was thinking of Mr. Sarrasin,' answered the Dictator. 'Forgive me for letting my thoughts drift. And the brother, what sort of man is this wonderful brother?'

'I have only seen the brother a very few times,' said Miss Ericson dubiously. 'I can hardly form an opinion. I do not think he is as nice as his brother, or, indeed, as nice as his brother believes him to be.'

' What is his record ? '

' He didn't get on with his father. He was sent against his will to China to work in the firm's offices in Shanghai. But he hated the business, and broke away and entered the Chinese army, I believe, and his father was furious and cut him off. Since then he has been all over the world, and served all sorts of causes. I believe he is a kind of soldier of fortune.'

The Dictator smiled, remembering Captain Sarrasin's own words.

' And has he made his fortune ? '

' Oh, no ; I believe not. But Gilbert behaved so well. When he came into the property he wanted to share it all with his disinherited brother, for whom he has the greatest affection.'

' A good fellow, your Gilbert Sarrasin.'

' The best. But the brother wouldn't take it, and it was with difficulty that Gilbert induced him to accept so much as would allow him a small certainty of income.'

'So. A good fellow, too, your Oisin Stewart Sarrasin, it would seem; at least in that particular.'

'Yes; of course. The brothers don't meet very often, for Captain Sarrasin——'

'Where does he take his title from?'

'He was captain in some Turkish irregular cavalry.'

'Turkish irregular cavalry? That must be a delightful corps,' the Dictator said with a smile.

'At least he was captain in several services,' Miss Ericson went on; 'but I believe that is the one he prefers and still holds. As I was going to say, Captain Sarrasin is almost always abroad.'

'Well, I feel curious to meet him. They are a strange pair of brothers.'

'They are, but we ought to talk of nothing

but you to-day. Ah, **my** dear, it is so good
to have you with me again.'

'Dear old aunt!'

'Let **me** see much **of** you **now** that you
have come back. Would it be any use asking
you to stop here?'

'Later, every use. Just at this moment I
mustn't. Till I see **how** things are going to
turn out I must live down there in London.
But my heart is here with you in this green
old garden, and where my heart is I hope to
bring **my** battered old body very often. I
will stop to luncheon with you if you will let
me.'

'Let you? My dear, I wish you were
always stopping here.' And the grey old lady
put her arms round the neck of the Dictator
and kissed him again.

CHAPTER IV

THE LANGLEYS

THAT same day there was a luncheon party at the new town house of the Langleys, Prince's Gate. The Langleys were two in number all told, father and daughter.

Sir Rupert Langley was a remarkable man, but his daughter, Helena Langley, was a much more remarkable woman. The few handfuls of people who considered them-selves to constitute the world in London had at one time talked much about Sir Rupert, but now they talked a great deal more about his daughter. Sir Rupert was once grimly amused, at a great party in a great house, to hear himself pointed out by a knowing youth as Helena Langley's father.

There was a time when people thought, and Sir Rupert thought with them, that Rupert Langley was to do great deeds in the world. He had entered political life at an early age, as all the Langleys had done since the days of Anne, and he made more than a figure there. He had travelled in Central Asia in days when travel there or anywhere else was not so easy as it is now, and he had published a book of his travels before he was three-and-twenty, a book which was highly praised, and eagerly read. He was saluted as a sort of coming authority upon Eastern affairs in a day when the importance of Eastern affairs was beginning to dawn dimly upon the insular mind, and he made several stirring speeches in the House of Commons which confirmed his reputation as a coming man. He was very dogmatic, very

determined in his opinions, very confident of
his own superior knowledge, and possessed of
a degree of knowledge which justified his confidence and annoyed his antagonists. He
formed a little party of his own, a party of
strenuous young Tories who recognised the
fact that the world was out of joint, but who
rejoiced in the conviction that they were born
for the express purpose of setting it right. In
Sir Rupert they found a leader after their own
heart, and they rallied around him and jibed
at their elders on the Treasury Bench in a way
that was quite distressing to the sensitive
organs of the party.

Sir Rupert and his adherents preached the
new Toryism of that day—the new Toryism
which was to work wonders, which was to
obliterate Radicalism by doing in a practical
Tory way, and conformably to the best traditions of the kingdom, all that Radicalism
dreamed of. Toryism, he used to say in those

hot-blooded, hot-headed days of his youth,
Toryism is the triumph of Truth, and the
phrase became a catchword and a watchword,
and frivolous people called his little party the
T.T.s—the Triumphers of Truth.   People
versed in the political history of that day and
hour will remember how the newspapers were
full of the T.T.s, and what an amazing re-
juvenescence of political force was supposed
to be behind them.

Then came a general election which carried
the Tory Party into power, and which proved
the strength of Langley and his party.   He
was offered a place in the new Government,
and accepted it—the Under-Secretaryship for
India.   Through one brilliant year he remained the most conspicuous member of the
Administration, irritating his colleagues by
daring speeches, by innovating schemes;
alarming timid party-men by a Toryism which
in certain aspects was scarcely to be distin-

guished from the reddest Radicalism. One brilliant year there was in which he blazed the comet of a season. Then, thwarted in some enterprise, faced by a refusal for some daring reform of Indian administration, he acted, as he had acted always, impetuously.

One morning the ' Times ' contained a long, fierce, witty, bitter letter from Rupert Langley assailing the Government, its adherents, and, above all, its leaders in the Lords. That same afternoon members coming to the Chamber found Langley sitting, no longer on the Treasury Bench, but in the corner seat of the second row below the gangway. It was soon known all over the House, all over town, all over England, that Rupert Langley had resigned his office. The news created no little amazement, some consternation in certain quarters of the Tory camp, some amusement among the Opposition sections. One or two of the extreme Radical papers made overtures to Langley to cross the floor of the House, and enter into alliance with men whose principles so largely resembled his own. These overtures even took the form of a definite appeal on the part of Mr. Wynter, M.P., then a rising Radical, who actually spent half an hour with Sir Rupert on the terrace, putting his case and the case of youthful Radicalism.

Sir Rupert only smiled at the suggestion, and put it gracefully aside. 'I am a Tory of the Tories,' he said; 'only my own people don't understand me yet. But they have got to find me out.' That was undoubtedly Sir Rupert's conviction, that he was strong enough to force the Government, to coerce his party, to compel recognition of his opinions and acceptance of his views. 'They cannot do without me,' he said to himself in his secret heart. He was met by disappointment. The party chiefs made no overtures to him to reconsider his decision, to withdraw his resignation. Another man was immediately put in his place, a man of mediocre ability, of commonplace mind, a man of routine, methodical, absolutely lacking in brilliancy or originality, a man who would do exactly what the Government wanted in the Government way. There was a more bitter blow still for Sir Rupert. There were in the Government certain members of his own little Adullamite party of the Opposition days, T.T.s who had been given office at his insistence, men whom he had discovered, brought forward, educated for political success.

It is certain that Sir Rupert confidently expected that these men, his comrades and followers, would endorse his resignation with their own, and that the Government would thus, by his action, find itself suddenly crippled, deprived of its young blood, its ablest Ministers. The confident expectation was not realised. The T.T.s remained where they were. The Government took advantage of the slight readjustment of places caused by Sir Rupert's resignation to give two of the most prominent T.T.s more important offices, and to those offices the T.T.s stuck like limpets.

Sir Rupert was not a man to give way readily, or readily to acknowledge that he was defeated. He bided his time, in his place below the gangway, till there came an Indian debate. Then, in a House which had been roused to intense excitement by vague rumours of his intention, he moved a resolution which was practically a vote of censure upon the Government for its Indian policy. Always a fluent, ready, ornate speaker, Sir Rupert was never better than on that desperate night. His attack upon the Government was merciless; every word seemed to sting like a poisoned arrow; his exposure of the

imbecilities and ineptitudes of the existing
system of administration was complete and
cruel; his scornful attack upon ' the Limpets '
sent the Opposition into paroxysms of
delighted laughter, and roused a storm of
angry protest from the crowded benches
behind the Ministry. That night was the
memorable event of the session. For long
enough after those who witnessed it carried
in their memories the picture of that pale,
handsome young man, standing up in that
corner seat below the gangway and assailing
the Ministry of which he had been the most
remarkable Minister with so much cold
passion, so much fierce disdain. ' By Jove !
he's smashed them !' cried Wynter, M.P.,
excitedly, when Rupert Langley sat down
after his speech of an hour and a quarter,
which had been listened to by a crowded
House amidst a storm of cheering and dis-
approval. Wynter was sitting on a lower

gangway seat, for every space of sitting room in the chamber was occupied that night, and he had made this remark to one of the Opposition leaders on the front bench, craning over to call it into his ear. The leader of the Opposition heard Wynter's remark, looked round at the excited Radical, and, smiling, shook his head. The excitement faded from Wynter's face. His chief was never wrong.

The usual exodus after a long speech did not take place when Rupert sat down. It was expected that the leader of the House would reply to Sir Rupert, but the expectation was not realised. To the surprise of almost everyone present the Government put up as their spokesman one of the men who had been most allied with Sir Rupert in the old T.T. party, Sidney Blenheim. Something like a frown passed over Sir Rupert's face as Blenheim rose; then he sat immovable, expressionless, while Blenheim made his speech. It was a very clever speech, delicately ironical, sharply cutting, tinged all through with an intolerable condescension, with a gallingly gracious recognition of Langley's merits, an irritating regret for his errors. There was a certain languidness in Blenheim's deportment, a certain air of sweetness in his face, which made his satire the more severe, his attack the more telling. People were as much surprised as if what looked like a dandy's cane had proved to be a sword of tempered steel. Whatever else that night did, it made Blenheim's reputation.

Langley did not carry a hundred men with him into the lobby against the Government. The Opposition, as a body, supported the Administration; a certain proportion of Radicals, a much smaller number of men from his own side, followed him to his fall. He returned to his seat after the numbers had been read out, and sat there as composedly as if nothing had happened, or as if the ringing cheers which greeted the Government triumph were so many tributes to his own success. But those who knew, or thought they knew, Rupert Langley well said that the hour in which he sat there must have been an hour of terrible suffering. After that great debate, the business of the rest of the evening fell rather flat, and was conducted in a House which rapidly thinned down to little short of emptiness. When it was at its emptiest, Rupert Langley rose, lifted his hat to the Speaker, and left the Chamber.

It would not be strictly accurate to say that he never returned to it that session; but practically the statement would be correct. He came back occasionally during the short remainder of the session, and sat in his new place below the gangway. Once or twice he put a question upon the paper; once or twice he contributed a short speech to some debate. He still spoke to his friends, with cold confidence, of his inevitable return to influence, to power, to triumph; he did not say how this would be brought about—he left it to be assumed.

Then paragraphs began to appear in the papers announcing Sir Rupert Langley's intention of spending the recess in a prolonged tour in India. Before the recess came Sir Rupert had started upon this tour, which was extended far beyond a mere investigation of the Indian Empire. When the House met again, in the February of the following year, Sir Rupert was not among the returned members. Such few of his friends as were in communication with him knew, and told their knowledge to others, that Sir Rupert was engaged in a voyage round the world. Not a voyage round the world in the hurried sense in which people occasionally made then, and frequently make now—a voyage round the world, scampering, like the hero of Jules Verne, across land and sea, fast as steam-engine can drag and steamship carry them. Sir Rupert intended to go round the world in the most leisurely fashion, stopping every-where, seeing everything, setting no limit to the time he might spend in any place that pleased him, fixing beforehand no limit to chain him to any place that did not please him. He proposed, his friends said, to go carefully over his old ground in Central Asia, to make himself a complete master of the problems of Australasian colonisation, and especially to make a very profound and exhaustive study of the strange civilisations of China and Japan. He intended further to give a very considerable time to a leisurely investigation of the South American Republics. 'Why,' said Wynter, M.P., when one of Sir Rupert's friends told him of these plans, 'why, such a scheme will take several years.' 'Very likely,' the friend answered; and Wynter said, 'Oh, by Jove!' and whistled.

The scheme did take several years. At various intervals Sir Rupert wrote to his constituents long letters spangled with stirring allusions to the Empire, to England's meteor flag, to the inevitable triumph of the New Toryism, to the necessity a sincere British statesman was under of becoming a complete master of all the possible problems of a daily-increasing authority. He made some sharp thrusts at the weakness of the Government, but accused the Opposition of a lack of patriotism in trading upon that weakness; he almost chaffed the leader in the Lower House and the leader in the Lords; he made no allusion to Sidney Blenheim, then rapidly advancing along the road of success. He concluded each letter by offering to resign his seat if his constituents wished it.

His constituents did not wish it—at least, not at first. The Conservative committee returned him a florid address assuring him of their confidence in his statesmanship, but expressing. the hope that he might be able speedily to return to represent them at Westminster, and the further hope that he might be able to see his way to reconcile his difficulties with the existing Government. To this address Sir Rupert sent a reply duly acknowledging its expression of confidence, but taking no notice of its suggestions. Time went on, and Sir Rupert did not return. He was heard of now and again; now in the court of some rajah in the North-West Provinces, now in the khanate of some Central Asian despot; now in South America, from which continent he sent a long letter to the 'Times,' giving an interesting account of the

latest revolution in the Gloria Republic, of
which he had happened to be an eye-witness;
now in Java; now in Pekin; now at the
Cape. He did not seem to pursue his idea
of going round the world on any settled con-
secutive plan.

Of his large means there could be no
doubt. He was probably one of the richest,
as he was certainly one of the oldest, baronets
in England, and he could afford to travel as
if he were an accredited representative of the
Queen—almost as if he were an American
Midas of the fourth or fifth class. But as to
his large leisure people began to say things.
It began to be hinted in leading articles that
it was scarcely fair that Sir Rupert's constituents should be disfranchised because it
pleased a disappointed politician to drift idly
about the world. These hints had their
effect upon the disfranchised constituents,
who began to grumble. The Conservative

Committee was goaded almost to the point of addressing a remonstrance to Sir Rupert, then in the interior of Japan, urging him to return or resign, when the need for any such action was taken out of their hands by a somewhat unexpected General Election. Sir Rupert telegraphed back to announce his intention of remaining abroad for the present, and of not, therefore, proposing to seek just then the suffrages of the electors. Sidney Blenheim succeeded in getting a close personal friend of his own, who was also his private secretary, accepted by the Conservative Committee, and he was returned at the head of the poll by a slightly decreased majority.

Sir Rupert remained away from England for several years longer. After he had gone round the world in the most thorough sense, he revisited many places where he had been before, and stayed there for longer periods.

It began to seem as if he did not really intend to return to England at all. His communications with his friends grew fewer and shorter, but wandering Parliamentarians in the recess occasionally came across him in the course of an extended holiday, and always found him affable, interested to animation in home politics, and always suggesting by his manner, though never in his speech, that he would some day return to his old place and his old fame. Of Sidney Blenheim he spoke with an equable, impartial composure.

At last one day he did come home. He had been in the United States during the closing years of the American Civil War, and in Washington, when peace was concluded, he had met at the English Ministry a young girl of great beauty, of a family that was old for America, that was wealthy, though not wealthy for America. He fell in love with her, wooed her, and was accepted. They

were married in Washington, and soon after
the marriage they returned to England.
They settled down for a while at the old home
of the Langleys, the home whose site had
been the home of the race ever since the
Conquest. Part of an old Norman tower still
held itself erect amidst the Tudor, Elizabethan, and Victorian additions to the ancient
place. It was called Queen's Langley now,
had been so called ever since the days when,
in the beginning of the Civil War, Henrietta
Maria had been besieged there during her
visit to the then baronet by a small party of
Roundheads, and had successfully kept them
off. Queen's Langley had been held during
the Commonwealth by a member of the family,
who had declared for the Parliament, but had
gone back to the head of the house when he
returned with his king at the Restoration.

At Queen's Langley Sir Rupert and his
wife abode for a while, and at Queen's

Langley a child was born to them, a girl child, who was christened after her mother, Helena. Then the taste for wandering which had become almost a passion with Sir Rupert took possession of Sir Rupert again. If he had expected to re-enter London in any kind of triumph he was disappointed. He had allowed himself to fall out of the race, and he found himself almost forgotten. Society, of course, received him almost rapturously, and his beautiful wife was the queen of a resplendent season. But politics seemed to have passed him by. The New Toryism of those youthful years was not very new Toryism now. Sidney Blenheim was a settled reactionary and a recognised celebrity. There was a New Toryism, with its new cave of strenuous, impetuous young men, and they, if they thought of Sir Rupert Langley at all, thought of him as old-fashioned, the hero or victim of a piece of ancient history.

Nevertheless, Sir Rupert had his thoughts of entering political life again, but in the meantime he was very happy. He had a steam yacht of his own, and when his little girl was three years old he and his wife went for a long cruise in the Mediterranean. And then his happiness was taken away from him. His wife suddenly sickened, died, unconscious, in his arms, and was buried at sea. Sir Rupert seemed like a broken man. From Alexandria he wrote to his sister, who was married to the Duke of Magdiel's third son, Lord Edmond Herrington, asking her to look after his child for him—the child was then with her aunt at Herrington Hall, in Argyll-shire—in his absence. He sold his yacht, paid off his crew, and disappeared for two years.

During those two years he was believed to have wandered all over Egypt, and to have passed much of his time the hermit-like

tenant of a tomb on the lovely, lonely island
of Phylæ, át the first cataract of the Nile.
At the end of the two years he wrote to his
sister that he was returning to Europe, to
England, to his own home, and his own
people. His little girl was then five years old.

He reappeared in England changed and
aged, but a strong man still, with a more
settled air of strength of purpose than he had
worn in his wild youth. He found his little
girl a pretty child, brilliantly healthy, brilliantly strong. The wind of the mountain,
of the heather, of the woods, had quickened
her with an enduring vitality very different
from that of the delicate fair mother for
whom his heart still grieved. Of course the
little Helena did not remember her father,
and was at first rather alarmed when Lady
Edmond Herrington told her that a new papa
was coming home for her from across the seas.
But the feeling of fear passed away after the

first meeting between father and child. The fascination which in his younger days Rupert Langley had exercised upon so many men and women, which had made him so much of a leader in his youth, affected the child powerfully. In a week she was as devoted to him as if she had never been parted from him.

Helena's education was what some people would call a strange education. She was never sent to school; she was taught and taught much at home, first by a succession of clever governesses, then by carefully chosen masters of many languages and many arts. In almost all things her father was her chief instructor. He was a man of varied aecomplishments; he was a good linguist, and his years of wandering had made his attainments in language really colloquial; he had a rich and various store of information gathered even more from personal experience than from

books. His great purpose in life appeared to
be to make his daughter as accomplished as
himself. People had said at first when he
returned that he would marry again, but the
assumption proved to be wrong. Sir Rupert
had made up his mind that he would never
marry again, and he kept to his determination.
There was an intense sentimentality in his
strong nature; the sentimentality which led
him to take his early defeat and the defection
of Sidney Blenheim so much to heart, had
made him vow, on the day when the body of
his fair young wife was lowered into the sea,
changeless fidelity to her memory. Undoubtedly it was somewhat of a grief to him
that there was no son to carry on his name;
but he bore that grief in silence. He
resolved, however, that his daughter should
be in every way worthy of the old line which
culminated in her; she should be a woman
worthy to surrender the ancient name to

some exceptional mortal; she should be worthy to be the wife of some great statesman.

In those years in which Helena Langley was growing up from childhood to womanhood, Sir Rupert returned to public life. The constituency in which Queen's Langley was situated was a Tory constituency which had been represented for nearly half a century by the same old Tory squire. The Tory squire had a grandson who was as uncompromisingly Radical as the squire was Tory; naturally he could not succeed, and would not contest the seat. Sir Rupert came forward, was eagerly accepted, and successfully returned. His reappearance in the House of Commons after so considerable an interval made some small excitement in Westminster, roused some comment in the press. It was fifteen years since he had left St. Stephen's; he thought curiously of the past as he took his place, not in that corner seat below the gangway, but on the second bench behind the Treasury Bench. His Toryism was now of a settled type; the Government, which had been a little apprehensive of his possible antagonism, found him a loyal and valuable supporter. He did not remain long behind the Treasury Bench. An important vacancy occurred in the Ministry; the post of Foreign Secretary was offered to and accepted by Sir Rupert. Years ago such a place would have seemed the highest goal of his ambition. Now he—accepted it. Once again he found himself a prominent man in the House of Commons, although under very different conditions from those of his old days.

In the meantime Helena grew in years and health, in beauty, in knowledge. Sir Rupert, as an infinite believer in the virtues of travel, took her with him every recess for extended expeditions to Europe, and, as she grew older, to other continents than Europe. By the time that she was twenty, she knew much of the world from personal experience ; she knew more of politics and political life than many politicians. After she was seventeen years old she began to make frequent appear-anecs in the Ladies' Gallery, and to take long walks on the Terrace with her father. Sir Rupert delighted in her companionship, she in his ; they were always happiest in each other's society. Sir Rupert had every reason to be proud of the graceful girl who united the beauty of her mother with the strength, the physical and mental strength, of her father.

It need surprise no one, it did not appear to surprise Sir Rupert, if such an education made Helena Langley what ill-natured people. called a somewhat eccentric young woman. Brought up on a manly system of education, having a man for her closest companion, learning much of the world at an early age, naturally tended to develop and sustain the strongly marked individuality of her character. Now, at three-and-twenty, she was one of the most remarkable girls in England, one of the best known girls in London. Her independence, both of thought and of action, her extended knowledge, her frankness of speech, her slightly satirical wit, her frequent and vehement enthusiasms for the most varied pursuits and pleasures, were much commented on, much admired by some, much disapproved of by others. She had many friends among women and more friends among men, and these were real friendships, not flirtations, nor love affairs of any kind. Whatever things Helena Langley did there was one thing she never did—she never flirted. Many men had been in love with her and had told their love, and had been laughed at or pitied according to the degree of their deserts, but no one of them could honestly say that Helena had in any way encouraged his love-making, or tempted him with false hopes, unless indeed the masculine frankness of her friendship was an encouragement and a treacherous temptation. One and all, she unhesitatingly refused her adorers. 'My father is the most interesting man I know,' she once said to a discomfited and slightly despairing lover. 'Till I find some other man as interesting as he is, I shall never think of marriage. And really I am sure you will not take it in bad part if I say that I do not find you as interesting a man as my father.' The discomfited adorer did not take it amiss; he smiled ruefully, and took his departure; but, to his credit be it spoken, he remained Helena's friend.

CHAPTER V

'MY GREAT DEED WAS TOO GREAT'

THE luncheon hour was an important epoch
of the day in the Langley house in Prince's
Gate. The Langley luncheons were an institution in London life ever since Sir Rupert
bought the big Queen Anne house and made
his daughter its mistress. As he said himself
good-humouredly, he was a mere Rōi
Fainéant in the place ; his daughter was the
Mayor of the Palace, the real ruling power.

Helena Langley ruled the great house with
the most gracious autocracy. She had everything her own way and did everything in her
own way. She was a little social Queen, with
a Secretary of State for her Prime Minister,

and she enjoyed her sovereignty exceedingly. One of the great events of her reign was the institution of what came to be known as the Langley luncheons.

These luncheons differed from ordinary luncheons in this, that those who were bidden to them were in the first instance almost always interesting people—people who had done something more than merely exist, people who had some other claim upon human recognition than the claim of ancient name or of immense wealth. In the second place, the people who were bidden to a Langley luncheon were of the most varied kind, people of the most different camps in social, in political life. At the Langley table statesmen who hated each other across the floor of the House sat side by side in perfect amity. The heir to the oldest dukedom in England met there the latest champion of the latest phase of demo-cratic socialism ; the great tragedian from the

Acropolis met the low comedian from the
Levity on terms of as much equality as if they
had met at the Macklin or the Call-Boy clubs ;
the President of the Royal Academy was
amused by, and afforded much amusement to,
the newest child of genius fresh from Paris,
with the slang of the Chat Noir upon his lips
and the scorn of *les vieux* in his heart. Whig
and Tory, Catholic and Protestant, millionaire
and bohemian, peer with a peerage old a
Runnymede and the latest working-man M.P.,
all came together under the regal republican-
ism of Langley House. Someone said that a
party at Langley House always suggested to
him the Day of Judgment.

On the afternoon of the morning on which
Sir Rupert's card was left at Paulo's Hotel,
various guests assembled for luncheon in
Miss Langley's Japanese drawing-room. The
guests were not numerous—the luncheons at
Langley House were never large parties.

Eight, including the host and hostess, was the number rarely exceeded; eight, including the host and hostess, made up the number in this instance. Mr. and Mrs. Selwyn, the distinguished and thoroughly respectable actor and actress, just returned from their tour in the United States; the Duke and Duchess of Deptford—the Duchess was a young and pretty American woman; Mr. Soame Rivers, Sir Rupert's private secretary; and Mr. Hiram Borringer, who had just returned from one expedition to the South Pole, and who was said to be organising another.

When the ringing of a chime of bells from a Buddhist's temple announced luncheon, and everyone had settled down in the great oak room, where certain of the ancestral Langleys, gentlemen and ladies of the last century, whom Reynolds and Gainsborough and Romney and Raeburn had painted, had been brought up from Queen's Langley at Helena's special wish, the company seemed to be under the special survey. There was one vice-admiral of the Red who was leaning on a Doric pillar, with a spy-glass in his hand, apparently wholly indifferent to a terrific naval battle that was raging in the background; all his shadowy attention seemed to be devoted to the mortals who moved and laughed below him. There was something in the vice-admiral which resembled Sir Rupert, but none of the lovely ladies on the wall were as beautiful as Helena.

Mrs. Selwyn spoke with that clear, bell-like voice which always enraptured an audience. Every assemblage of human beings was to her an audience, and she addressed them accordingly. Now, she practically took the stage, leaning forward between the Duke of Deptford and Hiram Borringer, and addressing Helena Langley.

' My dear Miss Langley,' she said, ' do you

know that something has surprised me to-day?'

'What is it?' Helena asked, turning away from Mr. Selwyn, to whom she had been talking.

'Why, I felt sure,' Mrs. Selwyn went on, 'to meet someone here to-day. I am quite disappointed—quite.'

Everyone looked at Mrs. Selwyn with interest. She had the stage all to herself, and was enjoying the fact exceedingly. Helena gazed at her with a note of interrogation in each of her bright eyes, and another in each corner of her sensitive mouth.

'I made perfectly sure that I should meet him here to-day. I said to Harry first thing this morning, when I saw the name in the paper, "Harry," I said, "we shall be sure to meet him at Sir Rupert's this afternoon. Now did I not, Harry?'

Mr. Selwyn, thus appealed to, admitted

that his wife had certainly made the remark she now quoted.

Mrs. Selwyn beamed gratitude and affection for his endorsement. Then she turned to Miss Langley again.

'Why isn't *he* here, my dear Miss Langley, why?' Then she added, 'You know you always have everybody before anybody else, don't you?'

Helena shook her head.

'I suppose it's very stupid of me,' she said, 'but, really, I'm afraid I don't know who your " he " is. Is your " he " a hero?'

Mrs. Selwyn laughed playfully. 'Oh, now your very words show that you do know whom I mean.'

'Indeed I don't.'

'Why, that wonderful man whom you admire so much, the illustrious exile, the hero of the hour, the new Napoleon.'

'I know whom you mean,' said Soame

Rivers. 'You mean the Dictator of
Gloria?'

'Of course. Whom else?' said Mrs.
Selwyn, clapping her hands enthusiastically.
The Duke gave a sigh of relief, and Hiram
Borringer, who had been rather silent, seemed
to shake himself into activity at the mention of
Gloria. Mr. Selwyn said nothing, but watched
his wife with the wondering admiration which
some twenty years of married life had done
nothing to diminish.

The least trace of increased colour came
into Helena's cheeks, but she returned Mrs.
Selwyn's smiling glances composedly.

'The Dictator,' she said. 'Why did you
expect to see him here to-day?'

'Why, because I saw his name in the
" Morning Post " this very morning. It said
he had arrived in London last night from
Paris. I felt morally certain that I should
meet him here to-day.'

'I am sorry you should be disappointed,' Helena said, laughing, 'but perhaps we shall be able to make amends for the disappointment another day. Papa called upon him this morning.'

Sir Rupert, sitting opposite his daughter, smiled at this. 'Did I really?' he asked. 'I was not aware of it.'

'Oh, yes, you did, papa; or, at least, I did for you.'

Sir Rupert's face wore a comic expression of despair. 'Helena, Helena, why?'

'Because he is one of the most interesting men existing.'

'And because he is down on his luck, too,' said the Duchess. 'I guess that always appeals to you.' The beautiful American girl had not shaken off all the expressions of her fatherland.

'But, I say,' said Selwyn, who seemed to think that the subject called for statesmanlike comment, 'how will it do for a pillar of the Government to be extending the hand of fellowship——'

'To a defeated man,' interrupted Helena. 'Oh, that won't matter one bit. The affairs of Gloria are hardly likely to be a grave international question for us, and in the meantime it is only showing a courtesy to a man who is at once an Englishman and a stranger.'

A slightly ironical 'Hear, hear,' came from Soame Rivers, who did not love enthusiasm.

Sir Rupert followed suit good-humouredly.

'Where is he stopping?' asked Sir Rupert.

'At Paulo's Hotel, papa.'

'Paulo's Hotel,' said Mrs. Selwyn; 'that seems to be quite the place for exiled potentates to put up at. The ex-King of Capri stopped there during his recent visit, and the chiefs from Mashonaland.'

'And Don Herrera de la Mancha, who claims the throne of Spain,' said the Duke.

'And the Rajah of Khandur,' added Mrs. Selwyn, ' and the Herzog of Hesse-Steinberg, and ever so many more illustrious personages. Why do they all go to Paulo's ? '

'I can tell you,' said Soame Rivers. 'Because Paulo's is one of the best hotels in London, and Paulo is a wonderful man. He knows how to make coffee in a way that wins a foreigner's heart, and he understands the cooking of all sorts of eccentric foreign dishes ; and, though he is as rich as a Chicago pig-dealer, he looks after everything himself, and isn't in the least ashamed of having been a servant himself. I think he was a Portuguese originally.'

'And our Dictator went there?' Mrs. Selwyn questioned.

Soame Rivers answered her, ' Oh, it is the right thing to do ; it poses a distinguished

exile immediately.   Quite the right thing.
He was well advised.'

'If only he had been as well advised in
other matters,' said Mr. Selwyn.

Then Hiram Borringer, who had hitherto
kept silent, after his wont, spoke.

'I knew him,' he said, 'some years ago,
when I was in Gloria.'

Everybody looked at once and with interest at the speaker.   Hiram seemed slightly
embarrassed at the attention he aroused; but
he was not allowed to escape from explanation.

'Did you really?' said Sir Rupert.   'How
very interesting!   What sort of man did you
find him?'

Helena said nothing, but she fixed her
dark eyes eagerly on Hiram's face and
listened, with slightly parted lips, all expectation.

'I found him a big man,' Hiram answered.

'I don't mean big in bulk, for he's not that;
but big in nature, the man to make an
empire and boss it.'

'A splendid type of man,' said Mrs.
Selwyn, clasping her hands enthusiastically.
'A man to stand at Cæsar's side and give
directions.'

'Quite so,' Hiram responded gravely;
'quite so, madam. I met him first just
before he was elected President, and that's
five years ago.'

'Rather a curious thing making an
Englishman President, wasn't it?' Mr. Selwyn
inquired. At Sir Rupert's Mr. Selwyn always
displayed a profound interest in all political
questions.

'Oh, he is a naturalised citizen of Gloria,
of course,' said Soame Rivers, deftly in-
sinuating his knowledge before Hiram could
reply.

'But I thought,' said the Duke, 'that in

those South American Republics, as in the United States, a man has to be born in the country to attain to its highest office.'

'That is so,' said Hiram. 'Though I fancy his friends in Gloria wouldn't have stuck at a trifle like that just then. But as a matter of fact he was actually born in Gloria.'

'Was he really?' said Sir Rupert. 'How curious!' To which Mr. Selwyn added, 'And how convenient;' while Mrs. Selwyn inquired how it happened.

'Why, you see,' said Hiram, 'his father was English Consul at Valdorado long ago, and he married a Spanish woman there, and the woman died, and the father seems to have taken it to heart, for he came home, bringing his baby boy with him. I believe the father died soon after he got home.'

Sir Rupert's face had grown slightly graver. Soame Rivers guessed that he was thinking of his own old loss. Helena felt a new thrill of interest in the man whose personality already so much attracted her. Like her, he had hardly known a mother.

'Then was that considered enough?' the Duke asked. 'Was the fact of his having been born there, although the son of an English father, enough, with subsequent naturalisation, to qualify him for the office of President?'

'It was a peculiar case,' said Hiram. 'The point had not been raised before. But, as he happened to have the army at his back, it was concluded then that it would be most convenient for all parties to yield the point. But a good deal has been made of it since by his enemies.'

'I should imagine so,' said Sir Rupert. 'But it really is a very curious position, and I should not like to say myself off-hand how it ought to be decided.'

'The big battalions decided it in his case,' said Mrs. Selwyn.

'Are they big battalions in Gloria?' inquired the Duke.

'Relatively, yes,' Hiram answered.   'It wasn't very much of an army at that time, even for Gloria; but it went solid for him. Now, of course, it's different.'

'How is it different?'   This question came from Mr. Selwyn, who put it with an air of profound curiosity.

Hiram explained.   'Why, you see; he introduced the conscription system.   He told me he was going to do so, on the plan of some Prussian statesman.'

'Stein,' suggested Soame Rivers.

'Very likely.   Every man to take service for a certain time.   Well, that made pretty well all Gloria soldiers; it also made him a heap of enemies, and showed them how to make themselves unpleasant.   I thought it

wasn't a good plan for him or them at the
time.'

'Did you tell him so?' asked Sir Rupert.

'Well, I did drop him a hint or two of my
ideas, but he wasn't the sort of man to take
ideas from anybody. Not that I mean at all
that my ideas were of any importance, but he
wasn't that sort of man.'

'What sort of man was he, Mr. Borringer?'
said Helena impetuously. 'What was he like,
mentally, physically, every way? That's
what we want to know.'

Hiram knitted his eyebrows, as he always
did when he was slightly puzzled. He did
not greatly enjoy haranguing the whole
company in this way, and he partly re-
gretted having confessed to any knowledge
of the Dictator. But he was very fond of
Helena, and he saw that she was sin-
cerely interested in the subject, so he went
on :

'Well, I seem to be spinning quite a yarn, and I'm not much of a hand at painting a portrait, but I'll do my best.'

'Shall we make it a game of twenty questions?' Mrs. Selwyn suggested. 'We all ask you leading questions, and you answer them categorically.'

Everyone laughed, and Soame Rivers suggested that they should begin by ascertaining his age, height, and fighting weight.

'Well,' said Hiram, 'I guess I can get out my facts without cross-examination.' He had lived a great deal in America, and his speech was full of American colloquialisms. For which reason the beautiful Duchess liked him much.

'He's not very tall, but you couldn't call him short; rather more than middling high; perhaps looks a bit taller than he is, he carries himself so straight. He would have made a good soldier.'

'He did make a good soldier,' the Duke suggested.

'That's true,' said Hiram thoughtfully. 'I was thinking of a man to whom soldiering was his trade, his only trade.'

'But you haven't half satisfied our curiosity,' said Mrs. Selwyn. 'You have only told us that he is a little over the medium height, and that he bears him stiffly up. What of his eyes, what of his hair—his beard? Does he discharge in either your straw-colour beard, your orange tawny beard, your purple-in-grain beard, or your French crown-coloured beard, your perfect yellow?'

Hiram looked a little bewildered. 'I beg your pardon, ma'am,' he said. The Duke came to the rescue.

'Mrs. Selwyn's Shakespearean quotation expresses all our sentiments, Mr. Borringer. Give us a faithful picture of the hero of the hour.'

'As for his hair and beard,' Hiram resumed, 'why, they are pretty much like most people's hair and beard—a fairish brown—and his eyes match them. He has very much the sort of favour you might expect from the son of a very fair-haired man and a dark woman. His father was as fair as a Scandinavian, he told me once. He was descended from some old Danish Viking, he said.'

'That helps to explain his belligerent Berserker disposition,' said Sir Rupert.

'A fine type,' said the Duke pensively, and Mr. Selwyn caught him up with 'The finest type in the world. The sort of men who have made our empire what it is;' and he added somewhat confusedly, for his wife's eyes were fixed upon him, and he felt afraid that he was overdoing his part, 'Hawkins, Frobisher, Drake, Rodney, you know.'

'But,' said Helena, who had been very silent, for her, during the interrogation of

Hiram, 'I do not feel as if I quite know all I want to know yet.'

'The noble thirst for knowledge does you credit, Miss Langley,' said Soame Rivers pertly.

Miss Langley laughed at him.

'Yes, I want to know all about him. He interests me. He has done something; he casts a shadow, as somebody has said somewhere. I like men who do something, who cast shadows instead of sitting in other people's shadows.'

Soame Rivers smiled a little sourly, and there was a suggestion of acerbity in his voice as he said in a low tone, as if more to himself than as a contribution to the general conversation, 'He has cast a decided shadow over Gloria.' He did not quite like Helena's interest in the dethroned Dictator.

'He made Gloria worth talking about!' Helena retorted. 'Tell me, Mr. Borringer, how did he happen to get to Gloria at all?

How did it come in his way to be President
and Dictator and all that?'

'Rebellion lay in his way and he found it,'
Mrs. Selwyn suggested, whereupon Soame
Rivers tapped her playfully upon the wrist,
carrying on the quotation with the words of
Prince Hal, 'Peace, chewit, peace.' Mr. Soame
Rivers was a very free-and-easy young gentle-
man, occasionally, and as he was a son of Lord
Riverstown, much might be forgiven to him.

Hiram, always slightly bewildered by the
quotations of Mrs. Selwyn and the badinage
of Soame Rivers, decided to ignore them
both, and to address himself entirely to Miss
Langley.

'Sorry to say I can't help you much, Miss
Langley. When I was in Gloria five years
ago I found him there, as I said, running for
President. He had been a nationalised citizen
there for some time, I reckon, but how he got
so much to the front I don't know.'

'Doesn't a strong man always get to the front?' the Duchess asked.

'Yes,' said Hiram, 'I guess that's so. Well, I happened to get to know him, and we became a bit friendly, and we had many a pleasant chat together. He was as frank as frank, told me all his plans. "I mean to make this little old place move," he said to me.'

'Well, he has made it move,' said Helena. She was immensely interested, and her eyes dilated with excitement.

'A little too fast, perhaps,' said Hiram meditatively. 'I don't know. Anyhow, he had things all his own way for a goodish spell.'

'What did he do when he had things his own way?' Helena asked impatiently.

'Well, he tried to introduce reforms——'

'Yes, I knew he would do that,' the girl said, with the proud air of a sort of owner-ship.

'You seem to have known all about him,' Mrs. Selwyn said, smiling loftily, sweetly, as at the romantic enthusiasm of youth.

'Well, so I do somehow,' Helena answered almost sharply ; certainly with impatience. She was not thinking of Mrs. Selwyn.

'Now, Mr. Borringer, go on—about his reforms.'

'He seemed to have gotten a kind of notion about making things English or American. He abolished flogging of criminals and all sorts of old-fashioned ways ; and he tried to reduce taxation ; and he put down a sort of remnant of slavery that was still hanging round ; and he wanted to give free land to all the emancipated folks ; and he wanted to have an equal suffrage to all men, and to do away with corruption in the public offices and the civil service ; and to compel the judges not to take bribes ; and all sorts of things. I am afraid he wanted to do a good deal too much reform for what you folks would call the governing classes out there. I thought so at the time. He was right, you know,' Hiram said meditatively, ' but, then, I am mightily afraid he was right in a wrong sort of way.'

'He was right, anyhow,' Helena said, triumphantly.

' S'pose he was,' said Hiram ; 'but things have to go slow, don't you see ? '

' Well, what happened ? '

' I don't rightly know how it all came about exactly ; but I guess all the privileged classes, as you call them here, got their backs up, and all the officials went dead against him——'

' My great deed was too great,' Helena said.

'What is that, Helena ? ' her father asked.

' It's from a poem by Mrs. Browning, about

another dictator; but more true of my
Dictator than of hers,' Helena answered.

'Well,' Hiram went on, 'the opposition
soon began to grumble——'

'Some people are always grumbling,' said
Soame Rivers. 'What should we do without
them? Where should we get our independent
opposition?'

'Where, indeed,' said Sir Rupert, with a
sigh of humorous pathos.

'Well,' said Helena, 'what did the opposition do?'

'Made themselves nasty,' answered Hiram.
'Stirred up discontent against the foreigner, as
they called him. He found his congress hard
to handle. There were votes of censure and
talks of impeachment, and I don't know what
else. He went right ahead, his own way,
without paying them the least attention.
Then they took to refusing to vote his necessary supplies for the army and navy. He

managed to get the money in spite of them;
but whether he lost his temper, or not, I can't
say, but he took it into his head to declare
that the constitution was endangered by the
machinations of unscrupulous enemies, and to
declare himself Dictator.'

'That was brave,' said Helena, enthusiastically.

'Rather rash, wasn't it?' sneered Soame
Rivers.

'It may have been rash, and it may not,'
Hiram answered meditatively. 'I believe he
was within the strict letter of the constitution,
which does empower a President to take such
a step under certain conditions. But the
opposition meant fighting. So they rebelled
against the Dictator, and that's how the
bother began. How it ended you all
know.'

'Where were the people all this time?'
Helena asked eagerly.

'I guess the people didn't understand much about it then,' Hiram answered.

'My great deed was too great,' Helena murmured once again.

'The usual thing,' said Soame Rivers. 'Victory to begin with, and the confidence born of victory; then defeat and disaster.'

'The story of those three days' fighting in Valdorado is one of the most rattling things in recent times,' said the Duke.

'Was it not?' said Helena. 'I read every word of it every day, and I did want him to win so much.'

'Nobody could be more sorry that you were disappointed than he, I should imagine,' said Mrs. Selwyn.

'What puzzles me,' said Mr. Selwyn, ' is why when they had got him in their power they didn't shoot him.'

'Ah, you see he was an Englishman by

family,' Sir Rupert explained; 'and though, of course, he had changed his nationality, I think the Congressionalists were a little afraid of arousing any kind of feeling in England.'

'As a matter of fact, of course,' said Soame Rivers, 'we shouldn't have dreamed of making any row if they had shot him or hanged him, for the matter of that.'

'You can never tell,' said the Duke. 'Somebody might have raised the Civis Romanus cry——

'Yes, but he wasn't any longer civis Romanus,' Soame Rivers objected.

'Do you think that would matter much if a cry was wanted against the Government?' the Duke asked, with a smile.

'Not much, I'm afraid,' said Sir Rupert. 'But whatever their reasons, I think the victors did the wisest thing possible in putting their man on board their big ironclad, the

"Almirante Cochrane," and setting him ashore at Cherbourg.'

'With a polite intimation, I presume, that if he again returned to the territory of Gloria he would be shot without form of trial,' added Soame Rivers.

'But he will return,' Helena said. 'He will, I am sure of it, and perhaps they may not find it so easy to shoot him then as they think now. A man like that is not so easily got rid of.'

Helena spoke with great animation, and her earnestness made Sir Rupert smile.

'If that is so,' said Soame Rivers, 'they would have done better if they had shot him out of hand.'

Helena looked slightly annoyed as she replied quickly, 'He is a strong man. I wish there were more men like him in the world.'

'Well,' said Sir Rupert, 'I suppose we shall all see him soon and judge for ourselves.

Helena seems to have made up her mind already. Shall we go upstairs?'

'My great deed was too great' held possession that day of the mind and heart of Helena Langley.

CHAPTER VI

' HERE IS MY THRONE—BID KINGS COME BOW TO IT '

LONDON, eager for a lion, lionised Ericson. That royal sport of lion-hunting, practised in old times by kings in Babylon and Nineveh, as those strange monuments in the British Museum bear witness, is the favourite sport of fashionable London to-day. And just at that moment London lacked its regal quarry. The latest traveller from Darkest Africa, the latest fugitive pretender to authority in France, had slipped out of the popular note and the favours of the Press. Ericson came in good time. There was a gap, and he filled it.

He found himself, to his amazement and his amusement, the hero of the hour. Invitations of all kinds showered upon him; the gates of great houses yawned wide to welcome him; had he been gifted like Kehama with the power of multiplying his personality, he could scarcely have been able to accept every invitation that was thrust upon him. But he did accept a great many; indeed, it might be said that he had to accept a great many. Had he had his own way, he might, perhaps, have buried himself in Hampstead, and enjoyed the company of his aunt and the mild society of Mr. Gilbert Sarrasin. But the impetuous, indomitable Hamilton would hear of no inaction. He insisted, copying a famous phrase of Lord Beaconsfield's, that the key of Gloria was in London. 'We must make friends,' he said; 'we must keep ourselves in evidence; we must never for a moment allow our claim to be forgotten, or our interests to be ignored. If we are ever to get back to Gloria we must make the most of our inevitable exile.'

The Dictator smiled at the enthusiasm of his young henchman. Hamilton was tremendously enthusiastic. A young Englishman of high family, of education, of some means, he had attached himself to Ericson years before at a time when Hamilton, fresh from the University, was taking that complement to a University career—a trip round the world, at a time when Ericson was just beginning that course of reform which had ended for the present in London and Paulo's Hotel. Hamilton's enthusiasm often proved to be practical. Like Ericson, he was full of great ideas for the advancement of mankind; he had swallowed all Socialisms, and had almost believed, before he fell in with Ericson, that he had elaborated the secret of social government. But his wide knowledge was of

service; and his devotion to the Dictator
showed itself of sterling stuff on that day in
the Plaza Nacional when he saved his life
from the insurgents. If the Dictator sometimes smiled at Hamilton's enthusiasm, he
often allowed himself to yield to it. Just for
the moment he was a little sick of the whole
business; the inevitable bitterness that tinges
a man's heart who has striven to be of
service, and who has been misunderstood,
had laid hold of him; there were times when
he felt that he would let the whole thing go
and make no further effort. Then it was that
Hamilton's enthusiasm proved so useful, that
Hamilton's restless energy in keeping in touch
with the friends of the fallen man roused him
and stimulated him.

He had made many friends now in
London. Both the great political parties
were civil to him, especially, perhaps, the
Conservatives. Being in power, they could

not make an overt declaration of their interest in him, but just then the Tory Party was experiencing one of those emotional waves which at times sweep over its consciousness, when it feels called upon to exalt the banner of progress; to play the old Roman part of lifting up the humble and casting down the proud; of showing a paternal interest in all manner of schemes for the redress of wrong and suffering everywhere. Somehow or other it had got it into its head that Ericson was a man after its own heart; that he was a kind of new Gordon; that his gallant determination to make the people of Gloria happy in spite of themselves was a proof of the application of Tory methods. Sir Rupert encouraged this idea. As a rule, his party were a little afraid of his advanced ideas; but on this occasion they were willing to accept them, and they manifested the friendliest interest in the Dictator's defeated schemes. Indeed, so friendly were they that many of the Radicals began to take alarm, and think that something must be wrong with a man who met with so cordial a reception from the ruling party.

Ericson himself met these overtures contentedly enough. If it was for the good of Gloria that he should return some day to carry out his dreams, then anything that helped him to return was for the good of Gloria too, and undoubtedly the friendliness of the Ministerialists was a very important factor in the problem he was engaged upon. He did not know at first how much Tory feeling was influenced by Sir Rupert; he did not know until later how much Sir Rupert was influenced by his daughter.

Helena had aroused in her father something of her own enthusiasm for the exiled Dictator. Sir Rupert had looked into the whole business more carefully, had recognised that it certainly would be very much better for the interests of British subjects under the green and yellow banner that Gloria should be ruled by an Englishman like Ericson than by the wild and reckless Junta, who at present upheld uncertain authority by martial law. England had recognised the Junta, of course; it was the *de facto* Government, and there was nothing else to be done. But it was not managing its affairs well; the credit of the country was shaken; its trade was gravely impaired; the very considerable English colony was loud in its protests against the defects of the new *régime.* Under these conditions Sir Rupert saw no reason for not extending the hand of friendship to the Dictator.

He did extend the hand of friendship. He met the Dictator at a dinner-party given in his honour by Mr. Wynter, M.P.: Mr. Wynter, who had always made it a point to

know everybody, and who was as friendly with
Sir Rupert as with the chieftains of his own
party. Sir Rupert had expressed to Wynter
a wish to meét Ericson; so when the dinner
came off he found himself placed at the right-
hand side of Ericson, who was at his host's
right-hand side. The two men got on well
from the first. Sir Rupert was attracted by
the fresh unselfishness of Ericson, by something still youthful, still simple, in a man who
had done and endured so much, and he
made himself agreeable, as he only knew how,
to his neighbour. Ericson, for his part, was
frankly pleased with Sir Rupert. He was a
little surprised, perhaps, at first to find that
Sir Rupert's opinions coincided so largely
with his own; that their views of government agreed on so many important par-
ticulars. He did not at first discover that it
was Ericson's unconstitutional act in en-
forcing his reforms, rather than the actual

reforms themselves, that aroused Sir Rupert's admiration. Sir Rupert was a good talker, a master of the manipulation of words, knowing exactly how much to say in order to convey to the mind of his listener a very decided impression without actually committing himself to any pledged opinion. Ericson was a shrewd man, but in such delicate dialectic he was not a match for a man like Sir Rupert.

Sir Rupert asked the Dictator to dinner, and the Dictator went to the great house in Queen's Gate and was presented to Helena, and was placed next to her at dinner, and thought her very pretty and original and attractive, and enjoyed himself very much. He found himself, to his half-unconscious surprise, still young enough and human enough to be pleased with the attention people were paying him—above all, that he was still young enough and human enough to be pleased with the very obvious homage of a charming young woman. For Helena's homage was very obvious indeed. Accustomed always to do what she pleased, and say what she pleased, Helena, at three-and-twenty, had a frankness of manner, a straightforwardness of speech, which her friends called original and her detractors called audacious. She would argue, unabashed, with the great leader of the party on some high point of foreign policy; she would talk to the great chieftain of Opposition as if he were her elder brother. People who did not understand her said that she was forward, that she had no reserve; even people who understood her, or thought they did, were sometimes a little startled by her careless directness. Soame Rivers once, when he was irritated by her, which occasionally happened, though he generally kept his irritation to himself, said that she had a 'slap on the back' way of treating her friends. The remark was not kind, but it happened to be fairly accurate, as unkind remarks sometimes are.

But from the first Helena did not treat the Dictator with the same brusque spirit of *camaraderie* which she showed to most of her friends. Her admiration for the public man, if it had been very enthusiastic, was very sincere. She had, from the first time that Ericson's name began to appear in the daily papers, felt a keen interest in the adventurous Englishman who was trying to introduce free institutions and advanced civilisation into one of the worm-eaten republics of the New World. As time went on, and Ericson's doings became more and more conspicuous, the girl's admiration for the lonely pioneer waxed higher and higher, till at last she conjured up for herself an image of heroic chivalry as romantic in its way as anything that could be evolved from the dreams of a sentimental schoolgirl. To reform the world —was not that always England's mission, if not especially the mission of her own party? —and here was an Englishman fighting for reform in that feverish place, and endeavouring to make his people happy and prosperous and civilised, by methods which certainly seemed to have more in common with the benevolent despotism of the Tory Party than with the theories of the Opposition. Bit by bit it came to pass that Helena Langley grew to look upon Ericson over there in that queer, ebullient corner of new Spain, as her ideal hero; and so it happened that when at last she met her hero in the flesh for the first time her frank audacity seemed to desert her.

Not that she showed in the slightest degree embarrassment when Sir Rupert first presented to her the grave man with the earnest eyes, whose pointed beard and brown hair were both slightly touched with grey. Only those who knew Helena well could possibly have told that she was not absolutely at her ease in the presence of the Dictator. Ericson himself thought her the most self-possessed young lady he had ever met, and to him, familiar as he was with the exquisite effrontery belonging to the New Castilian dames of Gloria, self-possession in young women was a recognised fact. Even Sir Rupert himself scarcely noticed anything that he would have called shyness in his daughter's demeanour as she stood talking to the Dictator, with her large fine eyes fixed in composed gaze upon his face. But Soame Rivers noticed a difference in her bearing; he was not her father, and he was accustomed to watch every tone of her speech and every movement of her eyes, and he saw that she was not entirely herself in the company of

the 'new man,' as he called Ericson; and
seeing it he felt a pang, or at least a prick, at
the heart, and sneered at himself immediately
in consequence. But he edged up to Helena
just before the pairing took place for dinner,
and said softly to her, so that no one else
could hear, 'You are shy to-night. Why?'
—and moved away smiling at the angry
flash of her eyes and the compression of her
mouth.

Possibly the words of Rivers may have
affected her more than she was willing to
admit; but she certainly was not as self-
composed as usual during that first dinner.
Her wit flashed vivaciously; the Dictator
thought her brilliant, and even rather bewil-
dering. If anyone had said to him that
Helena Langley was not absolutely at her
ease with him, he would have stared in
amazement. For himself, he was not at all
dismayed by the brilliant, beautiful girl who

sat next to him. The long habit of intercourse with all kinds of people, under all kinds of conditions, had given him the experience which enabled him to be at his ease under any circumstances, even the most unfamiliar, and certainly talking to Helena Langley was an experience that had no precedent in the Dictator's life. But he talked to her readily, with great pleasure; he felt a little surprise at her obvious willingness to talk to him and accept his judgment upon many things; but he set this down as one of the few agreeable conditions attendant upon being lionised, and accepted it gratefully. 'I am the newest thing,' he thought to himself, 'and so this child is interested in me and consequently civil to me. Probably she will have forgotten all about me the next time we meet; in the meanwhile she is very charming.' The Dictator had even been about to suggest to himself that he might possibly forget all about her ; but somehow this did not seem very likely, and he dismissed it.

He did not see very much of Helena that night after the dinner.   Many people came in, and Helena was surrounded by a little court of adorers, men of all ages and occupations, statesmen, soldiers, men of letters, all eagerly talking a kind of talk which was almost unintelligible to the Dictator.   In that bright Babel of voices, in that conversation which was full of allusions to things of which he knew nothing, and for which, if he had known, he would have cared less, the Dictator felt his sense of exile suddenly come strongly upon him like a great chill wave.   It was not that he could feel neglected.   A great statesman was talking to him, talking at much length confidentially, paying him the compliment of repeatedly inviting his opinion, and of deferring to his judgment.   There was not a man or woman in the room who was not anxious to be introduced to Ericson, who was not delighted when the introduction was accorded, and when he or she had taken his hand and exchanged a few words with him. But somehow it was Helena's voice that seemed to thrill in the Dictator's ears; it was Helena's face that his eyes wandered to through all that brilliant crowd, and it was with something like a sense of serious regret that he found himself at last taking her hand and wishing her good-night. Her bright eyes grew brighter as she expressed the hope that they should meet soon again. The Dictator bowed and withdrew. He felt in his heart that he shared the hope very strongly.

The hope was certainly realised. So notable a lion as the Dictator was asked everywhere, and everywhere that he went he met the Langleys. In the high political and social life in which the Dictator, to his entertainment, found himself, the hostilities of warring parties had little or no effect. In that rarefied air it was hard to draw the breath of party passion, and the Dictator came across the Langleys as often in the houses of the Opposition as in Ministerial mansions. So it came to pass that something almost approaching to an intimacy sprang up between John Ericson on the one part and Sir Rupert and Helena Langley on the other. Sir Rupert felt a real interest in the adventurous man with the eccentric ideas; perhaps his presence recalled something of Sir Rupert's own hot youth when he had had eccentric ideas and was looked upon with alarm by the steady-going. Helena made no concealment of her interest in the exile. She was always so frank in her friendships, so off-hand and boyish in her air of comradeship with many people, that her attitude towards the Dictator did not strike

any one, except Soame Rivers, as being in
the least marked—for her. Indeed, most of
her admirers would have held that she was
more reserved with the Dictator than with
others of her friends. Soame Rivers saw
that there was a difference in her bearing
towards the Dictator and towards the courtiers
of her little court, and he smiled cynically and
pretended to be amused.

Ericson's acquaintance with the Langleys
ripened into that rapid intimacy which is
sometimes possible in London. At the end of
a week he had met them many times and
had been twice to their house. Helena had
always insisted that a friendship which was
worth anything should declare itself at once,
should blossom quickly into being, and not
grow by slow stages. She offered the Dictator her friendship very frankly and very
graciously, and Ericson accepted very frankly
the gracious gift. For it delighted him, tired

as he was of all the strife and struggle of the last few years, to find rest and sympathy in the friendship of so charming a girl; the cordial sympathy she showed him came like a balm to the humiliation of his overthrow. He liked Helena, he liked her father; though he had known them but for a handful of days, it always delighted him to meet them; he always felt in their society that he was in the society of friends.

One evening, when Ericson had been little more than a month in London, he found himself at an evening party given by Lady Seagraves. Lady Seagraves was a wonderful woman—'the fine flower of our modern civilisation,' Soame Rivers called her. Everybody came to her house; she delighted in contrasts; life was to her one prolonged antithesis. Soame Rivers said of her parties that they resembled certain early Italian pictures, which gave you the mythological gods in one place, a battle in another, a scene of pastoral peace in a third. It was an astonishing amalgam.

Ericson arrived at Lady Seagraves' house rather late; the rooms were very full—he found it difficult to get up the great staircase. There had been some great Ministerial function, and the dresses of many of the men in the crowd were as bright as the women's. Court suits, ribands, and orders lent additional colour to a richly coloured scene. But even in a crowd where everybody bore some claim to distinction the arrival of the Dictator aroused general attention. Ericson was not yet sufficiently hardened to the experience to be altogether indifferent to the fact that everyone was looking at him; that people were whispering his name to each other as he slowly made his way from stair to stair; that pretty women paused in their upward or downward progress to look at him, and invariably with a look of admiration for his grave, handsome face.

When he got to the top of the stairs Ericson found his hostess, and shook hands with her. Lady Seagraves was an effusive woman, who was always delighted to see any of her friends; but she felt a special delight at seeing the Dictator, and she greeted him with a special effusiveness. Her party was choking with celebrities of all kinds, social, political, artistic, legal, clerical, dramatic; but it would not have been entirely triumphant if it had not included the Dictator. Lady Seagraves was very glad to see him indeed, and said so in her warm, enthusiastic way.

'I'm so glad to see you,' Lady Seagraves murmured. 'It was so nice of you to come. I was beginning to be desperately afraid that you had forgotten all about me and my poor little party.'

It was one of Lady Seagraves' graceful little affectations to pretend that all her parties were small parties, almost partaking of the nature of impromptu festivities. Ericson glanced around over the great room crammed to overflowing with a crowd of men and women who could hardly move, men and women most of whose faces were famous or beautiful, men and women all of whom, as Soame Rivers said, had their names in the play-bill; there was a smile on his face as he turned his eyes from the brilliant mass to Lady Seagraves' face.

'How could I forget a promise which it gives me so much pleasure to fulfil?' he asked. Lady Seagraves gave a little cry of delight.

'Now that's perfectly sweet of you! How did you ever learn to say such pretty things in that dreadful place? Oh, but of course; I forgot Spaniards pay compliments to perfection, and you have learnt the art from them, you frozen Northerner.'

Ericson laughed. 'I am afraid I should never rival a Spaniard in compliment,' he said. He never knew quite what to talk to Lady Seagraves about, but, indeed, there was no need for him to trouble himself, as Lady Seagraves could at all times talk enough for two more.

So he just listened while Lady Seagraves rattled on, sending his glance hither and thither in that glittering assembly, seeking almost unconsciously for one face. He saw it almost immediately; it was the face of Helena Langley, and her eyes were fixed on him. She was standing in the throng at some little distance from him, talking to Soame Rivers, but she nodded and smiled to the Dictator.

At that moment the arrival of the Duke and Duchess of Deptford set Ericson free from the ripple of Lady Seagraves' conversation. She turned to greet the new arrivals, and the Dictator began to edge his way through the press to where Helena was standing. Though she was only a little distance off, his progress was but slow progress. The rooms were tightly packed, and almost every person he met knew him and spoke to him, or shook hands with him, but he made his way steadily forward.

'Here comes the illustrious exile!' said Soame Rivers, in a low tone. 'I suppose nobody will have a chance of saying a word to you for the rest of the evening?'

Miss Langley glanced at him with a little frown. 'I am afraid I can scarcely hope that Mr. Ericson will consent to be monopolised by me for the whole of the evening,' she said; 'but I wish he would, for he is certainly the most interesting person here.'

Soame Rivers shrugged his shoulders

slightly. 'You always know someone who is the most interesting man in the world—for the time being,' he said.

Miss Langley frowned again, but she did not reply, for by this time Ericson had reached her, and was holding out his hand. She took it with a bright smile of welcome. Soame Rivers slipped away in the crowd, after nodding to Ericson.

'I am so glad that you have come,' Helena said. 'I was beginning to fear that you were not coming.'

'It is very kind of you,' the Dictator began, but Miss Langley interrupted him.

'No, no; it isn't kind of me at all; it is just natural selfishness. I want to talk to you about several things; and if you hadn't come I should have been disappointed in my purpose, and I hate being disappointed.'

The Dictator still persisted that any mark of interest from Miss Langley was kindness.

'What do you want to talk to me about particularly?' he asked.

'Oh, many things! But we can't talk in this awful crush. It's like trying to stand up against big billows on a stormy day. Come with me. There is a quieter place at the back, where we shall have a chance of peace.'

She turned and led the way slowly through the crowd, the Dictator following her obediently. Once again the progress was a slow one, for every man had a word for Miss Langley, and he himself was eagerly caught at as they drifted along. But at last they got through the greater crush of the centre rooms and found themselves in a kind of lull in a further saloon where a piano was, and where there were fewer people. Out of this room there was a still smaller one with several palms in it, and out of the palms arising a great bronze reproduction of the

Hermes of Praxiteles. Lady Seagraves playfully called this little room her Pagan parlour.
Here people who knew the house well found
their way when they wanted quiet conversation. There was nobody in it when Miss
Langley and the Dictator arrived. Helena
sat down on a sofa with a sigh of relief, and
Ericson sat down beside her.

'What a delightful change from all that
awful noise and glare!' said Helena. 'I am
very fond of this little corner, and I think
Lady Seagraves regards it as especially sacred
to me.'

'I am grateful for being permitted to
cross the hallowed threshold,' said the Dictator. 'Is this the tutelary divinity?' And
he glanced up at the bronze image.

'Yes,' said Miss Langley; 'that is a copy
of the Hermes of Praxiteles which was discovered at Olympia some years ago. It is
the right thing to worship.'

'One so seldom worships the right thing —at least, at the right time,' he said.

'I worship the right thing, I know,' she rejoined, 'but I don't quite know about the right time.'

'Your instincts would be sure to guide you right,' he answered, not indeed quite knowing what he was talking about.

'Why?' she asked, point blank.

'Well, I suppose I meant to say that you have nobler instincts than most other people.'

'Come, you are not trying to pay me a compliment? I don't want compliments; I hate and detest them. Leave them to stupid and uninteresting men.'

'And to stupid and uninteresting women?'

'Another try at a compliment!'

'No; I felt that.'

'Well, anyhow, I did not entice you in

here to hear anything about myself; I know all about myself.'

'Indeed,' he said straightforwardly, 'I do not care to pay compliments, and I should never think of wearying you with them. I believe I hardly quite knew what I was talking about just now.'

'Very well; it does not matter. I want to hear about you. I want to know all about you. I want you to trust in me and treat me as your friend.'

'But what do you want me to tell you?'

'About yourself and your projects and everything. Will you?'

The Dictator was a little bewildered by the girl's earnestness, her energy, and the perfect simplicity of her evident belief that she was saying nothing unreasonable. She saw reluctance and hesitation in his eyes.

'You are very young,' he began.

'Too young to be trusted?'

'No, I did not say *that*.'

'But your look said it.'

'My look then mistranslated my feeling.'

'What did you feel?'

'Surprise, and interest, and gratitude.'

She tossed her head impatiently.

'Do you think I can't understand?' she asked, in her impetuous way—her imperial way with most others, but only an impetuous way with him. For most others with whom she was familiar she was able to control and be familiar with, but she could only be impetuous with the Dictator. Indeed, it was the high tide of her emotion which carried her away so far as to fling her in mere impetuousness against him.

The Dictator was silent for a moment, and then he said: 'You don't seem much more than a child to me.'

'Oh! Why? Do you not know?—I am twenty-three!'

'I am twenty-three,' the Dictator murmured, looking at her with a kindly and half-melancholy interest. 'You are twenty-three! Well, there it is—do you not see, Miss Langley?'

'There what is?'

'There is all the difference. To be twenty-three seems to you to make you quite a grown-up person.'

'What else should it make me? I have been of age for two years. What am I but a grown-up person?'

'Not in my sense,' he said placidly. 'You see, I have gone through so much, and lived so many lives, that I begin to feel quite like an old man already. Why, I might have had a daughter as old as you.'

'Oh, stuff!' the audacious young woman interposed.

'Stuff? How do you know?'

'As if I hadn't read lives of you in all the

papers and magazines and I don't know what.
I can tell you your birthday if you wish, and
the year of your birth. You are quite young
—in my eyes.'

'You are kind to me,' he said, gravely,
'and I am quite sure that I look at my very
best in your eyes.'

'You do indeed,' she said fervently, gratefully.

'Still that does not prevent me from being
twenty years older than you.'

'All right ; but would you refuse to talk
frankly and sensibly about yourself?—
sensibly, I mean, as one talks to a friend and
not as one talks to a child. Would you refuse to talk in that way to a young man
merely because you were twenty years older
than he ?'

'I am not much of a talker,' he said, 'and
I very much doubt if I should talk to a young

man at all about my projects, unless, of course, to my friend Hamilton.'

Helena turned half away disappointed. It was of no use, then—she was not his friend. He did not care to reveal himself to her; and yet she thought she could do so much to help him. She felt that tears were beginning to gather in her eyes, and she would not for all the world that he should see them.

'I thought we were friends,' she said, giving out the words very much as a child might give them out—and, indeed, her heart was much more as that of a little child than she herself knew or than he knew then; for she had not the least idea that she was in love or likely to be in love with the Dictator. Her free, energetic, wild-falcon spirit had never as yet troubled itself with thoughts of such kind. She had made a hero for herself out of the Dictator—she almost adored him; but it was

with the most genuine hero-worship— or fetish
worship, if that be the better and harsher way
of putting it—and she had never thought of
being in love with him. Her highest ambition
up to this hour was to be his friend and to be
admitted to his confidence, and—oh, happy
recognition!—to be consulted by him. When
she said 'I thought we were friends,' she
jumped up and went towards the window to
hide the emotion which she knew was only too
likely to make itself felt.

The Dictator got up and followed her.
'We are friends,' he said.

She looked brightly round at him, but
perhaps he saw in her eyes that she had been
feeling a keen disappointment.

'You think my professed friendship mere
girlish inquisitiveness—you know you do,' she
said, for she was still angry.

'Indeed I do not,' he said earnestly. 'I
have had no friendship since I came back an

outcast to England—no friendship like that given to me by you——'

She turned round delightedly towards him.

'And by your father.'

And again, she could not tell why, she turned partly away.

'But the truth is,' he went on to say, 'I have no clearly defined plans as yet.'

'You don't mean to give in?' she asked eagerly.

He smiled at her impetuosity. She blushed slightly as she saw his smile.

'Oh, I know,' she exclaimed, 'you think me an impertinent schoolgirl, and you only laugh at me.'

'I do nothing of the kind. It is only too much of a pleasure to me to talk to you on terms of friendship. Look here, I wish we could do as people used to do in the old melodramas, and swear an eternal friendship.'

'I swear an eternal friendship to you,' she exclaimed, ' whether you like it or not,' and, obeying the wild impulse of the hour, she held out both her hands.

He took them both in his, held them for just one instant, and then let them go.

' I accept the friendship,' he said, with a quiet smile, ' and I reciprocate it with all my heart.'

Helena was already growing a little alarmed at her own impulsiveness and effusiveness. But there was something in the Dictator's quiet, grave, and protecting way which always seemed to reassure her. ' He will be sure to understand me,' was the vague thought in her mind.

Assuredly the Dictator now thought he did understand her. He felt satisfied that her enthusiasm was the enthusiasm of a generous girl's friendship, and that she thought about him in no other way. He had learned to like her companionship, and to think much of her fresh, courageous intellect, and even of her practical good sense. He had no doubt that he should find her advice on many things worth having. His battlefield just now and for some time to come must be in London—in the London of finance and diplomacy.

'Come and sit down again,' the Dictator said; 'I will tell you all I know—and I don't know much. I do not mean to give up, Miss Langley. I am not a man who gives up—I am not built that way.'

'Of course I knew,' Helena exclaimed triumphantly; 'I knew you would never give up. You couldn't.'

'I couldn't—and I do not believe I ought to give up. I am sure I know better how to provide for the future of Gloria than—than—well, than Gloria knows herself—just now. I believe Gloria will want me back.'

'Of course she will want you back when

she comes to her senses,' Helena said with sparkling eyes.

'I don't blame her for having a little lost her senses under the conditions—it was all too new, and I was too hasty. I was too much inspired by the ungoverned energy of the new broom. I should do better now if I had the chance.'

'You will have the chance—you must have it!'

'Do you promise it to me?' he asked with a kindly smile.

'I do—I can—I know it will come to you!'

'Well, I can wait,' he said quietly. 'When Gloria calls me to go back to her I will go.'

'But what do you mean by Gloria? Do you want a *plébiscite* of the whole population in your favour?'

'Oh no! I only mean this, that if the

large majority of the people whom I strove
to serve are of opinion they can do without
me—well, then, I shall do without them.
But if they call me I shall go to them,
although I went to my death and knew it
beforehand.'

'One may do worse things,' the girl said
proudly, 'than go knowingly to one's
death.'

'You are so young,' he said. 'Death
seems nothing to you. The young and the
generous are brave like that.'

'Oh,' she exclaimed, 'let my youth
alone!'

She would have liked to say, 'Oh, con-
found my youth!' but she did not give way
to any such unseemly impulse. She felt very
happy again, her high spirits all rallying
round her.

'Let your youth alone!' the Dictator said,
with a half-melancholy smile. 'So long as

time lets it alone—and even time will do that for some years yet.'

Then he stopped and felt a little as if he had been preaching a sermon to the girl.

'Come,' she broke in upon his moralisings, 'if I am so dreadfully young, at least I'll have the benefit of my immaturity. If I am to be treated as a child, I must have a child's freedom from conventionality.' She dragged forward a heavy armchair lined with the soft, mellowed, dull red leather which one sees made into cushions and sofa-pillows in the shops of Nuremberg's more artistic uphol- sterers, and then at its side on the carpet she planted a footstool of the same material and colour. 'There,' she said, 'you sit in that chair.'

'And you, what are you going to do?'

'Sit first, and I will show you.'

He obeyed her and sat in the great chair. 'Well, now?' he asked.

' I shall sit here at your feet.' She flung herself down and sat on the footstool.

' Here is my throne,' she said composedly ; ' bid kings come bow to it.'

'Kings come bowing to a banished Republican ? '

' You are my King,' she answered, ' and so I sit at your feet and am proud and happy. Now talk to me and tell me some more.'

But the talk was not destined to go any farther that night. Rivers and one or two others came lounging in. Helena did not stir from her lowly position. The Dictator remained as he was just long enough to show that he did not regard himself as having been disturbed. Helena flung a saucy little glance of defiance at the principal intruder.

' I know you were sent for me,' she said. ' Papa wants me ? '

' Yes,' the intruder replied ; ' if I had not

been sent I should never have ventured to follow you into this room.'

'Of course not—this is my special sanctuary. Lady Seagraves has dedicated it to me, and now I dedicate it to Mr. Ericson. I have just been telling him that, for all he is a Republican, he is *my* King.'

The Dictator had risen by this time.

'You are sent for?' he said.

'Yes—I am sorry.'

'So am I—but we must not keep Sir Rupert waiting.'

'I shall see you again—when?' she asked eagerly.

'Whenever you wish,' he answered. Then they shook hands, and Soame Rivers took her away.

Several ladies remarked that night that really Helena Langley was going quite beyond all bounds, and was overdoing her unconventionality quite too shockingly. She was actually throwing herself right at Mr. Ericson's head. Of course Mr. Ericson would not think of marrying a chit like that. He was quite old enough to be her father.

One or two stout dowagers shook their heads sagaciously, and remarked that Sir Rupert had a great deal of money, and that a large fortune got with a wife might come in very handy for the projects of a dethroned Dictator. 'And men are all so vain, my dear,' remarked one to another. 'Mr. Ericson doesn't look vain,' the other said meditatively. 'They are all alike, my dear,' rejoined the one. And so the matter was settled—or left unsettled.

Meanwhile the Dictator went home, and began to look over maps and charts of Gloria. He buried himself in some plans of street improvement, including a new and splendid opera house, of which he had actually laid the foundation before the crash came.

CHAPTER VII

THE PRINCE AND CLAUDIO

WHY did the Dictator bury himself in his maps and his plans and his improvements in the street architecture of a city which in all probability he was never to see more?

For one reason. Because his mind was on something else to-night, and he did not feel as if he were acting with full fidelity to the cause of Gloria if he allowed any subject to come even for an hour too directly between him and that. Little as he permitted himself to put on the airs of a patriot and philanthropist—much as he would have hated to exhibit himself or be regarded as a professional patriot, yet the devotion to that cause which he had himself created—the cause of a regene-

rated Gloria—was deep down in his very
heart. Gloria and her future were his day-
dream—his idol, his hobby, or his craze, if
you like; he had long been possessed by the
thought of a redeemed and regenerated Gloria.
To-night his mind had been thrown for a
moment off the track—and it was therefore
that he pulled out his maps and was endeavouring to get on to the track again.

But he could not help thinking of Helena
Langley. The girl embarrassed him—bewildered him. Her upturned eyes came between
him and his maps. Her frank homage was
just like that of a child. Yet she was not a
child, but a remarkably clever and brilliant
young woman, and he did not know whether
he ought to accept her homage. He was, for
all his strange career, somewhat conservative
in his notions about women. He thought that
there ought to be a sweet reserve about them
always. He rather liked the pedestal theory

about woman. The approaches and the devotion, he thought, ought to come from the man
always. In the case of Helena Langley, it
never occurred to him to think that her devotion was anything different from the devotion
of Hamilton ; but then a young man who is
one's secretary is quite free to show his devotion, while a young woman who is not one's
secretary is not free to show her devotion.
Ericson kept asking himself whether Sir
Rupert would not feel vexed when he heard
of the way in which his dear spoiled child
had been going on—as he probably would
from herself—for she evidently had not the
faintest notion of concealment. On the other
hand, what could Ericson do ? Give Helena
Langley an exposition of his theories concerning proper behaviour in unmarried
womanhood ? Why, how absurd and priggish
and offensive such a course of action would
be ! The girl would either break into

laughter at him or feel herself offended by his
attempt to lecture her. And who or what
had given him any right to lecture her?
What, after all, had she done? Sat on a footstool beside the chair of a public man whose
cause she sympathised with, and who was
quite old enough—or nearly so, at all events
—to be her father. Up to this time Ericson
was rather inclined to press the 'old enough
to be her father,' and to leave out the 'nearly
so.' Then, again, he reminded himself that
social ways and manners had very much
changed in London during his absence, and
that girls were allowed, and even encouraged,
to do all manner of things now which would
have been thought tomboyish, or even im-
proper, in his younger days. Why, he had
glanced at scores of leading articles and essays
written to prove that the London girl of the
close of the century was free to do things
which would have brought the deepest and

most comprehensive blush to the cheeks of the meek and modest maidens of a former generation.

Yes—but for all this change of manners it was certain that he had himself heard comments made on the impulsive unconventionality of Miss Langley. The comments were sometimes generous, sympathetic, and perhaps a little pitying—and of course they were sometimes ill-natured and spiteful. But, whatever their tone, they were all tuned to the one key—that Miss Langley was impulsively unconventional.

The Dictator was inclined to resent the intrusion of a woman into his thoughts. For years he had been in the habit of regarding women as trees walking. He had had a love disappointment early in life. His true love had proved a false true love, and he had taken it very seriously—taken it quite to heart. He was not enough of a modern London man to recognise the fact that something of the

kind happens to a good many people, and that
there are still a great many girls left to choose
from. He ought to have made nothing of it,
and consoled himself easily, but he did not.
So he had lost his ideal of womanhood, and
went through the world like one deprived of
a sense. The man is, on the whole, happiest
whose true love dies early, and leaves him with
an ideal of womanhood which never can
change. He is, if he be at all a true man,
thenceforth as one who walks under the
guidance of an angel. But Ericson's mind
was put out by the failure of his ideal. Hap-
pily he was a strong man by nature, with deep
impassioned longings and profound convie-
tions; and going on through life in his lonely,
overcrowded way, he soon became absorbed
in the entrancing egotism of devotion to a
great cause. He began to see all things in
life first as they bore on the regeneration of
Gloria—now as they bore on his restoration to

Gloria. So he had been forgetting all about women, except as ornaments of society, and occasionally as useful mechanisms in politics.

The memory of his false true love had long faded. He did not now particularly regret that she had been false. He did not regret it even for her own sake—for he knew that she has got on very well in life—had married a rich man—held a good position in society, and apparently had all her desires gratified. It was probable—it was almost certain—that he should meet her in London this season—and he felt no interest or curiosity about the meeting—did not even trouble himself by wondering whether she had been following his career with eyes in which old memories gleamed. But after her he had done no love-making and felt inclined for no romance. His ideal, as has been said, was gone—and he did not care for women without an ideal to pursue.

Every night, however late, when the Dictator had got back to his rooms Hamilton came to see him, and they read over letters and talked over the doings of the next day. Hamilton came this night in the usual course of things and Ericson was delighted to see him. He was sick of trying to study the street improvements of the metropolis of Gloria, and he was vexed at the intrusion of Helena Langley into his mind—for he did not suspect in the least that she had yet made any intrusion into his heart.

'Well, Hamilton, I hope you have been enjoying yourself?'

'Yes, Excellency—fairly enough. Do you know I had a long talk with Sir Rupert Langley about you?'

'Aye, aye. What does Sir Rupert say about me?'

'Well,' he says, Hamilton began distress-

edly, ' that you had better give up all notions
of Gloria and go in for English politics.'

The Dictator laughed; and at the same
time felt a little touched.   He could not help
remembering the declaration of his life's
policy he had just been making to Sir Rupert
Langley's daughter.

' What on earth do I know about English
politics ? '

' Oh, well; of course you could get it all
up easily enough, so far as that goes.'

' But doesn't Sir Rupert see that, so far as
I understand things at all, I should be in the
party opposed to him ? '

' Yes, he says that; but he doesn't seem
to mind.   He thinks you would find a field in
English politics; and he says the life of the
House of Commons is the life to which the
ambition of every true Englishman ought to
turn—and, you know—all that sort of thing.'

'And does he think that I have forgotten Gloria?'

'No ; but he has a theory about all South American States. He thinks they are all rotten, and that sort of thing. He insists that you are thrown away on Gloria.'

'Fancy a man being thrown away upon a country,' the Dictator said, with a smile. 'I have often heard and read of a country being thrown away upon a man, but never yet of a man being thrown away upon a country. I should not have wondered at such an opinion from an ordinary Englishman, who has no idea of a place the size of Gloria, where we could stow away England, France, and Germany in a little unnoticed corner. But Sir Rupert—who has been there! Give us out the cigars, Hamilton—and ring for some drinks.'

Hamilton brought out the cigars, and rang the bell.

'Well—anyhow—I have told you,' he said hesitatingly.

'So you have, boy, with your usual indomitable honesty. For I know what you think about all this.'

'Of course you do.'

'You don't want to give up Gloria?'

'Give up Gloria? Never—while grass grows and water runs!'

'Well, then, we need not say any more about that. Tell me, though, where was all this? At Lady Seagraves'?'

'No; it was at Sir Rupert's own house.'

'Oh, yes, I forgot; you were dining there?'

'Yes; I was dining there.'

'This was after dinner?'

'Yes; there were very few men there, and he talked all this to me in a confidential sort of way. Tell me, Excellency; what do you think of his daughter?'

The Dictator almost started. If the question had come out of his own inner consciousness it could not have illustrated more clearly the problem which was perplexing his heart.

'Why, Hamilton, I have not seen very much of her, and I don't profess to be much of a judge of young ladies. Why on earth do you want my opinion? What is your own opinion of her?'

'I think she is very beautiful.'

'So do I.'

'And awfully clever.'

'Right again—so do I.'

'And singularly attractive, don't you think?'

'Yes; very attractive indeed. But you know, my boy, that the attractions of young women have now little more than a purely historical interest for me. Still, I am quite prepared to go as far with you as to admit that Miss Langley is a most attractive young woman.'

'She thinks ever so much of *you*,' Hamilton said dogmatically.

'She has great sympathy with our cause,' the Dictator said.

'She would do anything *you* asked her to do.'

'My boy, I don't want to ask her to do anything.'

'Excellency, I want you to advise her to do something—for *me*.'

'For you, Hamilton? Is that the way?' The Dictator asked the question with a tone of infinite sympathy, and he stood up as if he were about to give some important order. Hamilton, on the other hand, collapsed into a chair.

'That is the way, Excellency.'

'You are in love with this child?'

'I am madly in love with this child, if you call her so.'

Ericson made some strides up and down the room, with his hands behind him. Then he suddenly stopped.

'Is this quite a serious business?' he asked, in a low, soft voice.

'Terribly serious for me, Excellency, if things don't turn out right. I have been hit very hard.'

The Dictator smiled.

'We get over such things,' he said.

'But I don't want to get over this; I don't mean to get over it.'

'Well,' Ericson said good-humouredly, and with quite recovered composure, 'it may not be necessary for you to get over it. Does the young lady want you to get over it?'

'I haven't ventured to ask her yet.'

'What do you mean to ask her?'

'Well, of course—if she will—have me.'

'Yes, naturally. But I mean when——'

'When do I mean to ask her?'

'No; when do you propose to marry her?'

'Well, of course, when we have settled ourselves again in Gloria, and .all is right there. You don't fancy I would do anything before we have made that all right?'

'But all that is a little vague,' the Dictator said; 'the time is somewhat indefinite. One does not quite know what the young lady might say.'

'She is just as enthusiastic about Gloria as I am, or as you are.'

'Yes, but her father. Have you said anything to him about this?'

'Not a word. I waited until I could talk of it to you, and get your promise to help me.'

'Of course I'll help you, if I can. But tell

me, how can I? What do you want me to
do? Shall I speak to Sir Rupert?'

'If you would speak to him after, I
should be awfully glad. But I don't so much
mind about him just yet; I want you to
speak to her!'

'To Miss Langley? To ask her to marry
you?'

'That's about what it comes to,' Hamilton
said courageously.

'But, my dear love-sick youth, would you
not much rather woo and win the girl for
yourself?'

'What I am afraid of,' Hamilton said
gravely, 'is that she would pretend not to take
me seriously. She would laugh and turn me
into ridicule, and try to make fun of the
whole thing. But if you tell her that it is
positively serious and a business of life and
death with me, then she will believe you, and
she *must* take it seriously and give you a

serious answer, or at least promise to give me a serious answer.'

'This is the oddest way of love-making, Hamilton.'

'I don't know,' Hamilton said ; 'we have Shakespeare's authority for it, haven't we? Didn't Don Pedro arrange for Claudio and Hero?'

'Well, a very good precedent,' Ericson said with a smile. 'Tell me about this to-morrow. Think over it and sleep over it in the meantime, and if you still think that you are willing to make your proposals through the medium of an envoy, then trust me, Hamilton, your envoy will do all he can to win for you your heart's desire.'

'I don't know how to thank you,' Hamilton exclaimed fervently.

'Don't try. I hate thanks. If they are sincere they tell their tale without words. I know you—everything about you is sincere.'

Hamilton's eyes glistened with joy and gratitude. He would have liked to seize his chief's hand and press it to his lips; but he forbore. The Dictator was not an effusive man, and effusiveness did not flourish in his presence. Hamilton confined his gratitude to looks and thoughts and to the dropping of the subject for the present.

'I have been pottering over these maps and plans,' the Dictator said.

'I am so glad,' Hamilton exclaimed, ' to find that your heart is still wholly absorbed in the improvement of Gloria.'

The Dictator remained for a few moments silent and apparently buried in thought. He was not thinking perhaps altogether of the projected improvements in the capital of Gloria. Hamilton had often seen him in those sudden and silent, but not sullen moods, and was always careful not to disturb him by asking any question or making any remark.

The Dictator had been sitting in a chair and pulling the ends of his moustache. At once he got up and went to where Hamilton was seated.

'Look here, Hamilton,' he said, in a tone of positive sternness, 'I want to be clear about all this. I want to help you—of course I want to help you—if you can really be helped. But, first of all, I must be certain—as far as human certainty can go—that you really know what you do want. The great curse of life is that men—and I suppose women too—I can't say—do not really know or trouble to know what they do positively want with all their strength and with all their soul. The man who positively knows what he does want and sticks to it has got it already. Tell me, do you really want to marry this young woman?'

'I do—with all my soul and with all my strength!'

'But have you thought about it—have you turned it over in your mind—have you come down from your high horse and looked at yourself, as the old joke puts it?'

'It's no joke for me,' Hamilton said dolefully.

'No, no, boy; I didn't mean that it was. But I mean, have you really looked at yourself and her? Have you thought whether she could make you happy?—have you thought whether you could make her happy? What do you know about her? What do you know about the kind of life which she lives? How do you know whether she could do without that kind of life—whether she could live any other kind of life? She is a London Society girl, she rides in the Row at a certain hour, she goes out to dinner-parties and to balls, she dances until all hours in the morning, she goes abroad to the regular place at the regular time, she spends a certain part of the winter visiting at the regulation country houses. Are you prepared to live that sort of life— or are you prepared to bear the responsibility of taking her out of it? Are you prepared to take the butterfly to live in the camp?'

'She isn't a butterfly——'

'No, no; never mind my bad metaphor. But she has been brought up in a kind of life which is second nature to her. Are you prepared to live that life with her? Are you sure—are you quite, quite sure—that she would be willing, after the first romantic outburst, to put up with a totally different life for the sake of you?'

'Excellency,' Hamilton said, smiling somewhat sadly, 'you certainly do your best to take the conceit out of a young man.'

'My boy, I don't think you have any self-conceit, but you may have a good deal of self-forgetfulness. Now I want you to call a halt and remember yourself. In this business of yours—supposing it comes to what you would consider at the moment a success——'

'At the moment?' Hamilton pleaded, in pained remonstrance.

'At the moment—yes. Supposing the thing ends successfully for you, one plan of life or other must necessarily be sacrificed— yours or hers. Which is it going to be? Don't make too much of her present enthusiasm. Which is it going to be?'

'I don't believe there will be any sacrifice needed,' Hamilton said, in an impassioned tone. 'I told you she loves Gloria as well as you or I could do.'

The Dictator shook his head and smiled pityingly.

'But if there is to be any sacrifice of any life,' Hamilton said, driven on perhaps by his chief's pitying smile, 'it shan't he hers. No, if she will have me after we have got back to Gloria, I'll live with her in London

every season and ride with her in the Row
every morning and afternoon, and take her,
by Jove! to all the dinners and balls she
cares about, and she shall have her heart's
desire, whatever it be.'

The Dictator's face was crossed by some
shadows. Pity was there and sympathy
was there—and a certain melancholy pleasure,
and, it may be, a certain disappointment.
He pulled himself together very quickly,
and was cool, genial, and composed, according to his usual way.

'All right, my boy,' he said, 'this is
genuine love at all events, however it may
turn out. You have answered my question
fairly and fully. I see now that you do
know what you want. That is one great
point, anyhow. I will do my very best to
get for you what you want. If it only rested
with me, Hamilton!' There was a positive
note of tenderness in his voice as he spoke

these words; and yet there was a kind of forlorn feeling in his heart as if the friend of his heart was leaving him. He felt a little as the brother Vult in Richter's exquisite and forgotten novel might have felt when he was sounding on his flute that final morning, and going out on his cold way never to see his brother again. The brother Walt heard the soft, sweet notes, and smiled tranquilly, believing that his brother was merely going on a kindly errand to help him, Walt, to happiness. But the flute-player felt that, come what might, they were, in fact, to be parted for ever.

CHAPTER VIII

' I WONDER WHY ? '

THE Dictator had had a good deal to do
with marrying and giving in marriage in the
Republic of Gloria. One of the social and
moral reforms he had endeavoured to bring
about was that which should secure to young
people the right of being consulted as to their
own inclinations before they were formally
and finally consigned to wedlock.   The
ordinary practice in Gloria was very much
like that which prevails in certain Indian
tribes—the family on either side arranged for
the young man and the maiden, made it a
matter of market bargain, settled it by com-
promise of price or otherwise, and then
brought the pair together and married them.

Ericson set his face against such a system, and tried to get a chance for the young people. He carried his influence so far that the parents on both sides among the official classes in the capital consulted him generally before taking any step, and then he frankly undertook the mediator's part, and found out whether the young woman liked the young man or not—whether she liked someone better or not. He had a sweet and kindly way with him which usually made both the youths and the maidens confidential—and he learned many a quiet heart-secret; and where he found that a suggested marriage would really not do, he told the parents as much, and they generally yielded to his influence and his authority. He had made happy many a pair of young lovers who, without his beneficent intervention, would have been doomed to 'spoil two houses,' as the old saying puts it.

Therefore, he did not feel much put out at the mere idea of intervening in another man's love affairs, or even the idea of carrying a proposal of marriage from another man.

Yet the Dictator was in somewhat thoughtful mood as he drove to Sir Rupert Langley's. He had taken much interest in Helena Langley. She had an influence over him which he told himself was only the influence of a clever child—told himself of this again and again. Yet there was a curious feeling of unfitness or dissatisfaction with the part he was going to play. Of course, he would do his very best for Hamilton. There was no man in the world for whom he cared half so much as he did for Hamilton. No—that is not putting it strongly enough—there was now no man in the world for whom he really cared but Hamilton. The Dictator's affections were curiously narrowed. He had almost no

friends whom he really loved but Hamilton—
and acquaintances were to him just all the
same, one as good as another, and no better.
He was a philanthropist by temperament, or
nature, or nerve, or something ; but while he
would have risked his life for almost any man,
and for any woman or child, he did not care
in the least for social intercourse with men,
women, and children in general.   He could
not talk to a child—children were a trouble
to him, because he did not know what to say
to them.   Perhaps this was one reason why
he was attracted by Helena Langley ; she
seemed so like the ideal child to whom one
can talk.   Then came up the thought in his
mind—must he lose Hamilton if Miss Langley
should consent to take him as her husband ?
Of course, Hamilton had declared that he
would never marry until the Dictator and he
had won back Gloria ; but how long would
that resolve last if Helena were to answer, Yes

—and Now? The Dictator felt lonely as his cab stopped at Sir Rupert Langley's door.

'Is Miss Langley at home?'

Yes, Miss Langley was at home. Of course, the Dictator knew that she would be, and yet in his heart he could almost have wished to hear that she was out. There is a mood of mind in which one likes any postponement. But the duty of friendship had to be done—and the Dictator was sorry for everybody.

The Dictator was met in the hall by the footman, and also by To-to. To-to was Helena's black poodle. The black poodle took to all Helena's friends very readily. Whom she liked, he liked. He had his ways, like his mistress—and he at once allowed Ericson to understand not only that Helena was at home, but that Helena was sitting just then in her own room, where she habitually received her friends. The footman told

the Dictator that Miss Langley was at home
—To-to told him what the footman could not
have ventured to do, that she was waiting for
him in her own drawing-room, and ready to
receive him.

Now, how did To-to contrive to tell him
that ?

Very easily, in truth. To-to had a keen,
healthy curiosity. He was always anxious to
know what was going on. The moment he
heard the bell ring at the great door, he
wanted to know who was coming in, and he
ran dowr the stairs and stood in the hall to
find out. When the door was opened, and
the visitor appeared, To-to instantly made up
his mind. If it was an unfamiliar figure, To-to
considered it an introduction in which he had
no manner of interest, and, without waiting
one second, he scampered back to rejoin his
mistress, and try to explain to her that
there was some very uninteresting man or

woman coming to call on her. But if it was somebody he knew, and whom he knew that his mistress knew, then there were two courses open to him. If Helena was not in her sitting-room, To-to welcomed the visitor in the most friendly and hospitable way, and then fell into the background, and took no further notice, but ranged the premises carelessly and on his own account. If, however, his mistress were in her drawing-room, then To-to invariably preceded the visitor up the stairs, going in front even of the footman, and ushered the new-comer into my lady's chamber. The process of reasoning on To-to's part must have been somewhat after this fashion. 'My business is to announce my lady's friends, the people whom I, with my exquisite intelligence, know to be people whom she wants to see. If I know that she is in her drawing-room ready to see them, then, of course, it is my duty and my pleasure to go before and announce them. But if I know, having just been there, that she is not yet there, then I have no function to perform. It is the business of some other creature—her maid very likely—to receive the news from the footman that someone is waiting to see her. That is a complex process with which I have nothing to do.' The favoured visitor, therefore—the visitor, that is to say, whom To-to favoured, believing him or her to be favoured by To-to's mistress—had to pass through what may be called two portals, or ordeals. First, he had to ask of the servant whether Miss Langley was at home. Being informed that she was at home, then it depended on To-to to let the visitor know whether Miss Langley was actually in her drawing-room waiting to receive him, or whether he was to be shown into the drawing-room and told that Miss Langley would be duly informed of his presence, and asked if he would be good enough to take a chair and wait for a moment. Never was To-to known to make the slightest mistake about the actual condition of things. Never had he run up in advance of the Dictator when his mistress was not seated in her drawing-room ready to receive her visitor. Never had he remained lingering in the hall and the passages when Miss Langley was in her room, and prepared for the reception. Evidently, To-to regarded himself as Helena's special functionary. The other attendants and followers—footmen, maids, and such like—might be allowed the privilege of saying whether Miss Langley was or was not at home to receive visitors; but the special and quite peculiar function of To-to was to make it clear whether Miss Langley was or was not at that very moment waiting in her own particular drawing-room to welcome them.

So the Dictator, who had not much time

to spare, being pressed with various affairs to attend to, was much pleased to find that To-to not merely welcomed him when the door was opened—a welcome which the Dictator would have expected from To-to's undisguised regard and even patronage—but that To-to briskly ran up the stairs in advance of the footman, and ran before him in through the drawing-room door when the footman had opened it. The Dictator loved the dog because of the creature's friendship for him and love for its mistress. The Dictator did not know how much he loved the dog because the dog was devoted to Helena Langley. On the stairs, as he went up, a sudden pang passed through the Dictator's heart. It might, perhaps, have brought him even clearer warning than it did. 'If I succeed in my mission'—it might have told him—'what is to become of *me*?' But, although the shot of pain did pass through him, he did not give it time to explain itself.

Helena was seated on a sofa. The moment she heard his name announced she jumped up and ran to meet him.

'I ought to have gone beyond the threshold,' she said, blushing, 'to meet my king.'

'So kind of you,' he said, rather stiffly, 'to stay in for me. You have so many engagements.'

'As if I would not give up any engagement to please you! And the very first time you expressed any wish to see me!'

'Well, I have come to talk to you about something very serious.'

She looked up amazed, her bright eyes broadening with wonder.

'Something that concerns the happiness of yourself, perhaps—of another person certainly.'

She drooped her eyes now, and her colour deepened and her breath came quickly.

The Dictator went to the point at once.

'I am bad at prefaces,' he said. 'I come to speak to you on behalf of my dear young friend and comrade, Ernest Hamilton.'

'Oh!' She drew herself up and looked almost defiantly at him.

'Yes; he asked me to come and see you.'

'What have I to do with Mr. Hamilton?'

'That you must teach me,' said Ericson, smiling rather sadly, and quoting from 'Hamlet.'

'I can teach you that very quickly—Nothing.'

'But you have not heard what I was going to say.'

'No. Well, you were quoting from Shakespeare—let me quote too. "Had I three ears I'd hear thee."' She drew herself back into her sofa. They were seated on the sofa side by side. He was leaning forward—she had drawn back. She was waiting in a sort of dogged silence.

'Hamilton is one of the noblest creatures I ever knew. He is my very dearest friend.'

A shade came over her face, and she shrugged her shoulders.

'I mean amongst men. I was not thinking of you.'

'No,' she answered, 'I am quite sure you were not thinking of me.'

She perversely pretended to misunderstand his meaning. He hardly noticed her words. 'Please go on,' she said, 'and tell me about Mr. Hamilton.'

'He is in love with you,' the Dictator said in a soft low voice, and as if he envied the man about whom that tale could be told.

'Oh!' she exclaimed impatiently, turning on the sofa as if in pain, 'I am sick of all this love-making! Why can't a young man like one without making an idiot of himself and falling in love with one? Why can't we let each other be happy all in our own way? It is all so horribly mechanical! You meet a man two or three times, and you dance with him, and you talk with him, and perhaps you like him—perhaps you like him ever so much —and then in a moment he spoils the whole thing by throwing his ridiculous offer of marriage right in your face! Why on earth should I marry Mr. Hamilton?'

'Don't take it too lightly, dear young lady —I know Hamilton to the very depth of his nature. This is a serious thing with him— he is not like the commonplace young masher of London Society; when he feels, he feels deeply—I know what has been his personal devotion to myself.'

'Then why does he not keep to that devotion? Why does he desert his post? What does he want of me? What do I want of him? I liked him chiefly because he was devoted to you—and now he turns right round and wants to be devoted to me! Tell

him from me that he was much better
employed with his former devotion—tell him
my advice was that he should stick to it.'

'You must give a more serious answer,'
the Dictator said gravely.

'Why didn't he come himself?' she asked
somewhat inconsequently, and going off on
another tack at once. 'I can't understand
how a man of any spirit can make love by
deputy.'

'Kings do sometimes,' the Dictator said.

Helena blushed again. Some thought was
passing through her mind which was not in
his. She had called him her king.

'Mr. Hamilton is not a king,' she said almost
angrily. She was on the point of blurting out,
'Mr. Hamilton is not *my* king,' but she recovered herself in good time. 'Even if he
were,' she went on, 'I should rather be proposed to in person as Katherine was by Henry
the Fifth.'

'You take this all too lightly,' Ericson pleaded. 'Remember that this young man's heart and his future life are wrapped up in your answer, and in *you*.'

'Tell him to come himself and get his answer,' she said with a scornful toss of her head. Something had risen up in her heart which made her unkind.

'Miss Langley,' Ericson said gravely, 'I think it would have been much better if Hamilton had come himself and made his proposal, and argued it out with you for himself. I told him so, but he would not be advised. He is too modest and fearful, although, I tell you, I have seen more than once what pluck he has in danger. Yes, I have seen how cool, how elate he can be with the bullets and the bayonets of the enemy all at work about him. But he is timid with *you*—because he loves you.'

' " He either fears his fate too much——" '
she began.

'You can't settle this thing by a quotation. I see that you are in a mood for quotations, and that shows that you are not very
serious. I shall tell you why he asked me,
and prevailed upon me, to come to you and
speak for him. There is no reason why I
should not tell you.'

' Tell me,' she said.

' I am old enough to have no hesitation in
telling a girl of your age anything.'

' Again !' Helena said. ' I do wish you
would let my age alone ! I thought we had
come to an honourable understanding to
leave my age out of the question.'

' I fear it can't well be left out of this
question. You see, what I was going to tell
you was that Hamilton asked me to break
this to you because he believes that I have
great influence with you.'

'Of course, you know you have.'

'Yes—but there was more.'

'What more?' She turned her head away.

'He is under the impression that you would do anything I asked you to do.'

'So I would, and so I will!' she exclaimed impetuously. 'If you ask me to marry Mr. Hamilton I will marry him! Yes —I *will*. If you, knowing what you do know, can wish your friend to marry me, and me to become his wife, I will accept his condescending offer! You know I do not love him—you know I never felt one moment's feeling of that kind for him—you know that I like him as I like twenty other young men —and not a bit more. You know this—at all events, you know it now when I tell you— and will you ask me to marry Mr. Hamilton now?'

'But is this all true? Is this really how you feel to him?'

'Zwischen uns sei Wahrheit,' Helena said scornfully. 'Why should I deceive you? If I loved Mr. Hamilton I could marry him, couldn't I?—seeing that he has sent you to ask me? I do not love him—I never could love him in that way. Now what do you ask me to do?'

'I am sorry for my poor young friend and comrade,' the Dictator answered sadly. 'I thought, perhaps, he might have had some reason to believe——'

'Did he tell you anything of the kind?'

'Oh, no, no; he is the last man in the world to say such a thing, or even to think it. One reason why he wished me to open the matter to you was that he feared, if he spoke to you about it himself, you would only laugh at him and refuse to give him a serious answer. He thought you would give me a serious answer.'

'What a very extraordinary and eccentric young man!'

'Indeed, he is nothing of the kind—although, of course, like myself, he has lived a good deal outside the currents of English feeling.'

'I should have thought,' she said gravely, 'that that was rather a question of the currents of common human feeling. Do the young women in Gloria like to be made love to by delegation?'

'Would it have made any difference if he had come himself?'

'No difference in the world—now or at any other time. But remember, I am a very loyal subject, and I admit the right of my King to hand me over in marriage. If you tell me to marry Mr. Hamilton, I will.'

'You are only jesting, Miss Langley, and this is not a jest.'

'I don't feel much in the mood for

jesting,' she answered. 'It would rather seem as if I had been made the subject of a jest——'

'Oh, you must not say that,' he interposed in an almost angry tone. 'You can't, and don't, think that either of him or of me.'

'No, I don't; I could not think it of *you* —and no, I could not think it of him either. But you must admit that he has acted rather oddly.'

'And I too, I suppose?'

'Oh, you—well, of course, you were naturally thinking of the interest, or, at least, the momentary wishes, of your friend.'

'Of my two friends—you are my friend. Did we not swear an eternal friendship the other night?'

'Now you *are* jesting.'

'I am not; I am profoundly serious. I thought perhaps this might be for the happiness of both.'

'Did you ever see anything in me which seemed to make such an idea likely?'

'You see, I have known you but for so short a time.'

'People who are worth knowing at all are known at once or never known,' she said promptly and very dogmatically.

'Young ladies do not wear their hearts upon their sleeves.'

'I am afraid I do sometimes—too much,' she said.

'I thought it at least possible.'

'Now you *know*. Well, are you going to ask me to marry your friend Mr. Hamilton?'

'No, indeed, Miss Langley. That would be a cruel injustice and wrong to him and to you. He must marry someone who loves him; you must marry someone whom you love. I am sorry for my poor friend—this will hurt him. But he cannot blame you,

and I cannot blame you. He has some comfort—he has Gloria to fight for some day.'

'Put it nicely—*very* nicely to him,'
Helena said, softening now that all was over.
'Tell him—won't you?—that I am ever so
fond of him; and tell him that this must not
make the least difference in our friendship.
No one shall ever know from me.'

'I will put it all as well as I can,' said the
Dictator; 'but I am afraid it must make a
difference to him. It made a difference to
me—when I was a young man of about his
age.'

'You were disappointed?' Helena asked,
in rather tremulous tone.

'More than that; I think I was deceived.
I was ever so much worse off than Hamilton,
for there was bitterness in my story, and
there can be none in his. But I have sur-
vived—as you see.'

'Is—she—still living?'

'Oh, yes; she married for money and rank, and has got both, and I believe she is perfectly happy.'

'And have you recovered—quite?'

'Quite; I fancy it must have been an unreal sort of thing altogether. My wound is quite healed—does not give me even a passing moment of pain, as very old wounds sometimes do. But I am not going to lapse into the sentimental. It was only the thought of Hamilton that brought all this up.'

'You are not sentimental?' Helena asked.

'I have not had time to be. Anyhow, no woman ever cared about me—in that way, I mean—no, not one.'

'Ah, you never can tell,' Helena said gently. He seemed to her somehow to have led a very lonely life; it came into her thoughts just then; she could not tell why. She was relieved when he rose to go, for she felt her sympathy for him beginning to be a little too strong, and she was afraid of betraying it. The interview had been a curious and a trying one for her. The Dictator left the room wondering how he could ever have been drawn into talking to a girl about the story of his lost love. 'That girl has a strange influence over me,' he thought. 'I wonder why?'

CHAPTER IX

THE PRIVATE SECRETARY

SOAME RIVERS was in some ways, and not a
few, a model private secretary for a busy
statesman. He was a gentleman by birth,
bringing-up, appearance, and manners; he
was very quick, adroit, and clever; he had a
wonderful memory, a remarkable faculty for
keeping documents and ideas in order; he
could speak French, German, Italian, and
Spanish, and conduct a correspondence in
these languages. He knew the political and
other gossip of most or all of the European
capitals, and of Washington and Cairo just
as well. He could be interviewed on behalf
of his chief, and could be trusted not to

utter one single word of which his chief could not approve. He would see any undesirable visitor, and in five minutes talk him over into the belief that it was a perfect grief to the Minister to have to forego the pleasure of seeing him in person. He was to be trusted with any secret which concerned his position, and no power on earth could surprise him into any look or gesture from which anybody could conjecture that he knew more than he professed to know. He was a younger son of very good family, and although his allowance was not large, it enabled him, as a bachelor, to live an easy and gentlemanly life. He belonged to some good clubs, and he always dined out in the season. He had nice little chambers in the St. James's Street region, and, of course, he spent the greater part of every day in Sir Rupert's house, or in the lobby of the House of Commons. It was understood that he was to be provided with a seat in Parliament at the earliest possible opportunity, not, indeed, so much for the good of the State as for the convenience of his chief, who, naturally, found it unsatisfactory to have to go out into the lobby in order to get hold of his private secretary. Rivers was devoted to his chief in his own sort of way. That way was not like the devotion of Hamilton to the Dictator; for it is very likely that, in his own secret soul, Rivers occasionally made fun of Sir Rupert, with his Quixotic ideas and his sentimentalisms, and his views of life. Rivers had no views on the subject of life or of anything else. But Hamilton himself could not be more careful of his chief's interests than was Rivers. Rivers had no beliefs and no prejudices. He was not an immoral man, but he had no prejudice in favour of morality; he was not cruel, but he had no objection to other people being as cruel as they liked, as cruel as the law would allow them to be, provided that their cruelty was not exercised on himself, or anyone he particularly cared about. He never in his life professed or felt one single impulse of what is called philanthropy. It was to him a matter of perfect indifference whether ten thousand people in some remote place did or did not perish by war, or fever, or cyclone, or inundation. Nor did he care in the least, except for occasional political purposes, about the condition of the poor in our rural villages or in the East End of London. He regarded the poor as he regarded the flies—that is, with entire indifference so long as they did not come near enough to annoy him. He did not care how they lived, or whether they lived at all. For a long time he could not bring himself to believe that Helena Langley really felt any strong interest in the poor. He could not believe that her professed zeal for their welfare was anything other than the graceful affectation of a pretty and clever girl.

But we all have our weaknesses, even the strongest of us, and Soame Rivers found, when he began to be much in companionship with Helena Langley, where the weak point was to be hit in his panoply of pride. To him love and affection and all that sort of thing were mere sentimental nonsense, encumbering a rising man, and as likely as not, if indulged in, to spoil his whole career. He had always made up his mind to the fact that, if he ever did marry, he must marry a woman with money. He would not marry at all unless he could have a house and entertain as other people in Society were in the habit of doing. As a bachelor he was all right. He could keep nice chambers; he could ride in the Row; he could have a valet; he could wear good clothes—and he was a man whom Nature had meant, and tailor recognised, for one to show

off good clothes.   But if he should ever marry
it was clear to him that he must have a house
like other people, and that he must give
dinner parties.   He did not reason this out in
his mind—he never reasoned anything out in
his mind—it was all clear and self-evident to
him.   Therefore, after a while, the question
began to arise—why should he not marry
Helena Langley?   He knew perfectly well
that if she wished to be married to him Sir
Rupert would not offer the slightest objection.
Any man whom his daughter really loved
Sir Rupert would certainly accept as a son-
in-law.   Rivers even fancied, not, perhaps,
altogether without reason, that Sir Rupert
personally would regard it as a convenient
arrangement if his daughter were to fall in
love with his secretary and get married to
him.   But above and beyond all this, Rivers,
as a practical philosopher, had broken down,
and he found himself in love with Helena

Langley. For herself, Helena never suspected it. She had grown to be very fond of Soame Rivers. He seemed to fill for her exactly the part that a good-tempered brother might have done. Indeed, not any brother, however good-natured, would have been as attentive to a sister as Rivers was to her. He had a quiet, unobtrusive way of putting his personal attentions as part of his official duty which absolutely relieved Helena's mind of any idea of lover-like consideration. At many a dinner party or evening party her father had to leave her prematurely, and go down to the House of Commons. It became to her a matter of course that in such a case Rivers was always sure to be there to put her into her carriage and see that she got safely home. There was nothing in it. He was her father's secretary—a gentleman, to be sure; a man of social position, as good as the best; but still, her father's secretary looking after

her because of his devotion to her father.
She began to like him every day more and
more for his devotion to her father. She did
not at first like his cynical ways—his trick of
making out that every great deed was really
but a small one, that every seemingly generous
and self-sacrificing action was actually inspired
by the very principle of selfishness ; that love
of the poor, sympathy with the oppressed,
were only with the better classes another
mode of amusing a weary social life. But she
soon made out a generous theory to satisfy
herself on that point.   Soame Rivers, she felt
sure, put on that panoply of cynicism only to
guard himself against the weakness of yielding
to a futile sensibility. He was very poor, she
thought. She had lordly views about money,
and she thought a man without a country-
house of his own must needs be wretchedly
poor, and she knew that Soame Rivers passed
all his holiday seasons in the country-houses

of other people. Therefore, she made out that Soame Rivers was very poor; and, of course, if he was very poor, he could not lend much practical aid to those who, in the East End or otherwise, were still poorer than he. So she assumed that he put on the mask of cynicism to hide the flushings of sensibility. She told him as much; she said she knew that his affected indifference to the interests of humanity was only a disguise put on to conceal his real feelings. At first he used to laugh at her odd, pretty conceits. After a while he came to encourage her in the idea, even while formally assuring her that there was nothing in it, and that he did not care a straw whether the poor were miserable or happy.

Chance favoured him. There were some poor people whom Helena and her father were shipping off to New Zealand. Sir Rupert, without Helena's knowledge, asked his secretary to look after them the night of their going aboard, as he could not be there himself. Helena, without consulting her father, drove down to the docks to look after her poor friends, and there she found Rivers installed in the business of protector. He did the work well—as he did every work that came to his hand. The emigrants thought him the nicest gentleman they had ever known. Helena said to him, 'Come now! I have found you out at last.' And he only said, 'Oh, nonsense! this is nothing.' But he did not more directly contradict her theory, and he did not say her father had sent him—for he knew Sir Rupert would never say that of himself.

Rivers found himself every day watching over Helena with a deepening interest and anxiety. Her talk, her companionship, were growing to be indispensable to him. He did not pay her compliments—indeed, some-

times they rather sparred at one another in a
pleasant schoolboy and schoolgirl sort of way.
But she liked his society, and felt herself
thoroughly companionable and comrade-like
with him, and she never thought of concealing
her liking. The result was that Soame
Rivers began to think it quite on the cards
that, if nothing should interpose, he might
marry Helena Langley—and that, too, before
very long. Then he should have in every
way his heart's desire.

If nothing should interpose? Yes, but
there was where the danger came in! If
nothing should interpose? But was it likely
that nothing and nobody would interpose?
The girl was well known to be a rich heiress;
she was the only child of a most distinguished
statesman; she would be very likely to have
Dukes and Marquises competing for her hand,
and where might Soame Rivers be then?
The young man sometimes thought that, if

through her unconventional and somewhat
romantic nature he could entangle her in a
love affair, he might be able to induce her to
get secretly married to him—before any of
the possible Dukes and Marquises had time
to put in a claim.   But, of course, there
would be always the danger of his turning
Sir Rupert hopelessly against him by any
trick of that kind, and he saw no use in having
the daughter on his side if he could not also
have the father.   Besides, he had a sore conviction that the girl would not do anything
to displease her father.   So he gave up the
idea of the romantic elopement, or the secret
marriage, and he reminded himself that, after
all, Helena Langley, with all her unconventional ways, was not exactly another Lydia
Languish.

Then the Dictator and Hamilton came on
the scene, and Rivers had many an unhappy
hour of it.   At first he was more alarmed

about Hamilton than about the Dictator. He could easily understand an impulsive girl's hero-worship for the Dictator, and he did not think much about it. The Dictator, he assured himself, must seem quite an elderly sort of person to a girl of Helena's age; but Hamilton was young and handsome, of good family, and undoubtedly rich. Hamilton and Helena fraternised very freely and openly in their adoration for Ericson, and Rivers thought moodily that that partnership of admiration for a third person might very well end in a partnership of still closer admiration for each other. So, although from the very first he disliked the Dictator, yet he soon began to detest Hamilton a great deal more.

His dislike of Ericson was not exclusively and altogether because of Helena's hero-worship. According to his way of thinking, all foreign adventure had something more or less vulgar in it, but that was especially objectionable in the case of an Englishman. What business had an Englishman—one who claims apparently to be an English gentleman —what business had he with a lot of South American Republicans? What did he want among such people? Why should he care about them? Why should he want to govern them? And if he did want to govern them, why did he not stay there and govern? The thing was in any case mere bravado, and melodramatic enterprise.

It was the morning after the day when the Dictator had proposed to Helena for poor Hamilton. Soame Rivers met Helena on the staircase.

'Of course,' he said, with an emphasis, ' *you* will be at luncheon to-day?'

'Why, of course?' she asked, carelessly.

'Well—your hero is coming—didn't you know?'

'I didn't know; and who is my hero?'

'Oh, come now !—the Dictator, of course.'

'*Is* he coming?' she asked, with a sudden gleam of genuine emotion flashing over her face.

'Yes; your father particularly wants him to meet Sir Lionel Rainey.'

'Oh, I didn't know. Well, yes—I shall be there, I suppose, if I feel well enough.'

'Are you not well?' Rivers asked, with a tone of somewhat artificial tenderness in his voice.

'Oh, yes, I am all right; but I might not feel quite up to the level of Sir Lionel Rainey. Only men, of course?'

'Only men.'

'Well, I shall think it over.'

'But you can't want to miss your Dictator?'

'My Dictator will probably not miss me,' the girl said in scornful tones which brought no comfort to the heart of Soame Rivers.

'You would be very sorry if he did not

miss you,' Soame Rivers said blunderingly.
Your cynical man of the world has his feelings and his angers.

'Very sorry!' Helena defiantly declared.

The Dictator came punctually at two—he
was always punctual. To-to was friendly,
but did not conduct him. He was shown at
once into the dining-room, where luncheon
was laid out. The room looked lonely to the
Dictator. Helena was not there.

'My daughter is not coming down to
luncheon,' Sir Rupert said.

'I am so sorry,' the Dictator said. 'Nothing serious, I hope?'

'Oh, no! a cold, or something like that—
she didn't tell me. She will be quite well, I
hope, to-morrow. You see how To-to keeps
her place?'

Ericson then saw that To-to was seated
resolutely on the chair which Helena usually
occupied at luncheon.

'But what is the use if she is not coming?' the Dictator suggested—not to disparage the intelligence of To-to, but only to find out, if he could, the motive of that undoubtedly sagacious animal's taking such a definite attitude.

'Well, To-to does not like the idea of anyone taking Helena's place except himself. Now, you will see; when we all settle down, and no one presumes to try for that chair, To-to will quietly drop out of it and allow the remainder of the performance to go undisturbed. He doesn't want to set up any claim to sit on the chair himself; all he wants is to assert and to protect the right of Helena to have that chair at any moment when she may choose to join us at luncheon.'

The rest of the party soon came in from various rooms and consultations. Soame Rivers was the first.

'Miss Langley not coming?' he said, with a glance at To-to.

'No,' Sir Rupert answered. 'She is a little out of sorts to-day—nothing much—but she won't come down just yet.'

'So To-to keeps her seat reserved, I see.'

The Dictator felt in his heart as if he and To-to were born to be friends.

The other guests were Lord Courtreeve and Sir Lionel Rainey, the famous Englishman who had settled himself down at the Court of the King of Siam, and taken in hand the railway and general engineering and military and financial arrangements of that monarch; and, having been somewhat hurt in an expedition against the Black Flags, was now at home, partly for rest and recovery, and partly in order to have an opportunity of enlightening his Majesty of Siam, who had a very inquiring mind, on the immediate condition of politics and housebuilding in England.

Sir Lionel said that, above all things, the King of Siam would be interested in learning something about Ericson and the condition of Gloria, for the King of Siam read everything he could get hold of about politics everywhere. Therefore, Sir Rupert had undertaken to invite the Dictator to this luncheon, and the Dictator had willingly undertaken to come. Soame Rivers had been showing Sir Lionel over the house, and explaining all its arrangements to him—for the King of Siam had thoughts of building a palace after the fashion of some first-class and up-to-date house in London. Sir Lionel was a stout man, rather above the middle height, but looking rather below it, because of his stoutness. He had a sharply turned-up dark moustache, and purpling cheeks and eyes that seemed too tightly fitted into the face for their own personal comfort.

Lord Courtreeve was a pale young man,

with a very refined and delicate face. He was
a member of the London County Council,
and was a chairman of a County Council in
his own part of the country. He was a strong
advocate of Local Option, and wore at his
courageous buttonhole the blue ribbon which
proclaimed his devotion to the cause of
temperance. He was an honoured and a
sincere member of the League of Social Purity.
He was much interested in the increase of
open spaces and recreation grounds for the
London poor. He was an unaffectedly good
young man, and if people sometimes smiled
quietly at him, they respected him all the
same. Soame Rivers had said of him that
Providence had invented him to be the chief
living argument in favour of the principle
of hereditary legislation.

Sir Lionel Rainey and Lord Courtreeve
did not get on at all. Sir Lionel had too
many odd and high-flavoured anecdotes about

life in Siam to be a congenial neighbour for
the champion of social purity. He had a way,
too, of referring everything to the lower
instincts of man, and roughly declining to
reckon in the least idea of any of man's, or
woman's, higher qualities. Therefore, the
Dictator did not take to him any more than
Lord Courtreeve did ; and Sir Rupert began
to think that his luncheon party was not well
mixed. Soame Rivers saw it too, and was
determined to get the company out of Siam.

' Do you find London society much changed
since you were here last, Sir Lionel ? ' he asked.

' Didn't come to London to study society,'
Sir Lionel answered, somewhat gruffly, for he
thought there was much more to be said
about Siam. ' I mean in that sort of way. I
want to get some notions to take back to the
King of Siam.'

'But might it not interest his Majesty to
know of any change, if there were any, in

London society during that time?' Rivers
blandly asked.

'No sir. His Majesty never was in England, and he could not be expected to take
any interest in the small and superficial
changes made in the tone or the talk of
society during a few years. You might as
well expect him to be interested in the fact
that whereas when I was here last the ladies
wore eel-skin dresses, now they wear full
skirts, and some of them, I am told, wear a
divided skirt.'

'But I thought such changes of fashion
might interest the King,' Rivers remarked
with an elaborate meekness.

'The King, sir, does not care about
divided skirts,' Sir Lionel answered, with scorn
and resentment in his voice.

'I must confess,' the Dictator said, glad
to be free of Siam, 'that I have been much
interested in observing the changes that have

been made in the life of England—I mean in the life of London—since I was living here.'

'We have all got so Republican,' Sir Rupert said sadly.

'And we all profess to be Socialists,' Soame Rivers added.

'There is much more done for the poor than ever there was before,' Lord Courtreeve pleaded.

'Because so many of the poor have got votes,' Rivers observed.

'Yes,' Sir Lionel struck in with a laugh, 'and you fellows all want to get into the House of Commons or the County Council, or some such place. By Jove! in my time a gentleman would not want to become a County Councillor.'

'I am not troubling myself about English politics,' the Dictator said. 'I do not care to vex myself about them. I should probably only end by forming opinions quite different from some of my friends here, and, as I have no mission for English political life, what would be the good of that? But I am much interested in English social life, and even in what is called Society. Now, what I want to know is how far docs society in London re-present social London, and still more, social England?'

'Not the least in the world,' Sir Rupert promptly replied.

'I am not quite so sure of that,' Soame Rivers interposed. 'I fancy most of the fellows try to take their tone from us.'

'I hope not,' the Dictator said.

'So do I,' added Sir Rupert emphatically; 'and I am quite certain they do not. What on earth do you know about it, Rivers?' he asked almost sharply.

'Why shouldn't I know all about it, if I took the trouble to find out?' Rivers answered languidly.

'Yes, yes. Of course you could,' Sir Rupert said benignly, correcting his awkward touch of anger as a painter corrects some sudden mistake in drawing. 'I didn't mean in the least to disparage your faculty of acquiring correct information on any subject. Nobody appreciates more than I do what you are capable of in that way—nobody has had so much practical experience of it. But what I mean is this—that I don't think you know a great deal of English social life outside the West End of London.'

'Is there anything of social life worth knowing to be known outside the West End of London?' Soame Rivers asked.

'Well, you see, the mere fact that you put the question shows that you can't do much to enlighten Mr. Ericson on the one point about which he asks for some enlightenment. He has been out of England for a great many years, and he finds some fault with our ways—or, at least, he asks for some explanation about them.'

'Yes, quite so. I am afraid I have forgotten the point on which Mr. Ericson desired to get information.' And Rivers smiled a bland smile without looking at Ericson. 'May I trouble you, Lord Courtreeve, for the cigarettes?'

'It was not merely a point, but a whole cresset of points—a cluster of points,' Ericson said, 'on every one of which I wished to have a tip of light. Is English social life to be judged of by the conversation and the canons of opinion which we find received in London society?'

'Certainly not,' Sir Rupert explained.

'Heaven forbid!' Lord Courtreeve added fervently.

'I don't quite understand,' said Soame Rivers.

'Well,' the Dictator explained, 'what I

mean is this. I find little or nothing prevailing in London society but cheap cynicism—the very cheapest cynicism—cynicism at a farthing a yard or thereabouts. We all admire healthy cynicism—cynicism with a great reforming and purifying purpose—the cynicism that is like a corrosive acid to an evil system ; but this West End London sham cynicism—what does that mean ? '

'I don't quite know what you mean,' Soame Rivers said.

'I mean this, wherever you go in London society—at all events, wherever I go—I notice a peculiarity that I think did not exist, at all events to such an extent, in my younger days. Everything is taken with easy ridicule. A divorce case is a joke. Marriage is a joke. Love is a joke. Patriotism is a joke. Everybody is assumed, as a matter of course, to have a selfish motive in everything. Is this the real feeling of London society, or is it only a fashion, a sham, a grimace?'

'I think it is a very natural feeling,' Soame Rivers replied, with the greatest promptitude.

'And represents the true feeling of what are called the better classes of London?'

'Why, certainly.'

'I think the thing is detestable, anyhow,' Lord Courtreeve interposed, 'and I am quite sure it does not represent the tone of English society.'

'So am I,' Sir Rupert added.

'But you must admit that it is the tone which does prevail,' the Dictator said pressingly, for he wanted very much to study this question down to its roots.

'I am afraid it is the prevailing social tone of London—I mean the West End,' Sir Rupert admitted reluctantly. 'But you know what a fashion there is in these things, as well as in others. The fashion in a woman's gown or a man's hat does not always represent the shape of a woman's body or the size of a man's head.'

' It sometimes represents the shape of the man's mind, and the size of the woman's heart,' said Rivers.

' Well, anyhow,' Sir Rupert persevered, ' we all know that a great deal of this sort of talk is talked for want of anything else to say, and because it amuses most people, and because anybody can talk cheap cynicism ; I believe that London society is healthy at the core.'

' But come now—let us understand ? ' Ericson asked ; ' how can the society be healthy at the core for which you yourself make the apology by saying that it parrots the jargon of a false and loathsome creed because it has nothing better to say, or because it hopes to be thought witty by parroting it ? Come, Sir Rupert, you won't maintain that ? '

' I will maintain,' Sir Rupert said, ' that London society is not as bad as it seems.'

' Oh, well, I have no doubt you are right in that,' the Dictator hastily replied. ' But what I think so melancholy to see is that degeneracy of social life in England—I mean in London—which apes a cynicism it doesn't feel.'

' But I think it does feel it,' Rivers struck in ; ' and very naturally and justly.'

' Then you think London society is really demoralised ? ' The Dictator spoke, turning on him rather suddenly.

' I think London society is just what it has always been,' Rivers promptly answered.

' Corrupt and cynical ? '

' Well, no. I should rather say corrupt and candid.'

' If that is London society, that certainly

is not English social life,' Lord Courtreeve declared emphatically, patting the table with his hand. 'It isn't even London social life. Come down to the East End, sir——'

'Oh, indeed, by Jove! I shall do nothing of the kind!' Rivers replied, as with a shudder. 'I think, of all the humbugs of London society, slumming is about the worst.'

'I was not speaking of that,' Lord Court-reeve said, with a slight flush on his mild face. 'Perhaps I do not think very differ-ently from you about some of it—some of it —although, Heaven be praised, not about all; but what I mean and was going to say when I was interrupted'—and he looked with a cer-tain modified air of reproach at Rivers—'what I was going to say when I was interrupted,' he repeated, as if to make sure that he was not going to be interrupted this time—'was, that if you would go down to the East End with me, I could show you in one day plenty of proofs that the heart of the English people is as sound and true as ever it was——'

'Very likely,' Rivers interposed saucily. 'I never said it wasn't.'

Lord Courtreeve gaped with astonishment.

'I don't quite grasp your meaning,' he stammered.

'I never said,' Soame Rivers replied deliberately, 'that the heart of the English people was not just as sound and true now as it ever was—I dare say it is just about the same—*même jeu*, don't you know?' and he took a languid puff at his cigarette.

'Am I to be glad or sorry of your answer?' Lord Courtreeve asked, with a stare.

'How can I tell? It depends on what you want me to say.'

'Well, if you mean to praise the great

heart of the English people now, and at other times——'

'Oh dear, no; I mean nothing of the kind.'

'I say, Rivers, this is all bosh, you know,' Sir Rupert struck in.

'I think we are all shams and frauds in our set—in our class,' Rivers said, composedly; 'and we are well brought up and educated and all that, don't you know? I really can't see why some cads who clean windows, or drive omnibuses, or sell vegetables in a donkey-cart, or carry bricks up a ladder, should be any better than we. Not a bit of it—if we are bad, they are worse, you may put your money on that.'

'Well, I think I have had my answer,' the Dictator said, with a smile.

'And what is your interpretation of the Oracle's answer?' Rivers asked.

'I should have to interpret the Oracle itself before I could be clear as to the meaning of its answer,' Ericson said composedly.

Soame Rivers knew pretty well by the words and by the tone that if he did not like the Dictator, neither did the Dictator very much like him.

'You must not mind Rivers and his cynicism,' Sir Rupert said, intervening somewhat hurriedly; 'he doesn't mean half he says.'

'Or say half he means,' Rivers added.

'But, as I was telling you, about the police organisation of Siam,' Sir Lionel broke out anew. And this time the others went back without resistance to a few moments more of Siam.

END OF THE FIRST VOLUME

Spottiswoode & Co. Printers, New-street Square, London.

CHATTO & WINDUS'S
LIST OF <u>528</u> POPULAR NOVELS
BY THE BEST AUTHORS.
Picture Covers, TWO SHILLINGS each.

BY EDMOND ABOUT.
The Fellah.

BY HAMILTON AÏDE.
Carr of Carrlyon.
Confidences

BY MARY ALBERT.
Brooke Finchley's Daughter.

BY MRS. ALEXANDER.
Maid, Wife, or Widow ?
Valerie's Fate.

BY GRANT ALLEN.
Strange Stories.
Philistia.
Babylon.
The Beckoning Hand.
In All Shades.
For Maimie's Sake.
The Devil's Die.
This Mortal Coil.
The Tents of Shem.
The Great Taboo.
Dumaresq's Daughter.

BY EDWIN LESTER ARNOLD.
Phra the Phœnician.

BY FRANK BARRTT.
A Recoiling Vengeance.
For Love and Honour.
John Ford ; & His Helpmate.
Honest Davie.
A Prodigal's Progress.
Folly Morrison.
Lieutenant Barnabas.
Found Guilty.
Fettered for Life.
Between Life and Death.
The Sin of Olga Zassoulich.
Little Lady Linton.

BY SHELSLEY BEAUCHAMP.
Grantley Grange.

BY BESANT AND RICE.
Ready-Money Mortiboy.
With Harp and Crown.
This Son of Vulcan.
My Little Girl.
The Case of Mr. Lucraft.
The Golden Butterfly.
By Celia's Arbour.
The Monks of Thelema.
'Twas in Trafalgar's Bay.
The Seamy Side.
The Ten Years' Tenant.
The Chaplain of the Fleet.

BY WALTER BESANT.
All Sorts and Conditions of Men
The Captains' Room.
All in a Garden Fair.
Dorothy Forster.
Uncle Jack.
Children of Gibeon.
World went very well then.
Herr Paulus.
For Faith and Freedom.
To Call her Mine.
The Bell of St. Paul's.
The Holy Rose.
Armorel of Lyonesse.
St. Katherine's by the Tower.

BY AMBROSE BIERCE.
In the Midst of Life.

BY FREDERICK BOYLE.
Camp Notes.
Savage Life.
Chronicles of No-Man's Land.

BY HAROLD BRYDGES.
Uncle Sam at Home.

BY ROBERT BUCHANAN.
The Shadow of the Sword.
A Child of Nature.
God and the Man.
Annan Water.
The New Abelard.
The Martyrdom of Madeline.
Love Me for Ever.
Matt : a Story of a Caravan.
Foxglove Manor.
The Master of the Mine.
The Heir of Linne

BY HALL CAINE.
The Shadow of a Crime.
A Son of Hagar.
The Deemster.

BY COMMANDER CAMERON.
Cruise of the 'Black Prince.'

BY MRS. LOVETT CAMERON.
Deceivers Ever.
Juliet's Guardian.

BY AUSTIN CLARE.
For the Love of a Lass.

BY MRS. ARCHER CLIVE.
Paul Ferroll.
Why Paul Ferroll Killed his Wife.

BY MACLAREN COBBAN.
The Cure of Souls.

BY C. ALLSTON COLLINS.
The Bar Sinister

BY WILKIE COLLINS.
Armadale.
After Dark.
No Name.
A Rogue's Life.
Antonina.
Basil.
Hide and Seek.
The Dead Secret.
Queen of Hearts.
My Miscellanies.
The Woman in White.
The Moonstone.
Man and Wife.
Poor Miss Finch.
Miss or Mrs ?
The New Magdalen.
The Frozen Deep
The Law and the Lady.
The Two Destinies.
The Haunted Hotel.
The Fallen Leaves.
Jezebel's Daughter.
The Black Robe.
Heart and Science.
'I say No.'
The Evil Genius.
Little Novels.
The Legacy of Cain.
Blind Love.

BY MORTIMER COLLINS.
Sweet Anne Page.
Transmigration.
From Midnight to Midnight.
A Fight with Fortune.

MORT. AND FRANCES COLLINS.
Sweet and Twenty.
Frances.
The Village Comedy.
You Play Me False.
Blacksmith and Scholar.

BY M. J. COLQUHOUN.
Every Inch a Soldier.

BY BUTTON COOK.
Leo.
Paul Foster's Daughter.

London : CHATTO & WINDUS, 214 Piccadilly, W.

BY C. EGBERT CRADDOCK.
The Prophet of the Great Smoky Mountains.

BY MATT CRIM.
Adventures of a Fair Rebel.

BY B. M. CROKER.
Pretty Miss Neville.
Proper Pride.
A Bird of Passage.
Diana Barrington.

BY WILLIAM CYPLES.
Hearts of Gold.

BY ALPHONSE DAUDET.
The Evangelist.

BY ERASMUS DAWSON.
The Fountain of Youth.

BY JAMES DE MILLE.
A Castle in Spain.

BY J. LEITH DERWENT.
Our Lady of Tears.
Circe's Lovers.

BY CHARLES DICKENS.
Sketches by Boz.
The Pickwick Papers.
Oliver Twist.
Nicholas Nickleby.

BY DICK DONOVAN.
The Man-hunter.
Caught at Last!
Tracked and Taken.
Who Poisoned Hetty Duncan?
The Man from Manchester.
A Detective's Triumphs.
In the Grip of the Law.
Wanted!
From Information Received.
Tracked to Doom.

BY MRS. ANNIE EDWARDES.
A Point of Honour.
Archie Lovell.

BY M. BETHAM-EDWARDS.
Felicia.
Kitty.

BY EDWARD EGGLESTON.
Roxy.

BY G. MANVILLE FENN.
The New Mistress.

BY PERCY FITZGERALD.
Bella Donna.
Polly.
The Second Mrs. Tillotson.
Seventy-five Brooke Street.
Never Forgotten.
The Lady of Brantome.
Fatal Zero.

BY PERCY FITZGERALD, &c.
Strange Secrets.

BY ALBANY DE FONBLANQUE.
Filthy Lucre.

BY R. E. FRANCILLON.
Olympia.
One by One.
Queen Cophetua.
A Real Queen.
King or Knave.
Romances of the Law.

BY HAROLD FREDERIC.
Seth's Brother's Wife.
The Lawton Girl.

PREFACED BY BARTLE FRERE.
Pandurang Hâri.

BY HAIN FRISWELL.
One of Two

BY EDWARD BARRETT.
The Capel Girls.

BY CHARLES GIBBON.
Robin Gray.
For Lack of Gold.
What will the World Say?
In Honour Bound.
In Love and War.
For the King
Queen of the Meadow.
In Pastures Green.
The Flower of the Forest.
A Heart's Problem.
The Braes of Yarrow.
The Golden Shaft.
Of High Degree.
The Dead Heart.
By Mead and Stream.
Heart's Delight.
Fancy Free.
Loving a Dream.
A Hard Knot.
Blood-Money.

BY WILLIAM GILBERT.
James Duke.
Dr. Austin's Guests.
The Wizard of the Mountain.

BY ERNEST GLANVILLE.
The Lost Heiress.
The Fossicker.

BY REV. S. BARING GOULD.
Eve.
Red Spider.

BY HENRY GREVILLE.
A Noble Woman.
Nikanor.

BY JOHN HABBERTON.
Brueton's Bayou.
Country Luck.

BY ANDREW HALLIDAY.
Every-Day Papers.

BY LADY DUFFUS HARDY.
Paul Wynter's Sacrifice.

BY THOMAS HARDY.
Under the Greenwood Tree

BY BRET HARTE.
An Heiress of Red Dog
The Luck of Roaring Camp
Californian Stories.
Gabriel Conroy.
Flip.
Maruja.
A Phyllis of the Sierras.

BY J. BERWICK HARWOOD.
The Tenth Earl.

BY JULIAN HAWTHORNE.
Garth.
Ellice Quentin.
Sebastian Strome.
Dust.
Fortune's Fool.
Beatrix Randolph.
Miss Cadogna.
Love—or a Name.
David Poindexter's Disappearance.
The Spectre of the Camera

BY SIR ARTHUR HELPS.
Ivan de Biron.

BY HENRY HERMAN.
A Leading Lady.

BY MRS. CASHEL HOEY.
The Lover's Creed.

BY MRS. GEORGE HOOPER.
The House of Raby.

BY TIGHE HOPKINS.
'Twixt Love and Duty.

BY MRS. HUNGERFORD.
In Durance Vile.
A Maiden all Forlorn.
A Mental Struggle.
Marvel.
A Modern Circe.

BY MRS. ALFRED HUNT.
Thornicroft's Model.
The Leaden Casket.
Self-Condemned.
That Other Person.

BY JEAN INGELOW.
Fated to be Free.

BY HARRIETT JAY.
The Dark Colleen.
The Queen of Connaught.

BY MARK KERSHAW.
Colonial Facts and Fictio

London: CHATTO & WINDUS, 214 *Piccadilly, W.*

TWO-SHILLING POPULAR NOVELS.

BY R. ASHE KING.
A Drawn Game.
'The Wearing of the Green.'
Passion's Slave.
Bell Barry.

BY JOHN LEYS.
The Lindsays.

BY E. LYNN LINTON.
Patricia Kemball.
Atonement of Leam Dundas.
The World Well Lost.
Under which Lord?
With a Silken Thread.
The Rebel of the Family.
'My Love!'
Ione.
Paston Carew.
Sowing the Wind.

BY HENRY W. LUCY.
Gideon Fleyce.

BY JUSTIN McCARTHY.
Dear Lady Disdain.
The Waterdale Neighbours.
My Enemy's Daughter.
A Fair Saxon.
Linley Rochford.
Miss Misanthrope.
Donna Quixote.
The Comet of a Season.
Maid of Athens.
Camiola: a Girl with Fortune.

BY HUGH MacCOLL.
Mr. Stranger's Sealed Packet.

BY MRS. MACDONELL.
Quaker Cousins.

BY KATHARINE S. MACQUOID.
The Evil Eye.
Lost Rose.

BY W. H. MALLOCK.
The New Republic.

BY FLORENCE MARRYAT.
Fighting the Air.
Written in Fire.
A Harvest of Wild Oats.
Open! Sesame!

BY J. MASTERMAN.
Half-a-dozen Daughters.

BY BRANDER MATTHEWS.
A Secret of the Sea.

BY LEONARD MERRICK.
The Man who was Good.

BY JEAN MIDDLEMASS.
Touch and Go.
Mr. Dorillion.

BY MRS. MOLESWORTH.
Hathercourt Rectory.

BY J. E. MUDDOCK.
Stories Weird and Wonderful.
The Dead Man's Secret.
From the Bosom of the Deep.

BY D. CHRISTIE MURRAY.
A Life's Atonement.
Joseph's Coat.
Val Strange.
A Model Father.
Coals of Fire.
Hearts.
By the Gate of the Sea.
The Way of the World.
A Bit of Human Nature.
First Person Singular.
Cynic Fortune.
Old Blazer's Hero.

BY D. CHRISTIE MURRAY AND HENRY HERMAN.
One Traveller Returns.
Paul Jones's Alias.
The Bishops' Bible.

BY HENRY MURRAY.
A Game of Bluff.

BY HUME NISBET.
'Bail Up!'
Dr. Bernard St. Vincent.

BY ALICE O'HANLON.
The Unforeseen.
Chance? or Fate?

BY GEORGES OHNET.
Doctor Rameau.
A Last Love.
A Weird Gift.

BY MRS. OLIPHANT.
Whiteladies.
The Primrose Path.
Greatest Heiress in England.

BY MRS. ROBERT O'RilLLY.
Phœbe's Fortunes.

BY OUIDA.
Held in Bondage.
Strathmore.
Chandos.
Under Two Flags.
Idalia.
Cecil Castlemaine's Gage.
Tricotrin.
Puck.
Folle Farine.
A Dog of Flanders.
Pascarèl.
Signa.
In a Winter City.
Ariadnê.
Moths.
Friendship.
Pipistrello.
Bimbi.
In Maremma.

BY OUIDA—continued.
Wanda.
Frescoes.
Princess Napraxine.
Two Little Wooden Shoes.
A Village Commune.
Othmar.
Guilderoy.
Ruffino.
Syrlin.
Wisdom, Wit, and Pathos.

BY MARGARET AGNES PAUL.
Gentle and Simple.

BY JAMES PAYN.
Lost Sir Massingberd.
A Perfect Treasure.
Bentinck's Tutor.
Murphy's Master.
A County Family.
At Her Mercy.
A Woman's Vengeance.
Cecil's Tryst.
The Clyffards of Clyffe.
The Family Scapegrace.
The Foster Brothers
The Best of Husbands.
Found Dead.
Walter's Word.
Halves.
Fallen Fortunes.
What He Cost Her.
Humorous Stories.
Gwendoline's Harvest.
Like Father, Like Son.
A Marine Residence.
Married Beneath Him.
Mirk Abbey.
Not Wooed, but Won.
£200 Reward.
Less Black than Painted.
By Proxy.
High Spirits.
Under One Roof.
Carlyon's Year.
A Confidential Agent.
Some Private Views.
A Grape from a Thorn.
From Exile.
Kit: a Memory.
For Cash Only
The Canon's Ward.
The Talk of the Town.
Holiday Tasks.
Glow-worm Tales.
The Mystery of Mirbridge.
The Burnt Million.
The Word and the Will.
A Prince of the Blood.
Sunny Stories.

BY C. L. PIRKIS.
Lady Lovelace.

BY EDGAR A. POE.
The Mystery of Marie Roget

London: CHATTO & WINDUS. 214 *Piccadilly.* W.

BY MRS. CAMPBELL PRAED.
The Romance of a Station
The Soul of Countess Adrian.

BY E. C. PRICE.
Valentina.
Gerald.
Mrs. Lancaster's Rival.
The Foreigners.

BY RICHARD PRYCE.
Miss Maxwell's Affections.

BY CHARLES READE.
It is Never Too Late to Mend.
Hard Cash.
Peg Woffington.
Christie Johnstone.
Griffith Gaunt.
Put Yourself in His Place.
The Double Marriage.
Love Me Little, Love Me Long.
Foul Play.
The Cloister and the Hearth.
The Course of True Love.
The Autobiography of a Thief.
A Terrible Temptation.
The Wandering Heir.
A Simpleton.
A Woman-Hater.
Singleheart and Doubleface.
Good Stories of Men &c.
The Jilt.
A Perilous Secret.
Readiana.

BY MRS. J. H. RIDDELL.
Her Mother's Darling.
The Uninhabited House.
Weird Stories.
Fairy Water.   [Party.
Prince of Wales's Garden
Mystery in Palace Gardens.
The Nun's Curse.
Idle Tales

BY F. W. ROBINSON.
Women are Strange.
The Hands of Justice.

BY JAMES RUNCIMAN.
Skippers and Shellbacks.
Grace Balmaign's Sweetheart.
Schools and Scholars.

BY W. CLARK RUSSELL.
Round the Galley Fire.
On the Fo'k'sle Head.
In the Middle Watch.
A Voyage to the Cape.
A Book for the Hammock.
Mystery of the 'Ocean Star.'
Romance of Jenny Harlowe.
An Ocean Tragedy.
My Shipmate Louise.
Alone on a Wide Wide Sea.

BY ALAN ST. AUBYN.
A Fellow of Trinity.
The Junior Dean.

BY GEORGE AUGUSTUS SALA.
Gaslight and Daylight.

BY JOHN SAUNDERS.
Guy Waterman.
The Lion in the Path.
The Two Dreamers.

BY KATHARINE SAUNDERS.
Joan Merryweather.
The High Mills.
Margaret and Elizabeth.
Sebastian.
Heart Salvage.

BY GEORGE R. SIMS.
Rogues and Vagabonds.
The Ring o' Bells.
Mary Jane's Memoirs.
Mary Jane Married.
Tales of To-day.
Dramas of Life.
Tinkletop's Crime.
Zeph: a Circus Story.

BY ARTHUR SKETCHLEY.
A Match in the Dark.

BY HAWLEY SMART.
Without Love or Licence.

BY T. W. SPEIGHT.
The Mysteries of Heron Dyke.
The Golden Hoop.
By Devious Ways.
Hoodwinked.
Back to Life.

BY R. A. STERNDALE.
The Afghan Knife.

BY R. LOUIS STEVENSON.
New Arabian Nights.
Prince Otto

BY BERTHA THOMAS.
Proud Maisie.
The Violin-player.
Cressida.

BY WALTER THORNBURY.
Tales for the Marines.
Old Stories Re-told.

BY ANTHONY TROLLOPE.
The Way We Live Now.
Mr. Scarborough's Family.
The Golden Lion of Granpère.
The American Senator.
Frau Frohmann.
Marion Fay.
Kept in the Dark.
The Land-Leaguers.
John Caldigate.

BY FRANCES E. TROLLOPE
Anne Furness.
Mabel's Progress.
Like Ships upon the Sea.

BY T. ADOLPHUS TROLLOP
Diamond Cut Diamond.

BY J. T. TROWBRIDGE.
Farnell's Folly

BY IVAN TURGENIEFF, &c
Stories from Foreign Nov

BY MARK TWAIN.
Tom Sawyer.
A Tramp Abroad.
The Stolen White Elephan
Pleasure Trip on Continen
The Gilded Age.
Huckleberry Finn.
Life on the Mississippi.
The Prince and the Paupe
Mark Twain's Sketches.
A Yankee at the Court
   King Arthur.

BY SARAH TYTLER.
Noblesse Oblige.
Citoyenne Jacqueline.
The Huguenot Family.
What She Came Through.
Beauty and the Beast.
The Bride's Pass.
Saint Mungo's City.
Disappeared.
Lady Bell.
Buried Diamonds.
The Blackhall Ghosts.

BY C. C. FRASER-TYLER
Mistress Judith.

BY ARTEMUS WARD.
Artemus Ward Complete.

BY MRS. F. H. WILLIAMSO
A Child Widow.

BY J. S. WINTER.
Cavalry Life.
Regimental Legends.

BY H. F. WOOD.
Passenger from Scotland Y
Englishman of the Rue C

BY LADY WOOD.
Sabina.

BY CELIA PARKER WOOLL
Rachel Armstrong.

BY EDMUND YATES.
Castaway.
The Forlorn Hope.
Land at Last.

London: CHATTO & WINDUS, 214 *Piccadilly, W.*

A List of Books

PUBLISHED BY

CHATTO & WINDUS

214, Piccadilly, London, W.

Sold by all Booksellers, or sent post-free for the published price by the Publishers.

ABOUT.—THE FELLAH: An Egyptian Novel. By EDMOND ABOUT. Translated by Sir RANDAL ROBERTS. Post 8vo, illustrated boards, **2s.**

ADAMS (W. DAVENPORT), WORKS BY.
A DICTIONARY OF THE DRAMA. Being a comprehensive Guide to the Plays, Playwrights, Players, and Playhouses of the United Kingdom and America. Crown 8vo half-bound, **12s. 6d.** [*Preparing.*
QUIPS AND QUIDDITIES. Selected by W. D. ADAMS. Post 8vo, cloth limp, **2s. 6d.**

AGONY COLUMN (THE) OF "THE TIMES," from 1800 to 1870. Edited, with an Introduction, by ALICE CLAY. Post 8vo, cloth limp, **2s. 6d.**

AIDE (HAMILTON), WORKS BY. Post 8vo, illustrated boards, **2s.** each.
CARR OF CARRLYON. | **CONFIDENCES.**

ALBERT.—BROOKE FINCHLEY'S DAUGHTER. By MARY ALBERT. Post 8vo, picture boards, **2s.**; cloth limp, **2s. 6d.**

ALDEN.—A LOST SOUL. By W. L. ALDEN. Fcap. 8vo, cl. bds., **1s. 6d.**

ALEXANDER (MRS.), NOVELS BY. Post 8vo, illustrated boards, **2s.** each.
MAID, WIFE, OR WIDOW? | **VALERIE'S FATE.**

ALLEN (F. M.).—GREEN AS GRASS. By F. M. ALLEN, Author of "Through Green Glasses." Frontispiece by J. SMYTH. Cr. 8vo, cloth ex., **3s. 6d.**

ALLEN (GRANT), WORKS BY. Crown 8vo, cloth extra, **6s.** each.
THE EVOLUTIONIST AT LARGE. | **COLIN CLOUT'S CALENDAR.**

Crown 8vo, cloth extra, **3s. 6d.** each ; post 8vo, illustrated boards, **2s.** each.
PHILISTIA.	**FOR MAIMIE'S SAKE.**	**THE TENTS OF SHEM.**
BABYLON.	**IN ALL SHADES.**	**THE GREAT TABOO.**
STRANGE STORIES.	**THE DEVIL'S DIE.**	**DUMARESQ'S DAUGHTER.**
BECKONING HAND.	**THIS MORTAL COIL.**	

Crown 8vo, cloth extra, **3s. 6d.** each.
THE DUCHESS OF POWYSLAND. | **BLOOD ROYAL.**
IVAN GREET'S MASTERPIECE, &c. With a Frontispiece. [*Shortly.*

AMERICAN LITERATURE, A LIBRARY OF, from the Earliest Settlement to the Present Time. Compiled and Edited by EDMUND CLARENCE STEDMAN and ELLEN MACKAY HUTCHINSON. Eleven Vols., royal 8vo, cloth extra, **£6 12s.**

ARCHITECTURAL STYLES, A HANDBOOK OF. By A. ROSENGARTEN. Translated by W. COLLETT-SANDARS. With 639 Illusts. Cr. 8vo, cl. ex., **7s. 6d.**

ART (THE) OF AMUSING: A Collection of Graceful Arts, GAMES, Tricks, Puzzles, and Charades. By FRANK BELLEW. 300 Illusts Cr. 8vo, cl. ex., **4s. 6d.**

ARNOLD (EDWIN LESTER), WORKS BY.
THE WONDERFUL ADVENTURES OF PHRA THE PHŒNICIAN. With Introduction by Sir EDWIN ARNOLD, and 12 Illustrations by H. M. PAGET. Crown 8vo, cloth extra, **3s. 6d.**; post 8vo, illustrated boards, **2s.**
THE CONSTABLE OF ST. NICHOLAS. Crown 8vo, cloth **3s. 6d.** *Sh ll...*

ARTEMUS WARD'S WORKS. With Portrait and Facsimile. Crown 8vo, cloth extra, **7s. 6d.**—Also a POPULAR EDITION, post 8vo, picture boards, **2s.**
THE GENIAL SHOWMAN: Life and Adventures of ARTEMUS WARD. By EDWARD P. HINGSTON. With a Frontispiece. Crown 8vo, cloth extra, **3s. 6d.**

ASHTON (JOHN), WORKS BY. Crown 8vo, cloth extra, **7s. 6d.** each.
HISTORY OF THE CHAP-BOOKS OF THE 18th CENTURY. With 334 Illusts.
SOCIAL LIFE IN THE REIGN OF QUEEN ANNE. With 85 Illustrations.
HUMOUR, WIT, AND SATIRE OF SEVENTEENTH CENTURY. With 82 Illusts.
ENGLISH CARICATURE AND SATIRE ON NAPOLEON THE FIRST. 115 Illusts.
MODERN STREET BALLADS. With 57 Illustrations.

BACTERIA.— A SYNOPSIS OF THE BACTERIA AND YEAST FUNGI AND ALLIED SPECIES. By W. B. GROVE, B.A. With 87 Illustrations. Crown 8vo, cloth extra, **3s. 6d.**

BARDSLEY (REV. C. W.), WORKS BY.
ENGLISH SURNAMES: Their Sources and Significations. Cr. 8vo, cloth, **7s. 6d.**
CURIOSITIES OF PURITAN NOMENCLATURE. Crown 8vo, cloth extra, **6s.**

BARING GOULD (S., Author of "John Herring," &c.), NOVELS BY. Crown 8vo, cloth extra, **3s. 6d.** each; post 8vo, illustrated boards, **2s.** each.
RED SPIDER. | EVE.

BARRETT (FRANK, Author of "Lady Biddy Fane,") NOVELS BY. Post 8vo, illustrated boards, **2s.** each; cloth, **2s. 6d.** each.
FETTERED FOR LIFE. | A PRODIGAL'S PROGRESS.
THE SIN OF OLGA ZASSOULICH. | JOHN FORD; and HIS HELPMATE.
BETWEEN LIFE AND DEATH. | A RECOILING VENGEANCE.
FOLLY MORRISON. | HONEST DAVIE. | FOUND GUILTY.
LIEUT. BARNABAS. | FOR LOVE AND HONOUR.
LITTLE LADY LINTON.

BEACONSFIELD, LORD: A Biography. By T. P. O'CONNOR, M.P. Sixth Edition, with an Introduction. Crown 8vo, cloth extra, **5s.**

BEAUCHAMP.—GRANTLEY GRANGE: A Novel. By SHELSLEY BEAUCHAMP. Post 8vo, illustrated boards, **2s.**

BEAUTIFUL PICTURES BY BRITISH ARTISTS: A Gathering of Favourites from our Picture Galleries, beautifully engraved on Steel. With Notices of the Artists by SYDNEY ARMYTAGE, M.A. Imperial 4to, cloth extra, gilt edges, **21s.**

BECHSTEIN.—AS PRETTY AS SEVEN, and other German Stories. Collected by LUDWIG BECHSTEIN. With Additional Tales by the Brothers GRIMM, and 98 Illustrations by RICHTER. Square 8vo, cloth extra, **6s. 6d.**; gilt edges, **7s. 6d.**

BEERBOHM.—WANDERINGS IN PATAGONIA; or, Life among the Ostrich Hunters. By JULIUS BEERBOHM. With Illusts. Cr. 8vo, cl. extra, **3s. 6d.**

BENNETT (W. C., LL.D.), WORKS BY. Post 8vo, cloth limp, **2s.** each.
A BALLAD HISTORY OF ENGLAND. | SONGS FOR SAILORS.

BESANT (WALTER), NOVELS BY.
Cr. 8vo. cl. ex., **3s. 6d.** each; post 8vo, illust. bds., **2s.** each; cl. limp, **2s. 6d.** each.
ALL SORTS AND CONDITIONS OF MEN. With Illustrations by FRED. BARNARD.
THE CAPTAINS' ROOM, &c. With Frontispiece by E. J. WHEELER.
ALL IN A GARDEN FAIR. With 6 Illustrations by HARRY FURNISS.
DOROTHY FORSTER. With Frontispiece by CHARLES GREEN.
UNCLE JACK, and other Stories. | CHILDREN OF GIBEON.
THE WORLD WENT VERY WELL THEN. With 12 Illustrations by A. FORESTIER.
HERR PAULUS: His Rise, his Greatness, and his Fall.
FOR FAITH AND FREEDOM. With Illustrations by A. FORESTIER and F. WADDY.
TO CALL HER MINE, &c. With 9 Illustrations by A. FORESTIER.
THE BELL OF ST. PAUL'S.
THE HOLY ROSE, &c. With Frontispiece by F. BARNARD.
ARMOREL OF LYONESSE: A Romance of To-day. With 12 Illusts. by F. BARNARD.
ST. KATHERINE'S BY THE TOWER. With 12 page Illustrations by C. GREEN.
Crown 8vo, cloth extra, **3s. 6d.** each.
VERBENA CAMELLIA STEPHANOTIS, &c. Frontispiece by GORDON BROWNE.
THE IVORY GATE: A Novel. [Shortly.
FIFTY YEARS AGO. With 144 Plates and Woodcuts. Crown 8vo, cloth extra, **5s.**
THE EULOGY OF RICHARD JEFFERIES. With Portrait. Cr. 8vo, cl. extra, **6s.**
THE ART OF FICTION. Demy 8vo, **1s.**
LONDON. With 124 Illustrations. Demy 8vo, cloth extra, **18s.**
THE REBEL QUEEN: A Novel. Three Vols., crown 8vo. [Shortly.

BESANT (WALTER) AND JAMES RICE, NOVELS BY.
Cr. 8vo, cl. ex., **3s. 6d.** each ; post 8vo, illust. bds., **2s.** each; cl. limp, **2s. 6d.** each.

READY-MONEY MORTIBOY.	BY CELIA'S ARBOUR.
MY LITTLE GIRL.	THE CHAPLAIN OF THE FLEET.
WITH HARP AND CROWN.	THE SEAMY SIDE.
THIS SON OF VULCAN.	THE CASE OF MR. LUCRAFT, &c.
THE GOLDEN BUTTERFLY.	'TWAS IN TRAFALGAR'S BAY, &c.
THE MONKS OF THELEMA.	THE TEN YEARS' TENANT, &c.

*** There is also a LIBRARY EDITION of the above Twelve Volumes, handsomely set in new type, on a large crown 8vo page, and bound in cloth extra. **6s.** each

BEWICK (THOMAS) AND HIS PUPILS. By Austin Dobson. With 95 Illustrations. Square 8vo, cloth extra, **6s.**

BIERCE.—IN THE MIDST OF LIFE : Tales of Soldiers and Civilians, By Ambrose Bierce. Crown 8vo, cloth extra, **6s.**; post 8vo, illustrated boards, **2s.**

BLACKBURN'S (HENRY) ART HANDBOOKS.
ACADEMY NOTES, separate years, from 1875–1887, 1889–1892, each **1s.**
ACADEMY NOTES, 1893. With Illustrations. **1s.**
ACADEMY NOTES, 1875–79. Complete in One Vol., with 600 Illusts. Cloth limp, **6s.**
ACADEMY NOTES, 1880–84. Complete in One Vol. with 700 Illusts. Cloth limp, **6s.**
GROSVENOR NOTES, 1877. **6d.**
GROSVENOR NOTES, separate years, from 1878 to 1890, each **1s.**
GROSVENOR NOTES, Vol. I., 1877–82. With 300 Illusts. Demy 8vo, cloth limp, **6s.**
GROSVENOR NOTES, Vol II., 1883–87. With 300 Illusts. Demy 8vo, cloth limp, **6s.**
THE NEW GALLERY, 1888–1892. With numerous Illustrations, each **1s.**
THE NEW GALLERY, 1893. With Illustrations. **1s.**
THE NEW GALLERY, Vol. I., 1888–1892. With 250 Illusts. Demy 8vo, cloth, **6s.**
ENGLISH PICTURES AT THE NATIONAL GALLERY. 114 Illustrations. **1s.**
OLD MASTERS AT THE NATIONAL GALLERY. 128 Illustrations. **1s. 6d.**
ILLUSTRATED CATALOGUE TO THE NATIONAL GALLERY. 242 Illusts. cl., **3s.**
THE PARIS SALON, 1893. With Facsimile Sketches. **3s.**
THE PARIS SOCIETY OF FINE ARTS, 1893. With Sketches. **3s. 6d.** [*Shortly.*

BLAKE (WILLIAM) : India-proof Etchings from his Works by William Bell Scott. With descriptive Text. Folio, half-bound boards, **21s.**

BLIND (MATHILDE). Poems by. Crown 8vo, cloth extra, **5s.** each.
THE ASCENT OF MAN.
DRAMAS IN MINIATURE. With a Frontispiece by Ford Madox Brown.
SONGS AND SONNETS. Fcap. 8vo, vellum and gold.

BOURNE (H. R. FOX), WORKS BY.
ENGLISH MERCHANTS: Memoirs in Illustration of the Progress of British Commerce. With numerous Illustrations. Crown 8vo, cloth extra, **7s. 6d.**
ENGLISH NEWSPAPERS: The History of Journalism. Two Vols., demy 8vo, cl., **25s.**
THE OTHER SIDE OF THE EMIN PASHA RELIEF EXPEDITION. Crown 8vo, cloth extra, **6s.**

BOWERS.—LEAVES FROM A HUNTING JOURNAL. By George Bowers. Oblong folio, half-bound, **21s.**

BOYLE (FREDERICK), WORKS BY. Post 8vo, illustrated boards, **2s.** each.
CHRONICLES OF NO-MAN'S LAND. | CAMP NOTES.
SAVAGE LIFE. Crown 8vo, cloth extra, **3s. 6d.**; post 8vo, picture boards, **2s.**

BRAND'S OBSERVATIONS ON POPULAR ANTIQUITIES ; chiefly illustrating the Origin of our Vulgar Customs, Ceremonies, and Superstitions. With the Additions of Sir Henry Ellis, and Illustrations. Cr. 8vo, cloth extra, **7s. 6d.**

BREWER (REV. DR.), WORKS BY.
THE READER'S HANDBOOK OF ALLUSIONS, REFERENCES, PLOTS, AND STORIES. Fifteenth Thousand. Crown 8vo, cloth extra, **7s. 6d.**
AUTHORS AND THEIR WORKS, WITH THE DATES: Being the Appendices to ' The Reader's Handbook,' separately printed. Crown 8vo, cloth limp, **2s.**
A DICTIONARY OF MIRACLES. Crown 8vo, cloth extra, **7s. 6d.**

BREWSTER (SIR DAVID), WORKS BY. Post 8vo cl. ex. **4s. 6d.** each.
MORE WORLDS THAN ONE: Creed of Philosopher and Hope of Christian. Plates.
THE MARTYRS OF SCIENCE: Galileo, Tycho Brahe, and Kepler. With Portraits.
LETTERS ON NATURAL MAGIC. With numerous Illustrations.

BRILLAT-SAVARIN.—GASTRONOMY AS A FINE ART. By Brillat-Savarin. Translated by R. E. Anderson, M.A. Post 8vo, half-bound, **2s.**

BRET HARTE, WORKS BY.

LIBRARY EDITION. In Seven Volumes, crown 8vo, cloth extra, **6s.** each.
BRET HARTE'S COLLECTED WORKS. Arranged and Revised by the Author.
Vol. I. COMPLETE POETICAL AND DRAMATIC WORKS. With Steel Portrait.
Vol. II. LUCK OF ROARING CAMP—BOHEMIAN PAPERS—AMERICAN LEGENDS.
Vol. III. TALES OF THE ARGONAUTS—EASTERN SKETCHES.
Vol. IV. GABRIEL CONROY. | Vol. V. STORIES—CONDENSED NOVELS, &c.
Vol. VI. TALES OF THE PACIFIC SLOPE.
Vol.VII. TALES OF THE PACIFIC SLOPE—II. With Portrait by JOHN PETTIE, R A.

THE SELECT WORKS OF BRET HARTE, in Prose and Poetry. With Introductory
Essay by J. M. BELLEW, Portrait of Author, and 50 Illusts. Cr. 8vo, cl. ex., **7s. 6d.**
BRET HARTE'S POETICAL WORKS. Hand-made paper & buckram. Cr.8vo, **4s.6d.**
THE QUEEN OF THE PIRATE ISLE. With 28 original Drawings by KATE
GREENAWAY, reproduced in Colours by EDMUND EVANS. Small 4to, cloth, **5s.**

Crown 8vo, cloth extra, **3s. 6d.** each.
A WAIF OF THE PLAINS. With 60 Illustrations by STANLEY L. WOOD.
A WARD OF THE GOLDEN GATE. With 59 Illustrations by STANLEY L. WOOD
A SAPPHO OF GREEN SPRINGS, &c. With Two Illustrations by HUME NISBET
COLONEL STARBOTTLE'S CLIENT, AND SOME OTHER PEOPLE. With a
Frontispiece by FRED. BARNARD.
SUSY: A Novel. With Frontispiece and Vignette by J. A. CHRISTIE.
SALLY DOWS, &c. With 47 Illustrations by W. D. ALMOND, &c.

Post 8vo, illustrated boards, **2s.** each.
GABRIEL CONROY. | THE LUCK OF ROARING CAMP, &c.
AN HEIRESS OF RED DOG, &c. | CALIFORNIAN STORIES.
        Post 8vo, illustrated boards, **2s.** each; cloth limp, **2s. 6d.** each.
FLIP. | MARUJA. | A PHYLLIS OF THE SIERRAS.
            Fcap. 8vo picture cover, **1s.** each.
THE TWINS OF TABLE MOUNTAIN. | JEFF BRIGGS'S LOVE STORY.
SNOW-BOUND AT EAGLE'S. |

BRYDGES.—UNCLE SAM AT HOME. By HAROLD BRYDGES. Post
8vo, illustrated boards, **2s.**; cloth limp, **2s. 6d.**

BUCHANAN'S (ROBERT) WORKS. Crown 8vo, cloth extra, **6s.** each.

SELECTED POEMS OF ROBERT BUCHANAN. With Frontispiece by T. DALZIEL.
THE EARTHQUAKE; or, Six Days and a Sabbath.
THE CITY OF DREAM: An Epic Poem. With Two Illustrations by P. MACNAB.
THE WANDERING JEW: A Christmas Carol. Second Edition.
THE OUTCAST: A Rhyme for the Time. With 15 Illustrations by RUDOLF BLIND,
PETER MACNAB, and HUME NISBET. Small demy 8vo, cloth extra, **8s.**
ROBERT BUCHANAN'S COMPLETE POETICAL WORKS. With Steel-plate Por-
trait. Crown 8vo, cloth extra, **7s. 6d.**

Crown 8vo, cloth extra, **3s. 6d.** each; post 8vo, illustrated boards, **2s.** each.
THE SHADOW OF THE SWORD. | LOVE ME FOR EVER. Frontispiece.
A CHILD OF NATURE. Frontispiece. | ANNAN WATER. | FOXGLOVE MANOR.
GOD AND THE MAN. With 11 Illus- | THE NEW ABELARD.
trations by FRED. BARNARD. | MATT: A Story of a Caravan. Front.
THE MARTYRDOM OF MADELINE. | THE MASTER OF THE MINE. Front.
With Frontispiece by A. W. COOPER. | THE HEIR OF LINNE.

BURTON (CAPTAIN).—THE BOOK OF THE SWORD: Being a
History of the Sword and its Use in all Countries, from the Earliest Times. By
RICHARD F. BURTON. With over 400 Illustrations. Square 8vo, cloth extra, **32s.**

BURTON (ROBERT).

THE ANATOMY OF MELANCHOLY: A New Edition, with translations of the
Classical Extracts. Demy 8vo, cloth extra, **7s. 6d.**
MELANCHOLY ANATOMISED. Being an Abridgment, for popular use, of BURTON's
ANATOMY OF MELANCHOLY. Post 8vo, cloth limp, **2s. 6d.**

CAINE (T. HALL), NOVELS BY. Crown 8vo, cloth extra, **3s. 6d.** each;
post 8vo, illustrated boards, **2s.** each; cloth limp, **2s. 6d.** each.
SHADOW OF A CRIME. | A SON OF HAGAR. | THE DEEMSTER.

CAMERON (COMMANDER).—THE CRUISE OF THE "BLACK
PRINCE" PRIVATEER. By V. LOVETT CAMERON, R.N., C.B. With Two Illustrations by P. MACNAB. Crown 8vo, cloth extra, **5s.**; post 8vo, illustrated boards, **2s.**

CAMERON (MRS. H. LOVETT), NOVELS BY. Post 8vo, illust. bds., **2s.** each.
JULIET'S GUARDIAN. | DECEIVERS EVER.

CARLYLE (THOMAS) ON THE CHOICE OF BOOKS. With Life by R. H. SHEPHERD, and Three Illustrations. Post 8vo, cloth extra, **1s. 6d.**
CORRESPONDENCE OF THOMAS CARLYLE AND R. W. EMERSON, 1834 to 1872. Edited by C. E. NORTON. With Portraits. Two Vols., crown 8vo, cloth, **24s.**

CARLYLE (JANE WELSH), LIFE OF. By Mrs. ALEXANDER IRELAND. With Portrait and Facsimile Letter. Small demy 8vo, cloth extra, **7s. 6d.**

CHAPMAN'S (GEORGE) WORKS. Vol. I. contains the Plays complete, including the doubtful ones. Vol. II., the Poems and Minor Translations, with an Introductory Essay by ALGERNON CHARLES SWINBURNE. Vol. III., the Translations of the Iliad and Odyssey. Three Vols., crown 8vo, cloth extra, **6s.** each.

CHATTO AND JACKSON.—A TREATISE ON WOOD ENGRAVING, Historical and Practical. By WILLIAM ANDREW CHATTO and JOHN JACKSON. With an Additional Chapter by HENRY G. BOHN, and 450 fine Illusts. Large 4to, hf.-bd., **28s.**

CHAUCER FOR CHILDREN: A Golden Key. By Mrs. H. R. HAWEIS. With 8 Coloured Plates and 30 Woodcuts. Small 4to, cloth extra, **6s.**
CHAUCER FOR SCHOOLS. By Mrs. H. R. HAWEIS. Demy 8vo, cloth limp, **2s. 6d.**

CLARE.—FOR THE LOVE OF A LASS: A Tale of Tynedale. By AUSTIN CLARE. Post 8vo, picture boards, **2s.**; cloth limp, **2s. 6d.**

CLIVE (MRS. ARCHER), NOVELS BY. Post 8vo, illust. boards, **2s.** each.
PAUL FERROLL. | WHY PAUL FERROLL KILLED HIS WIFE.

CLODD.—MYTHS AND DREAMS. By EDWARD CLODD, F.R.A.S. Second Edition, Revised. Crown 8vo, cloth extra, **3s. 6d.**

COBBAN (J. MACLAREN), NOVELS BY.
THE CURE OF SOULS. Post 8vo, illustrated boards, **2s.**
THE RED SULTAN. Three Vols., crown 8vo. [*Shortly.*

COLEMAN (JOHN), WORKS BY.
PLAYERS AND PLAYWRIGHTS I HAVE KNOWN. Two Vols., 8vo, cloth, **24s.**
CURLY: An Actor's Story. With 21 Illusts. by J. C. DOLLMAN. Cr. 8vo, cl., **1s. 6d.**

COLERIDGE.—THE SEVEN SLEEPERS OF EPHESUS. By M. E. COLERIDGE. Fcap. 8vo, cloth, **1s. 6d.**

COLLINS (C. ALLSTON).—THE BAR SINISTER. Post 8vo, 2s.

COLLINS (MORTIMER AND FRANCES), NOVELS BY.
Crown 8vo, cloth extra, **3s. 6d.** each; post 8vo, illustrated boards, **2s.** each.
FROM MIDNIGHT TO MIDNIGHT. | BLACKSMITH AND SCHOLAR.
TRANSMIGRATION. | YOU PLAY ME FALSE. | A VILLAGE COMEDY.
Post 8vo, illustrated boards, **2s.** each.
SWEET ANNE PAGE. | FIGHT WITH FORTUNE. | SWEET & TWENTY. | FRANCES.

COLLINS (WILKIE), NOVELS BY.
Cr. 8vo, cl. ex., **3s. 6d.** each; post 8vo, illust. bds., **2s.** each; cl. limp, **2s. 6d.** each.
ANTONINA. With a Frontispiece by Sir JOHN GILBERT, R.A.
BASIL. Illustrated by Sir JOHN GILBERT, R.A., and J. MAHONEY.
HIDE AND SEEK. Illustrated by Sir JOHN GILBERT, R.A., and J. MAHONEY.
AFTER DARK. Illustrations by A. B. HOUGHTON. | THE TWO DESTINIES.
THE DEAD SECRET. With a Frontispiece by Sir JOHN GILBERT, R.A.
QUEEN OF HEARTS. With a Frontispiece by Sir JOHN GILBERT, R.A.
THE WOMAN IN WHITE. With Illusts. by Sir J. GILBERT, R.A., and F. A. FRASER
NO NAME. With Illustrations by Sir J. E. MILLAIS, R.A., and A. W. COOPER.
MY MISCELLANIES. With a Steel-plate Portrait of WILKIE COLLINS.
ARMADALE. With Illustrations by G. H. THOMAS.
THE MOONSTONE. With Illustrations by G. DU MAURIER and F. A. FRASER.
MAN AND WIFE. With Illustrations by WILLIAM SMALL.
POOR MISS FINCH. Illustrated by G. DU MAURIER and EDWARD HUGHES.
MISS OR MRS.? With Illusts. by S. L. FILDES, R.A., and HENRY WOODS, A.R.A.
THE NEW MAGDALEN. Illustrated by G. DU MAURIER and C. S. REINHARDT.
THE FROZEN DEEP. Illustrated by G. DU MAURIER and J. MAHONEY.
THE LAW AND THE LADY. Illusts. by S. L. FILDES, R.A., and SYDNEY HALL.
THE HAUNTED HOTEL. Illustrated by ARTHUR HOPKINS.
THE FALLEN LEAVES. | HEART AND SCIENCE. | THE EVIL GENIUS.
JEZEBEL'S DAUGHTER. | "I SAY NO." | LITTLE NOVELS.
THE BLACK ROBE. | A ROGUE'S LIFE. | THE LEGACY OF CAIN.
BLIND LOVE. With Preface by WALTER BESANT, and Illusts. by A. FORESTIER.

COLLINS (JOHN CHURTON, M.A.), BOOKS BY.
ILLUSTRATIONS OF TENNYSON. Crown 8vo, cloth extra, **6s.**

COLMAN'S HUMOROUS WORKS: "Broad Grins," "My Nightgown and Slippers," and other Humorous Works of GEORGE COLMAN. With Life by G. B. BUCKSTONE, and Frontispiece by HOGARTH. Crown 8vo, cloth extra, **7s. 6d.**

COLMORE.—A VALLEY OF SHADOWS. By G. COLMORE, Author of "A Conspiracy of Silence." Two Vols., crown 8vo.

COLQUHOUN.—EVERY INCH A SOLDIER: A Novel. By M. J. COLQUHOUN. Post 8vo, illustrated boards, **2s.**

CONVALESCENT COOKERY: A Family Handbook. By CATHERINE RYAN. Crown 8vo, **1s.**; cloth limp, **1s. 6d.**

CONWAY (MONCURE D.), WORKS BY.
DEMONOLOGY AND DEVIL-LORE. 65 Illustrations. Two Vols., 8vo, cloth **28s.**
A NECKLACE OF STORIES. 25 Illusts. by W. J. HENNESSY. Sq. 8vo, cloth, **6s.**
PINE AND PALM: A Novel. Two Vols., crown 8vo, cloth extra, **21s.**
GEORGE WASHINGTON'S RULES OF CIVILITY. Fcap. 8vo, Jap. vellum, **2s. 6d.**

COOK (DUTTON), NOVELS BY.
PAUL FOSTER'S DAUGHTER. Cr. 8vo, cl. ex., **3s. 6d.**; post 8vo, illust. boards, **2s.**
LEO. Post 8vo, illustrated boards, **2s.**

COOPER (EDWARD H.)—GEOFFORY HAMILTON. Two Vols.

CORNWALL.—POPULAR ROMANCES OF THE WEST OF ENG-LAND; or, The Drolls, Traditions, and Superstitions of Old Cornwall. Collected by ROBERT HUNT, F.R.S. Two Steel-plates by GEO. CRUIKSHANK. Cr. 8vo, cl., **7s. 6d.**

COTES.—TWO GIRLS ON A BARGE. By V. CECIL COTES. With 44 Illustrations by F. H. TOWNSEND. Crown 8vo, cloth extra, **3s. 6d.**

CRADDOCK.—THE PROPHET OF THE GREAT SMOKY MOUN-TAINS. By CHARLES EGBERT CRADDOCK. Post 8vo, illust bds., **2s.**; cl limp, **2s. 6d.**

CRIM.—ADVENTURES OF A FAIR REBEL. By MATT CRIM. With a Frontispiece. Crown 8vo, cloth extra, **3s. 6d.**; post 8vo, illustrated boards, **2s.**

CROKER (B.M.), NOVELS BY. Crown 8vo, cloth extra, **3s. 6d.** each; post 8vo, illustrated boards, **2s.** each; cloth limp, **2s. 6d.** each.

PRETTY MISS NEVILLE.	DIANA BARRINGTON.
A BIRD OF PASSAGE.	PROPER PRIDE.
A FAMILY LIKENESS. Three Vols., crown 8vo.	

CRUIKSHANK'S COMIC ALMANACK. Complete in TWO SERIES: The FIRST from 1835 to 1843; the SECOND from 1844 to 1853. A Gathering of the BEST HUMOUR of THACKERAY, HOOD, MAYHEW, ALBERT SMITH, A'BECKETT, ROBERT BROUGH, &c. With numerous Steel Engravings and Woodcuts by CRUIKSHANK, HINE, LANDELLS, &c. Two Vols., crown 8vo, cloth gilt, **7s. 6d.** each.
THE LIFE OF GEORGE CRUIKSHANK. By BLANCHARD JERROLD. With 84 Illustrations and a Bibliography. Crown 8vo, cloth extra, **7s. 6d.**

CUMMING (C. F. GORDON), WORKS BY. Demy 8vo, cl. ex., **8s. 6d.** each.
IN THE HEBRIDES. With Autotype Facsimile and 23 Illustrations.
IN THE HIMALAYAS AND ON THE INDIAN PLAINS. With 42 Illustrations.
TWO HAPPY YEARS IN CEYLON. With 28 Illustrations.
VIA CORNWALL TO EGYPT. With Photogravure Frontis. Demy 8vo, cl., **7s. 6d.**

CUSSANS.—A HANDBOOK OF HERALDRY; with Instructions for Tracing Pedigrees and Deciphering Ancient MSS., &c. By JOHN E. CUSSANS. With 408 Woodcuts and 2 Coloured Plates. New edition, revised, crown 8vo, cloth, **6s.**

CYPLES (W.)—HEARTS of GOLD. Cr. 8vo, cl., **3s. 6d.**; post 8vo, bds., **2s.**

DANIEL.—MERRIE ENGLAND IN THE OLDEN TIME. By GEORGE DANIEL. With Illustrations by ROBERT CRUIKSHANK. Crown 8vo, cloth extra, **3s. 6d.**

DAUDET.—THE EVANGELIST; or, Port Salvation. By ALPHONSE DAUDET. Crown 8vo, cloth extra, **3s. 6d.**; post 8vo, illustrated boards, **2s.**

DAVENANT.—HINTS FOR PARENTS ON THE CHOICE OF A PRO-FESSION FOR THEIR SONS. By F. DAVENANT, M.A. Post 8vo **1s.**; cl., **1s. 6d.**

DAVIES (DR. N. E. YORKE-), WORKS BY.
Crown 8vo, **1s.** each; cloth limp, **1s. 6d.** each
ONE THOUSAND MEDICAL MAXIMS AND SURGICAL HINTS.
NURSERY HINTS: A Mother's Guide in Health and Disease.
FOODS FOR THE FAT: A Treatise on Corpulency, and a Dietary for its Cure.
AIDS TO LONG LIFE. Crown 8vo, **2s.**; cloth limp, **2s. 6d.**

DAVIES' (SIR JOHN) COMPLETE POETICAL WORKS, for the first time Collected and Edited, with Memorial-Introduction and Notes, by the Rev. A. B. GROSART, D.D. Two Vols., crown 8vo, cloth boards, **12s.**

DAWSON.—THE FOUNTAIN OF YOUTH: A Novel of Adventure. By ERASMUS DAWSON, M.B. Edited by PAUL DEVON. With Two Illustrations by HUME NISBET. Crown 8vo, cloth extra, **3s. 6d.**; post 8vo, illustrated boards, **2s.**

DE GUERIN.—THE JOURNAL OF MAURICE DE GUERIN. Edited by G. S. TREBUTIEN. With a Memoir by SAINTE-BEUVE. Translated from the 20th French Edition by JESSIE P. FROTHINGHAM. Fcap. 8vo, half-bound, **2s. 6d.**

DE MAISTRE.—A JOURNEY ROUND MY ROOM. By XAVIER DE MAISTRE. Translated by HENRY ATTWELL. Post 8vo, cloth limp, **2s. 6d.**

DE MILLE.—A CASTLE IN SPAIN. By JAMES DE MILLE. With a Frontispiece. Crown 8vo, cloth extra, **3s. 6d.**; post 8vo, illustrated boards, **2s.**

DERBY (THE).—THE BLUE RIBBON OF THE TURF: A Chronicle of the RACE FOR THE DERBY, from Diomed to Donovan With Brief Accounts of THE OAKS. By LOUIS HENRY CURZON Crown 8vo, cloth limp, **2s. 6d.**

DERWENT (LEITH), NOVELS BY. Cr 8vo.cl., **3s.6d.** ea.; post 8vo,bds.,**2s.**ea.
OUR LADY OF TEARS. | CIRCE'S LOVERS.

DICKENS (CHARLES), NOVELS BY. Post 8vo. illustrated boards, **2s.** each.
SKETCHES BY BOZ. | NICHOLAS NICKLEBY.
THE PICKWICK PAPERS. | OLIVER TWIST.
THE SPEECHES OF CHARLES DICKENS, 1841-1870. With a New Bibliography. Edited by RICHARD HERNE SHEPHERD. Crown 8vo, cloth extra, **6s.**—Also a SMALLER EDITION, in the *Mayfair Library*, post 8vo, cloth limp, **2s. 6d.**
ABOUT ENGLAND WITH DICKENS. By ALFRED RIMMER. With 57 Illustrations by C. A. VANDERHOOF, ALFRED RIMMER, and others. Sq. 8vo, cloth extra, **7s. 6d.**

DICTIONARIES.

A DICTIONARY OF MIRACLES: Imitative, Realistic, and Dogmatic. By the Rev. E. C BREWER, LL.D. Crown 8vo, cloth extra, **7s. 6d.**
THE READER'S HANDBOOK OF ALLUSIONS, REFERENCES, PLOTS, AND STORIES. By the Rev. E. C. BREWER, LL.D. With an ENGLISH BIBLIOGRAPHY. Fifteenth Thousand. Crown 8vo, cloth extra **7s. 6d.**
AUTHORS AND THEIR WORKS, WITH THE DATES. Cr. 8vo, cloth limp, **2s.**
FAMILIAR SHORT SAYINGS OF GREAT MEN. With Historical and Explanatory Notes. By SAMUEL A. BENT, A M. Crown 8vo, cloth extra, **7s. 6d.**
SLANG DICTIONARY: Etymological, Historical, and Anecdotal. Cr. 8vo, cl., **6s. 6d.**
WOMEN OF THE DAY: A Biographical Dictionary. By F. HAYS. Cr. 8vo, cl., **5s.**
WORDS, FACTS, AND PHRASES: A Dictionary of Curious, Quaint, and Out-of-the-Way Matters. By ELIEZER EDWARDS. Crown 8vo. cloth extra, **7s. 6d.**

DIDEROT.—THE PARADOX OF ACTING. Translated, with Annotations, from Diderot's "Le Paradoxe sur le Comédien," by WALTER HERRIES POLLOCK. With a Preface by HENRY IRVING. Crown 8vo, parchment, **4s. 6d.**

DOBSON (AUSTIN), WORKS BY.
THOMAS BEWICK & HIS PUPILS. With 95 Illustrations. Square 8vo, cloth, **6s.**
FOUR FRENCHWOMEN. Fcap. 8vo, hf.-roxburghe, with a Portrait, **2s. 6d.**— Also, a Library Edition, with 4 Portraits, crown 8vo, buckram, gilt top, **6s.**
EIGHTEENTH CENTURY VIGNETTES. Crown 8vo, buckram, gilt top, **6s.**

DOBSON (W. T.)—POETICAL INGENUITIES AND ECCENTRICITIES. Post 8vo, cloth limp, **2s. 6d.**

DONOVAN (DICK), DETECTIVE STORIES BY.
Post 8vo. illustrated boards, **2s.** each: cloth limp, **2s. 6d.** each.
THE MAN-HUNTER. | WANTED! | A DETECTIVE'S TRIUMPHS.
CAUGHT AT LAST! | IN THE GRIP OF THE LAW.
TRACKED AND TAKEN. | FROM INFORMATION RECEIVED.
WHO POISONED HETTY DUNCAN? |
Crown 8vo, cloth extra, **3s. 6d.** each ; post 8vo, illustrated boards, **2s.** each ; cloth limp, **2s. 6d.** each.
THE MAN FROM MANCHESTER. With 23 Illustrations.
TRACKED TO DOOM. With 6 full-page Illustrations by GORDON BROWNE.

DOYLE (CONAN).—THE FIRM OF GIRDLESTONE. By A. CONAN DOYLE, Author of "Micah Clarke." Crown 8vo, cloth extra, **3s. 6d.**

DRAMATISTS, THE OLD. With Vignette Portraits. Cr. 8vo, cl. ex., **6s.** per Vol.
BEN JONSON'S WORKS. With Notes Critical and Explanatory, and a Biographical Memoir by WM. GIFFORD. Edited by Col. CUNNINGHAM. Three Vols.
CHAPMAN'S WORKS. Complete in Three Vols. Vol. I. contains the Plays complete; Vol. II., Poems and Minor Translations, with an Introductory Essay by A. C. SWINBURNE ; Vol. III., Translations of the Iliad and Odyssey.
MARLOWE'S WORKS. Edited, with Notes, by Col. CUNNINGHAM. One Vol.
MASSINGER'S PLAYS. From GIFFORD'S Text. Edit by Col. CUNNINGHAM OneVol.

DUNCAN (SARA JEANNETTE), WORKS BY.
Crown 8vo, cloth extra, **7s. 6d.** each.
A SOCIAL DEPARTURE: How Orthodocia and I Went round the World by Ourselves. With 111 Illustrations by F. H. TOWNSEND.
AN AMERICAN GIRL IN LONDON. With 80 Illustrations by F. H. TOWNSEND.
THE SIMPLE ADVENTURES OF A MEMSAHIB. Numerous Illusts. [*Preparing.*

DYER.—THE FOLK-LORE OF PLANTS. By Rev. T. F. THISELTON
DYER, M.A. Crown 8vo, cloth extra, **6s.**

EARLY ENGLISH POETS. Edited, with Introductions and Annotations, by Rev. A. B. GROSART, D.D. Crown 8vo, cloth boards, **6s.** per Volume.
FLETCHER'S (GILES) COMPLETE POEMS. One Vol.
DAVIES' (SIR JOHN) COMPLETE POETICAL WORKS. Two Vols.
HERRICK'S (ROBERT) COMPLETE COLLECTED POEMS. Three Vols.
SIDNEY'S (SIR PHILIP) COMPLETE POETICAL WORKS. Three Vols.

EDGCUMBE.—ZEPHYRUS : A Holiday in Brazil and on the River Plate.
By E. R. PEARCE EDGCUMBE. With 41 Illustrations. Crown 8vo, cloth extra, **5s.**

EDWARDES (MRS. ANNIE), NOVELS BY:
A POINT OF HONOUR. Post 8vo, illustrated boards, **2s.**
ARCHIE LOVELL. Crown 8vo, cloth extra, **3s. 6d.** ; post 8vo, illust. boards, **2s.**

EDWARDS (ELIEZER).—WORDS, FACTS, AND PHRASES : A
Dictionary of Curious, Quaint, and Out-of-the-Way Matters. By ELIEZER EDWARDS.
Crown 8vo, cloth extra, **7s. 6d.**

EDWARDS (M. BETHAM-), NOVELS BY.
KITTY. Post 8vo, illustrated boards, **2s.** ; cloth limp, **2s. 6d.**
FELICIA. Post 8vo, illustrated boards, **2s.**

EGERTON.—SUSSEX FOLK & SUSSEX WAYS. By Rev. J. C. EGERTON.
With Introduction by Rev. Dr. H. WACE, and 4 Illustrations. Cr. 8vo, cloth ex., **5s.**

EGGLESTON (EDWARD).—ROXY : A Novel. Post 8vo, illust. bds., 2s.

ENGLISHMAN'S HOUSE, THE : A Practical Guide to all interested in
Selecting or Building a House ; with Estimates of Cost, Quantities, &c. By C. J.
RICHARDSON. With Coloured Frontispiece and 600 Illusts. Crown 8vo, cloth, **7s. 6d.**

EWALD (ALEX. CHARLES, F.S.A.), WORKS BY.
THE LIFE AND TIMES OF PRINCE CHARLES STUART, Count of Albany
(THE YOUNG PRETENDER). With a Portrait. Crown 8vo, cloth extra, **7s. 6d.**
STORIES FROM THE STATE PAPERS. With an Autotype Crown 8vo, cloth, **6s.**

EYES, OUR : How to Preserve Them from Infancy to Old Age. By
JOHN BROWNING, F.R.A.S. With 70 Illusts. Eighteenth Thousand. Crown 8vo, **1s.**

FAMILIAR SHORT SAYINGS OF GREAT MEN. By SAMUEL ARTHUR
BENT, A.M. Fifth Edition, Revised and Enlarged. Crown 8vo, cloth extra, **7s. 6d.**

FARADAY (MICHAEL), WORKS BY. Post 8vo, cloth extra, **4s. 6d.** each
THE CHEMICAL HISTORY OF A CANDLE: Lectures delivered before a Juvenil
Audience. Edited by WILLIAM CROOKES, F.C.S. With numerous Illustrations
**ON THE VARIOUS FORCES OF NATURE, AND THEIR RELATIONS T
EACH OTHER.** Edited by WILLIAM CROOKES, F.C.S. With Illustrations.

FARRER (J. ANSON), WORKS BY.
MILITARY MANNERS AND CUSTOMS. Crown 8vo, cloth extra, **6s.**
WAR: Three Essays, reprinted from "Military Manners." Cr. 8vo, **1s.** ; cl., **1s. 6d.**

FENN G. MANVILLE NOVELS BY

FIN-BEC.—THE CUPBOARD PAPERS: Observations on the Art of Living and Dining. By FIN-BEC. Post 8vo, cloth limp, **2s. 6d.**

FIREWORKS, THE COMPLETE ART OF MAKING; or, The Pyrotechnist's Treasury. By THOMAS KENTISH. With 267 Illustrations. Cr. 8vo, cl., **5s.**

FITZGERALD (PERCY, M.A., F.S.A.), WORKS BY.
THE WORLD BEHIND THE SCENES. Crown 8vo, cloth extra, **3s. 6d.**
LITTLE ESSAYS: Passages from Letters of CHARLES LAMB. Post 8vo, cl., **2s. 6d.**
A DAY'S TOUR: Journey through France and Belgium. With Sketches. Cr. 4to. **1s.**
FATAL ZERO. Crown 8vo, cloth extra, **3s. 6d.**: post 8vo, illustrated boards, **2s.**
 Post 8vo, illustrated boards, **2s.** each.
BELLA DONNA. | LADY OF BRANTOME. | THE SECOND MRS. TILLOTSON.
POLLY. | NEVER FORGOTTEN. | SEVENTY-FIVE BROOKE STREET.
LIFE OF JAMES BOSWELL (of Auchinleck). With an Account of his Sayings, Doings, and Writings; and Four Portraits. Two Vols., demy 8vo, cloth, **24s.**

FLAMMARION.—URANIA: A Romance. By CAMILLE FLAMMARION. Translated by AUGUSTA RICE STETSON. With 87 Illustrations by DE BIELER, MYRBACH, and GAMBARD. Crown 8vo, cloth extra, **5s.**

FLETCHER'S (GILES, B.D.) COMPLETE POEMS: Christ's Victorie in Heaven, Christ's Victorie on Earth, Christ's Triumph over Death, and Minor Poems. With Notes by Rev. A. B. GROSART, D.D. Crown 8vo, cloth boards, **6s.**

FLUDYER (HARRY) AT CAMBRIDGE: A Series of Family Letters. Post 8vo, picture cover, **1s.**; cloth limp, **1s. 6d.**

FONBLANQUE (ALBANY).—FILTHY LUCRE. Post 8vo, illust. bds., **2s.**

FRANCILLON (R. E.), NOVELS BY.
 Crown 8vo, cloth extra, **3s. 6d.** each: post 8vo, illustrated boards, **2s.** each.
ONE BY ONE. | QUEEN COPHETUA. | A REAL QUEEN. | KING OR KNAVE?
OLYMPIA. Post 8vo, illust. bds., **2s.** | ESTHER'S GLOVE. Fcap. 8vo, pict. cover, **1s.**
ROMANCES OF THE LAW. Crown 8vo, cloth, **6s.**; post 8vo, illust. boards, **2s.**
ROPES OF SAND. 3 vols., crown 8vo.

FREDERIC (HAROLD), NOVELS BY.
SETH'S BROTHER'S WIFE. Post 8vo, illustrated boards, **2s.**
THE LAWTON GIRL. Cr. 8vo, cloth ex., **6s.**: post 8vo, illustrated boards, **2s.**

FRENCH LITERATURE, A HISTORY OF. By HENRY VAN LAUN. Three Vols., demy 8vo, cloth boards, **7s. 6d.** each.

FRERE.—PANDURANG HARI; or, Memoirs of a Hindoo. With Preface by Sir BARTLE FRERE. Crown 8vo, cloth, **3s. 6d.**; post 8vo, illust. bds., **2s.**

FRISWELL (HAIN).—ONE OF TWO: A Novel. Post 8vo, illust. bds., **2s.**

FROST (THOMAS), WORKS BY. Crown 8vo, cloth extra, **3s. 6d.** each.
CIRCUS LIFE AND CIRCUS CELEBRITIES. | LIVES OF THE CONJURERS.
THE OLD SHOWMEN AND THE OLD LONDON FAIRS.

FRY'S (HERBERT) ROYAL GUIDE TO THE LONDON CHARITIES. Showing their Name, Date of Foundation, Objects, Income, Officials, &c. Edited by JOHN LANE. Published Annually. Crown 8vo, cloth, **1s. 6d.**

GARDENING BOOKS. Post 8vo, **1s.** each; cloth limp, **1s. 6d.** each.
A YEAR'S WORK IN GARDEN AND GREENHOUSE: Practical Advice as to the Management of the Flower, Fruit, and Frame Garden. By GEORGE GLENNY.
HOUSEHOLD HORTICULTURE. By TOM and JANE JERROLD. Illustrated.
THE GARDEN THAT PAID THE RENT. By TOM JERROLD.
OUR KITCHEN GARDEN: The Plants we Grow, and How we Cook Them. By TOM JERROLD. Crown 8vo, cloth, 1s. 6d.
MY GARDEN WILD, AND WHAT I GREW THERE. By FRANCIS G. HEATH. Crown 8vo, cloth extra, gilt edges. **6s.**

GARRETT.—THE CAPEL GIRLS: A Novel. By EDWARD GARRETT. Crown 8vo, cloth extra, **3s. 6d.**; post 8vo, illustrated boards, **2s.**

GENTLEMAN'S ANNUAL, THE. Published Annually in Novembe
The 1892 Annual, written by T. W. SPEIGHT, is entitled "**THE LOUD TRAGEDY.**"

GERMAN POPULAR STORIES.
and Translated by EDGAR TAYLOR. Wit
Plates after GEORGE CRUIKSHANK. Squ

GIBBON (CHARLES), NOVELS BY.
Crown 8vo, cloth extra, **3s. 6d.** each ; post 8vo, illustrated boards, **2s.** each.

ROBIN GRAY. | LOVING A DREAM.	THE GOLDEN SHAFT.
THE FLOWER OF THE FOREST.	OF HIGH DEGREE.

Post 8vo, illustrated boards, **2s.** each.

THE DEAD HEART.	IN LOVE AND WAR.
FOR LACK OF GOLD.	A HEART'S PROBLEM.
WHAT WILL THE WORLD SAY?	BY MEAD AND STREAM.
FOR THE KING. | A HARD KNOT.	THE BRAES OF YARROW.
QUEEN OF THE MEADOW.	FANCY FREE. | IN HONOUR BOUN
IN PASTURES GREEN.	HEART'S DELIGHT. | BLOOD-MONE

GIBNEY (SOMERVILLE).—SENTENCED! Cr. 8vo, 1s. ; cl, 1s. 6

GILBERT (WILLIAM), NOVELS BY. Post 8vo, illustrated boards, **2s.** ea

DR. AUSTIN'S GUESTS.	JAMES DUKE, COSTERMONGER.
THE WIZARD OF THE MOUNTAIN.	

GILBERT (W. S.), ORIGINAL PLAYS BY. Two Series, **2s. 6d.** eac
The FIRST SERIES contains: The Wicked World—Pygmalion and Galatea
Charity—The Princess—The Palace of Truth—Trial by Jury.
The SECOND SERIES: Broken Hearts—Engaged—Sweethearts—Gretchen—Da
Druce—Tom Cobb—H.M.S. " Pinafore "—The Sorcerer—Pirates of Penzanc

EIGHT ORIGINAL COMIC OPERAS written by W. S. GILBERT. Containin
The Sorcerer—H.M.S. "Pinafore"—Pirates of Penzance—Iolanthe—Patience
Princess Ida—The Mikado—Trial by Jury. Demy 8vo, cloth limp, **2s. 6d.**
THE "GILBERT AND SULLIVAN" BIRTHDAY BOOK: Quotations for Eve
Day in the Year, Selected from Plays by W. S. GILBERT set to Music by Sir
SULLIVAN. Compiled by ALEX. WATSON. Royal 16mo, Jap. leather, **2s. 6d.**

GLANVILLE (ERNEST), NOVELS BY.
Crown 8vo, cloth extra, **3s. 6d.** each ; post 8vo, illustrated boards, **2s.** each.
THE LOST HEIRESS: A Tale of Love, Battle, and Adventure. With 2 Illusts
THE FOSSICKER: A Romance of Mashonaland. With 2 Illusts. by HUME NIS

GLENNY.—A YEAR'S WORK IN GARDEN AND GREENHOUS
Practical Advice to Amateur Gardeners as to the Management of the Flower. Fru
and Frame Garden. By GEORGE GLENNY. Post 8vo. 1s. ; cloth limp, **1s. 6d.**

GODWIN.—LIVES OF THE NECROMANCERS. By WILLIAM GC
WIN. Post 8vo. cloth limp, **2s.**

GOLDEN TREASURY OF THOUGHT, THE: An Encyclopæc
QUOTATIONS. Edited by THEODORE TAYLOR. Crown 8vo. cloth gilt, **7s. 6d.**

GOODMAN.—THE FATE OF HERBERT WAYNE. By E. J. GOC
MAN, Author of "Too Curious." Crown 8vo, cloth, **3s. 6d.**

GOWING.—FIVE THOUSAND MILES IN A SLEDGE: A Midwin
Journey Across Siberia. By LIONEL F. GOWING. With 30 Illustrations by C.
UREN, and a Map by E. WELLFR. Large crown 8vo, cloth extra, **8s.**

GRAHAM. — THE PROFESSOR'S WIFE: A Story By LE
GRAHAM Fcap. 8vo, picture cover. **1s.**

GREEKS AND ROMANS, THE LIFE OF THE, described fro
Antique Monuments By ERNST GUHL and W. KONER Edited by Dr. F. HUEFFE
With 545 Illustrations Large crown 8vo, cloth extra. **7s. 6d.**

GREENWOOD (JAMES), WORKS BY Cr. 8vo. cloth extra, **3s. 6d.** eac

THE WILDS OF LONDON.	LOW-LIFE DEEPS.

GREVILLE (HENRY), NOVELS BY: ·
NIKANOR. Translated by ELIZA E. CHASE. With 8 Illustrations. Cro
cloth extra, **6s.**; post 8vo, illustrated boards, **2s.**
A NOBLE WOMAN. Crown 8vo. cloth extra. **5s.**; post 8vo. illustrated boar

I   · A Novel   B. CECIL

HABBERTON (JOHN, Author of "Helen's Babies"), NOVELS BY.
Post 8vo, illustrated boards **2s.** each; cloth limp, **2s. 6d.** each.

BRUETON'S BAYOU.	**COUNTRY LUCK.**

HAIR, THE: Its Treatment in Health, Weakness, and Disease. Translated from the German of Dr. J. PINCUS. Crown 8vo, **1s.**; cloth, **1s. 6d.**

HAKE (DR. THOMAS GORDON), POEMS BY. Cr. 8vo, cl. ex., **6s.** each.
NEW SYMBOLS. | **LEGENDS OF THE MORROW.** | **THE SERPENT PLAY.**
MAIDEN ECSTASY. Small 4to, cloth extra, **8s.**

HALL.—SKETCHES OF IRISH CHARACTER. By Mrs. S. C. HALL. With numerous Illustrations on Steel and Wood by MACLISE, GILBERT, HARVEY, and GEORGE CRUIKSHANK. Medium 8vo, cloth extra, **7s. 6d.**

HALLIDAY (ANDR.).—EVERY-DAY PAPERS. Post 8vo, bds., **2s.**

HANDWRITING, THE PHILOSOPHY OF. With over 100 Facsimiles and Explanatory Text. By DON FELIX DE SALAMANCA. Post 8vo, cloth limp, **2s. 6d.**

HANKY-PANKY: Easy Tricks, White Magic, Sleight of Hand, &c. Edited by W. H CREMER. With 200 Illustrations. Crown 8vo, cloth extra, **4s. 6d.**

HARDY (LADY DUFFUS). — PAUL WYNTER'S SACRIFICE. **2s.**

HARDY (THOMAS). — UNDER THE GREENWOOD TREE. By THOMAS HARDY, Author of "Far from the Madding Crowd." With Portrait and 15 Illustrations. Crown 8vo, cloth extra, **3s. 6d.**; post 8vo, illustrated boards, **2s.**

HARPER.—THE BRIGHTON ROAD: Old Times and New on a Classic Highway. By CHARLES G. HARPER. With a Photogravure Frontispiece and 90 Illustrations. Demy 8vo, cloth extra, **16s.**

HARWOOD.—THE TENTH EARL. By J. BERWICK HARWOOD. Post 8vo, illustrated boards, **2s.**

HAWEIS (MRS. H. R.), WORKS BY. Square 8vo, cloth extra, **6s.** each.
THE ART OF BEAUTY. With Coloured Frontispiece and 91 Illustrations.
THE ART OF DECORATION. With Coloured Frontispiece and 74 Illustrations.
CHAUCER FOR CHILDREN. With 8 Coloured Plates and 30 Woodcuts.
THE ART OF DRESS. With 32 Illustrations. Post 8vo, **1s.**; cloth, **1s. 6d.**
CHAUCER FOR SCHOOLS. Demy 8vo. cloth limp, **2s. 6d.**

HAWEIS (Rev. H. R., M.A.). —AMERICAN HUMORISTS: WASHINGTON IRVING, OLIVER WENDELL HOLMES, JAMES RUSSELL LOWELL, ARTEMUS WARD, MARK TWAIN, and BRET HARTE. Third Edition. Crown 8vo, cloth extra, **6s.**

HAWLEY SMART.—WITHOUT LOVE OR LICENCE: A Novel. By HAWLEY SMART. Crown 8vo. cloth extra, **3s. 6d.**; post 8vo, illustrated boards, **2s.**

HAWTHORNE. —OUR OLD HOME. By NATHANIEL HAWTHORNE. Annotated with Passages from the Author's Note-book, and Illustrated with 31 Photogravures. Two Vols., crown 8vo buckram, gilt top, **15s.**

HAWTHORNE (JULIAN), NOVELS BY.
Crown 8vo, cloth extra, **3s. 6d.** each; post 8vo, illustrated boards, **2s.** each.

GARTH.	**ELLICE QUENTIN.**	**BEATRIX RANDOLPH.**	**DUST.**
SEBASTIAN STROME.		**DAVID POINDEXTER.**	
FORTUNE'S FOOL.		**THE SPECTRE OF THE CAMERA.**	

Post 8vo, illustrated boards, **2s.** each.
MISS CADOGNA. | **LOVE—OR A NAME.**
MRS. GAINSBOROUGH'S DIAMONDS. Fcap. 8vo. illustrated cover, **1s.**

HEATH.—MY GARDEN WILD, AND WHAT I GREW THERE. By FRANCIS GEORGE HEATH. Crown 8vo, cloth extra, gilt edges, **6s.**

HELPS (SIR ARTHUR), WORKS BY. Post 8vo, cloth limp, **2s. 6d.** each.
ANIMALS AND THEIR MASTERS. | **SOCIAL PRESSURE.**
IVAN DE BIRON: A Novel. Cr. 8vo, cl. extra, **3s. 6d.**; post 8vo, illust. bds., **2s.**

HENDERSON.—AGATHA PAGE: A Novel. By ISAAC HENDERSON. Crown 8vo, cloth extra, **3s. 6d.**

HENTY.—RUJUB, THE JUGGLER. By G. A. HENTY. Three Vols.

HERRICK'S (ROBERT) HESPERIDES, NOBLE NUMBERS, AN
COMPLETE COLLECTED POEMS. With Memorial-Introduction and Notes by t
Rev. A. B. GROSART, D.D. ; Steel Portrait, &c. Three Vols., crown 8vo, cl. bds., 1

HERTZKA.—FREELAND : A Social Anticipation. By Dr. THEOD
HERTZKA. Translated by ARTHUR RANSOM. Crown 8vo, cloth extra, 6s.

HESSE-WARTEGG.—TUNIS : The Land and the People. By Cheval
ERNST VON HESSE-WARTEGG. With 22 Illustrations. Cr. 8vo, cloth extra, 3s. (

HILL.—TREASON-FELONY : A Novel. By JOHN HILL. Two Vols.

HINDLEY (CHARLES), WORKS B
TAVERN ANECDOTES AND SAYINGS: Including
Coffee Houses, Clubs, &c. With Illustrations. C
THE LIFE AND ADVENTURES OF A CHEAP JAC

HOEY.—THE LOVER'S CREED. By Mrs. CASHEL HOEY. P

HOLLINGSHEAD (JOHN).—NIAGARA SPRAY. Crown 8v

HOLMES.—THE SCIENCE OF VOICE PRODUCTION AI
·PRESERVATION. By GORDON HOLMES, M.D. Crown 8vo, 1s. ; clot

HOLMES (OLIVER WENDELL), WORKS BY.
THE AUTOCRAT OF THE BREAKFAST-TABLE. Illustrated by J. GORD
THOMSON. Post 8vo, cloth limp, 2s. 6d.—Another Edition, in smaller type, w
an Introduction by G. A. SALA. Post 8vo, cloth limp, 2s.
THE AUTOCRAT OF THE BREAKFAST-TABLE and THE PROFESSOR AT TI
BREAKFAST-TABLE. In One Vol. Post 8vo, half-bound, 2s.

HOOD'S (THOMAS) CHOICE WORKS, in Prose and Verse. With L
of the Author, Portrait, and 200 Illustrations. Crown 8vo, cloth extra, 7s. 6d
HOOD'S WHIMS AND ODDITIES. With 85 Illustrations. Post 8vo, printed
laid paper and half-bound, 2s.

HOOD (TOM).—FROM NOWHERE TO THE NORTH POLE :
Noah's Arkæological Narrative. By TOM HOOD. With 25 Illustrations by W. BRUNI
and E. C. BARNES. Square 8vo, cloth extra, gilt edges, 6s.

HOOK'S (THEODORE) CHOICE HUMOROUS WORK
Ludicrous Adventures, Bons Mots, Puns, and Hoaxes. With
Portraits, Facsimiles, and Illustrations. Crown 8vo, cloth extra,

HOOPER.—THE HOUSE OF RABY : A Novel. B
HOOPER. Post 8vo, illustrated boards, 2s.

HOPKINS.—"'TWIXT LOVE AND DUTY :" A No
HOPKINS. Post 8vo, illustrated boards, 2s.

HORNE. — ORION : An Epic Poem. By RICHA
With Photographic Portrait by SUMMERS. Tenth Edition.

HORSE (THE) AND HIS RIDER : An Anecdotic
MANBY." Crown 8vo, cloth extra, 6s.

HUNGERFORD (MRS.), Author of "Molly Bawn," NOVELS B
Post 8vo, illustrated boards, 2s. each ; cloth limp, 2s. 6d. each.
A MAIDEN ALL FORLORN. | IN DURANCE VILE. | A MENTAL STRUGG
MARVEL. | A MODERN CIRCE.
LADY VERNER'S FLIGHT. Two Vols., crown 8vo.

HUNT.—ESSAYS BY LEIGH HUNT : A TALE FOR A CHIMNE
&c. Edited by EDMUND OLLIER. Post 8vo, printed on laid paper and h

HUNT (MRS. ALFRED), NOVELS BY.
Crown 8vo, cloth extra, 3s. 6d. each ; post 8vo, illustrated boards, 2s. each.
THE LEADEN CASKET. | SELF-CONDEMNED. | THAT OTHER PERSO
THORNICROFT'S MODEL. Post 8vo, illustrated boards, 2s.
MRS. JULIET. Three Vols., crown 8vo.

HUTCHISON.—HINTS ON COLT-BREAKING. By W. M. HUTCHIS
With 25 Illustrations. Crown 8vo, cloth extra, 3s. 6d.

HYDROPHOBIA : An Account of M. PASTEUR's System ; Techniqu
his Method, and Statistics. By RENAUD SUZOR, M.B. Crown 8vo, cloth extra,

IDLER (THE) : A Monthly Magazine. Edited by

INGELOW (JEAN).—FATED TO BE FREE. Post 8vo, illustrated bds., 2s.

INDOOR PAUPERS. By One of Them. Crown 8vo, 1s.; cloth, 1s. 6d.

INNKEEPER'S HANDBOOK (THE) AND LICENSED VICTUALLER'S MANUAL. By J. Trevor-Davies. Crown 8vo, 1s.; cloth, 1s. 6d.

IRISH WIT AND HUMOUR, SONGS OF. Collected and Edited by A. Perceval Graves. Post 8vo, cloth limp, 2s. 6d.

JAMES.—A ROMANCE OF THE QUEEN'S HOUNDS. By Charles James. Post 8vo, picture cover, 1s.; cloth limp, 1s. 6d.

JANVIER.—PRACTICAL KERAMICS FOR STUDENTS. By Catherine A. Janvier. Crown 8vo, cloth extra, 6s.

JAY (HARRIETT), NOVELS BY. Post 8vo, illustrated boards, 2s. each.
THE DARK COLLEEN. | THE QUEEN OF CONNAUGHT.

JEFFERIES (RICHARD), WORKS BY. Post 8vo, cloth limp, 2s. 6d. each.
NATURE NEAR LONDON. | THE LIFE OF THE FIELDS. | THE OPEN AIR.
*** Also the Hand-made Paper Edition, crown 8vo, buckram, gilt top, 6s. each.
THE EULOGY OF RICHARD JEFFERIES. By Walter Besant. Second Edition. With a Photograph Portrait. Crown 8vo, cloth extra, 6s.

JENNINGS (H. J.), WORKS BY.
CURIOSITIES OF CRITICISM. Post 8vo, cloth limp, 2s. 6d.
LORD TENNYSON: A Biographical Sketch. With a Photograph. Cr. 8vo, cl., 6s.

JEROME.—STAGELAND. By Jerome K. Jerome. With 64 Illustrations by J. Bernard Partridge. Square 8vo, picture cover, 1s.; cloth limp, 2s.

JERROLD.—THE BARBER'S CHAIR; & THE HEDGEHOG LETTERS. By Douglas Jerrold. Post 8vo, printed on laid paper and half-bound, 2s.

JERROLD (TOM), WORKS BY. Post 8vo, 1s. each; cloth limp, 1s. 6d. each.
THE GARDEN THAT PAID THE RENT.
HOUSEHOLD HORTICULTURE: A Gossip about Flowers. Illustrated.
OUR KITCHEN GARDEN: The Plants, and How we Cook Them. Cr. 8vo, cl., 1s. 6d.

JESSE.—SCENES AND OCCUPATIONS OF A COUNTRY LIFE. By Edward Jesse. Post 8vo, cloth limp, 2s.

JONES (WILLIAM, F.S.A.), WORKS BY. Cr. 8vo, cl. extra, 7s. 6d. each.
FINGER-RING LORE: Historical, Legendary, and Anecdotal. With nearly 300 Illustrations. Second Edition, Revised and Enlarged.
CREDULITIES, PAST AND PRESENT. Including the Sea and Seamen, Miners, Talismans, Word and Letter Divination, Exorcising and Blessing of Animals, Birds, Eggs, Luck, &c. With an Etched Frontispiece.
CROWNS AND CORONATIONS: A History of Regalia. With 100 Illustrations.

JONSON'S (BEN) WORKS. With Notes Critical and Explanatory, and a Biographical Memoir by William Gifford. Edited by Colonel Cunningham. Three Vols., crown 8vo, cloth extra, 6s. each.

JOSEPHUS, THE COMPLETE WORKS OF. Translated by Whiston. Containing "The Antiquities of the Jews" and "The Wars of the Jews." With 5 Illustrations and Maps. Two Vols., demy 8vo, half-bound, 12s. 6d.

KEMPT.—PENCIL AND PALETTE: Chapters on Art and Artists. By Robert Kempt. Post 8vo, cloth limp, 2s. 6d.

KERSHAW.— COLONIAL FACTS AND FICTIONS: Humorous Sketches. By Mark Kershaw. Post 8vo, illustrated boards, 2s.; cloth, 2s. 6d.

KEYSER.— CUT BY THE MESS: A Novel. By Arthur Keyser. Crown 8vo, picture cover, 1s.; cloth limp, 1s. 6d.

KING (R. ASHE), NOVELS BY. Cr. 8vo, cl., 3s. 6d. ea.; post 8vo, bds., 2s. ea.
A DRAWN GAME. | "THE WEARING OF THE GREEN."
Post 8vo, illustrated boards, 2s. each.
PASSION'S SLAVE. | BELL BARRY.

KNIGHT.—THE PATIENT'S VADE MECUM : How to Get Mo
Benefit from Medical Advice. By WILLIAM KNIGHT, M.R.C.S., and EDWA
KNIGHT, L.R.C.P. Crown 8vo, **1s.**; cloth limp, **1s. 6d.**

LAMB'S (CHARLES) COMPLETE WORKS, in Prose and Vers
including "Poetry for Children" and "Prince Dorus." Edited, with Notes a
Introduction, by R. H. SHEPHERD. With Two Portraits and Facsimile of a pa
of the "Essay on Roast Pig." Crown 8vo, half-bound, **7s. 6d.**
THE ESSAYS OF ELIA. Post 8vo, printed on laid paper and half-bound, **2s.**
LITTLE ESSAYS: Sketches and Characters by CHARLES LAMB, selected from
Letters by PERCY FITZGERALD. Post 8vo, cloth limp, **2s. 6d.**
THE DRAMATIC ESSAYS OF CHARLES LAMB. With Introduction and No'
by BRANDER MATTHEWS, and Steel-plate Portrait. Fcap. 8vo, hf.-bd., **2s. 6d**

LANDOR.—CITATION AND EXAMINATION OF WILLIAM SHAK
PEARE, &c., before Sir THOMAS LUCY, touching Deer-stealing, 19th September, 15
To which is added, **A CONFERENCE OF MASTER EDMUND SPENSER** with 1
Earl of Essex, touching the State of Ireland, 1595. By WALTER SAVAGE LAND
Fcap 8vo, half-Roxburghe, **2s. 6d.**

LANE.—THE THOUSAND AND ONE NIGHTS, commonly called
England **THE ARABIAN NIGHTS' ENTERTAINMENTS.** Translated from
Arabic, with Notes, by EDWARD WILLIAM LANE. Illustrated by many hund
Engravings from Designs by HARVEY. Edited by EDWARD STANLEY POOLE. Wit
Preface by STANLEY LANE-POOLE. Three Vols., demy 8vo, cloth extra, **7s. 6d.** ea

LARWOOD (JACOB), WORKS BY.
THE STORY OF THE LONDON PARKS. With Illusts. Cr. 8vo, cl. extra, **3s.**
ANECDOTES OF THE CLERGY: The Antiquities, Humours, and Eccentricitie
the Cloth. Post 8vo, printed on laid paper and half-bound, **2s.**
Post 8vo, cloth limp, **2s. 6d.** each.
FORENSIC ANECDOTES. | THEATRICAL ANECDOTES.

LEIGH (HENRY S.), WORKS BY.
CAROLS OF COCKAYNE. Printed on hand-made paper, b
JEUX D'ESPRIT. Edited by HENRY S. LEIGH. Post 8vo,

LEYS (JOHN).—THE LINDSAYS : A Romance. Po

LIFE IN LONDON ; or, The History of JERRY
INTHIAN TOM. With CRUIKSHANK'S Coloured Illustratior
7s. 6d.

LINTON (E. LYNN), WORKS BY.   Post 8vo, cloth limp, **2s. 6d.** each.
WITCH STORIES. | OURSELVES: ESSAYS ON WOMEN
Crown 8vo, cloth extra, **3s. 6d.** each; post 8vo, illustrated boards, **2s.** each.
SOWING THE WIND. | UNDER WHICH LORD?
PATRICIA KEMBALL. | "MY LOVE!" | IONE.
ATONEMENT OF LEAM DUNDAS. | PASTON CAREW, Millionaire & Mi
THE WORLD WELL LOST. |
Post 8vo, illustrated boards, **2s.** each.
THE REBEL OF THE FAMILY. | WITH A SILKEN THREAD.
FREESHOOTING: Extracts from the Works of Mrs. LYNN LINTON. Post 8vo, cl
2s. 6d.

LONGFELLOW'S POETICAL WORKS. With numerous Illustrati
on Steel and Wood. Crown 8vo, cloth extra, **7s. 6d.**

LUCY.—GIDEON FLEYCE : A Novel. By HENRY W. L
8vo, cloth extra, **3s. 6d.**; post 8vo, illustrated boards, **2s.**

LUSIAD (THE) OF CAMOENS. Translated into Englis
Verse by ROBERT FFRENCH DUFF. With 14 Plates. Demy 8vo, clo

MACALPINE (AVERY), NOVELS BY.
TERESA ITASCA. Crown 8vo, cloth extra, **1s.**
BROKEN WINGS. With 6 Illusts. by W. J. HENNESSY. Crown 8vo, cloth extra

MACCOLL (HUGH), NOVELS BY.
MR. STRANGER'S SEALED PACKET. Crown 8vo, cloth extra, **5s.**; post 8vo, 1
trated boards, **2s.**
EDNOR WHITLOCK. Crown 8vo, cloth extra, **6s.**

McCARTHY (JUSTIN, M.P.), WORKS BY.

A HISTORY OF OUR OWN TIMES, from the Accession of Queen Victoria to the General Election of 1880. Four Vols. demy 8vo, cloth extra, **12s.** each.—Also a POPULAR EDITION, in Four Vols., crown 8vo, cloth extra, **6s.** each.—And a JUBILEE EDITION, with an Appendix of Events to the end of 1886, in Two Vols., large crown 8vo, cloth extra, **7s. 6d.** each.

A SHORT HISTORY OF OUR OWN TIMES. One Vol., crown 8vo, cloth extra, **6s.** —Also a CHEAP POPULAR EDITION, post 8vo, cloth limp, **2s. 6d.**

A HISTORY OF THE FOUR GEORGES. Four Vols. demy 8vo, cloth extra, **12s.** each. [Vols. I. & II. *ready.*]

Cr. 8vo, cl. extra, **3s. 6d.** each; post 8vo, illust. bds., **2s.** each; cl. limp, **2s. 6d.** each.

THE WATERDALE NEIGHBOURS.	MISS MISANTHROPE.
MY ENEMY'S DAUGHTER.	DONNA QUIXOTE.
A FAIR SAXON.	THE COMET OF A SEASON.
LINLEY ROCHFORD.	MAID OF ATHENS.
DEAR LADY DISDAIN.	CAMIOLA: A Girl with a Fortune

THE DICTATOR. Three Vols., crown 8vo. [*Shortly*]

"THE RIGHT HONOURABLE." By JUSTIN McCARTHY, M.P., and Mrs. CAMPBELL-PRAED. Fourth Edition. Crown 8vo, cloth extra, **6s.**

McCARTHY (JUSTIN H.), WORKS BY.

THE FRENCH REVOLUTION. Four Vols., 8vo, **12s.** each. [Vols. I. & II. *ready.*]
AN OUTLINE OF THE HISTORY OF IRELAND. Crown 8vo, **1s.**; cloth, **1s. 6d.**
IRELAND SINCE THE UNION: Irish History, 1798-1886 Crown 8vo, cloth, **6s.**
HAFIZ IN LONDON: Poems. Small 8vo, gold cloth, **3s. 6d.**
HARLEQUINADE: Poems. Small 4to, Japanese vellum, **8s.**
OUR SENSATION NOVEL. Crown 8vo, picture cover, **1s.**; cloth limp, **1s. 6d.**
DOOM! An Atlantic Episode. Crown 8vo, picture cover, **1s.**
DOLLY: A Sketch. Crown 8vo, picture cover, **1s.**; cloth limp, **1s. 6d.**
LILY LASS: A Romance. Crown 8vo, picture cover, **1s.**; cloth limp, **1s. 6d.**
THE THOUSAND AND ONE DAYS: Persian Tales. Edited by JUSTIN H. McCARTHY. With 2 Photogravures by STANLEY L. WOOD. Two Vols., crown 8vo, half-bound, **12s.**

MACDONALD (GEORGE, LL.D.), WORKS BY.

WORKS OF FANCY AND IMAGINATION. Ten Vols., cl. extra, gilt edges, in cloth case, **21s.** Or the Vols. may be had separately, in grolier cl., at **2s. 6d.** each.
Vol. I. WITHIN AND WITHOUT.—THE HIDDEN LIFE.
,, II. THE DISCIPLE —THE GOSPEL WOMEN —BOOK OF SONNETS.—ORGAN SONGS.
,, III. VIOLIN SONGS.—SONGS OF THE DAYS AND NIGHTS.—A BOOK OF DREAMS.—ROADSIDE POEMS.—POEMS FOR CHILDREN.
,, IV. PARABLES.—BALLADS.—SCOTCH SONGS.
,, V. & VI. PHANTASTES: A Faerie Romance. | Vol. VII. THE PORTENT.
,, VIII. THE LIGHT PRINCESS —THE GIANT'S HEART.—SHADOWS.
,, IX. CROSS PURPOSES.—THE GOLDEN KEY.—THE CARASOYN.—LITTLE DAYLIGHT
,, X. THE CRUEL PAINTER.—THE WOW O' RIVVEN.—THE CASTLE.—THE BROKEN SWORDS.—THE GRAY WOLF.—UNCLE CORNELIUS.

POETICAL WORKS OF GEORGE MACDONALD. Collected and arranged by the Author. 2 vols., crown 8vo, buckram, **12s.**
A THREEFOLD CORD. Edited by GEORGE MACDONALD. Post 8vo, cloth, **5s.**
HEATHER AND SNOW: A Novel. 2 vols., crown 8vo. [*Shortly.*]

MACGREGOR. — PASTIMES AND PLAYERS: Notes on Popular
Games. By ROBERT MACGREGOR. Post 8vo, cloth limp, **2s. 6d.**

MACKAY.—INTERLUDES AND UNDERTONES; or, Music at Twilight.
By CHARLES MACKAY, LL.D. Crown 8vo, cloth extra, **6s.**

MACLISE PORTRAIT GALLERY (THE) OF ILLUSTRIOUS LITER-
ARY CHARACTERS: 85 PORTRAITS; with Memoirs — Biographical, Critical, Bibliographical, and Anecdotal—illustrative of the Literature of the former half of the Present Century, by WILLIAM BATES, B.A. Crown 8vo, cloth extra, **7s. 6d.**

MACQUOID (MRS.), WORKS BY. Square 8vo, cloth extra, **7s. 6d.** each.

IN THE ARDENNES. With 50 Illustrations by THOMAS R. MACQUOID.
PICTURES AND LEGENDS FROM NORMANDY AND BRITTANY. With 34 Illustrations by THOMAS R. MACQUOID.
THROUGH NORMANDY. With 92 Illustrations by T. R. MACQUOID, and a Map.
THROUGH BRITTANY. With 35 Illustrations by T. R. MACQUOID, and a Map.
ABOUT YORKSHIRE. With 67 Illustrations by T. R. MACQUOID.

Post 8vo, illustrated boards, **2s.** each.

MAGIC LANTERN, THE, and its Management: including full Practi
Directions for producing the Limelight, making Oxygen Gas, and preparing Lan
Slides. By T. C. HEPWORTH. With 10 Illustrations. Cr. 8vo, **1s.**; cloth, **1s.**

MAGICIAN'S OWN BOOK, THE: Performances with Cups and Bal
Eggs, Hats, Handkerchiefs, &c. All from actual Experience. Edited by W.
CREMER. With 200 Illustrations. Crown 8vo, cloth extra, **4s. 6d.**

MAGNA CHARTA: An Exact Facsimile of the Original in the Brit
Museum, 3 feet by 2 feet, with Arms and Seals emblazoned in Gold and Colours,

MALLOCK (W. H.), WORKS BY.
THE NEW REPUBLIC. Post 8vo, picture cover, **2s.**; cloth limp, **2s. 6d.**
THE NEW PAUL & VIRGINIA: Positivism on an Island. Post 8vo, cloth, **2s.**
POEMS. Small 4to, parchment, **8s.**
IS LIFE WORTH LIVING? Crown 8vo, cloth extra, **6s.**
A ROMANCE OF THE NINETEENTH CENTURY. Crown 8vo, cloth, **6s.**

MALLORY'S (SIR THOMAS) MORT D'ART
King Arthur and of the Knights of the Round Table. (
MONTGOMERIE RANKING. Post 8vo, cloth limp, **2s.**

MARK TWAIN, WORKS BY. Crown 8vo, cloth extra, **7s. 6d.** each.
THE CHOICE WORKS OF MARK TWAIN. Revised and Corrected throug
by the Author. With Life, Portrait, and numerous Illustrations.
ROUGHING IT, and INNOCENTS AT HOME. With 200 Illusts. by F. A. FRAS
MARK TWAIN'S LIBRARY OF HUMOUR. With 197 Illustrations.
Crown 8vo, cloth extra (illustrated), **7s. 6d.** each; post 8vo, illust. boards, **2s.** eac
THE INNOCENTS ABROAD; or, New Pilgrim's Progress. With 234 Illustrati
(The Two-Shilling Edition is entitled MARK TWAIN'S PLEASURE TRIP.
THE GILDED AGE. By MARK TWAIN and C. D. WARNER. With 212 Illustrati
THE ADVENTURES OF TOM SAWYER. With 111 Illustrations.
A TRAMP ABROAD. With 314 Illustrations.
THE PRINCE AND THE PAUPER. With 190 Illustrations.
LIFE ON THE MISSISSIPPI. With 300 Illustrations.
ADVENTURES OF HUCKLEBERRY FINN. With 174 Illusts. by E. W. KEMB
A YANKEE AT THE COURT OF KING ARTHUR. With 220 Illusts. by BE
MARK TWAIN'S SKETCHES. Post 8vo, illustrated boards, **2s.**
THE STOLEN WHITE ELEPHANT, &c. Cr. 8vo, cl., **6s.**; post 8vo, illust. bds.
THE AMERICAN CLAIMANT. With 81 Illustrations by HAL HURST and
BEARD. Crown 8vo, cloth extra, **3s. 6d.**

MARLOWE'S WORKS. Including his Translations. Edited, with
and Introductions, by Col. CUNNINGHAM. Crown 8vo, cloth extra, **6s.**

MARRYAT (FLORENCE), NOVELS BY. Post 8vo, illust. boards,
A HARVEST OF WILD OATS. | FIGHTING THE AIR.
OPEN! SESAME! | WRITTEN IN FIRE.

MASSINGER'S PLAYS. From the Text of W
by Col CUNNINGHAM Crown 8vo cloth extra. **6s.**

MASTERMAN.—HALF-A-DOZEN DAUGHT
MASTERMAN. Post 8vo, illustrated boards, **2s.**

MATTHEWS.—A SECRET OF THE SE
Post 8vo, illustrated boards, **2s.**; cloth limp,

MAYHEW.—LONDON CHARACTERS AND THE HUMOROUS
OF LONDON LIFE. By HENRY MAYHEW. With Illusts. Crown 8vo, cloth, **3**

MENKEN.—INFELICIA: Poems by ADAH ISAACS MENKEN.
Illustrations by F. E. LUMMIS and F. O. C. DARLEY. Small 4to, cloth extra, **7**

MERRICK.—THE MAN WHO WAS GOOD. By LEONARD ME
Author of "Violet Moses," &c. Post 8vo, illustrated boards, **2s.**

MEXICAN MUSTANG (ON A), through Texas to the Rio Grand
A. E. SWEET and J. ARMOY KNOX. With 265 Illusts Cr. 8vo, cloth extra,

MIDDLEMASS (JEAN), NOVELS BY. Post 8v
TOUCH AND GO. | MR. DORILL

MILLER.—PHYSIOLOGY FOR THE YOUNG;

MILTON (J. L.), WORKS BY. Post 8vo, **1s.** each ; cloth, **1s. 6d.** each.
THE HYGIENE OF THE SKIN. With Directions for Diet, Soaps, Baths, &c.
THE BATH IN DISEASES OF THE SKIN.
THE LAWS OF LIFE, AND THEIR RELATION TO DISEASES OF THE SKIN.
THE SUCCESSFUL TREATMENT OF LEPROSY. Demy 8vo, **1s.**

MINTO (WM.)—WAS SHE GOOD OR BAD? Cr. 8vo, **1s.** ; cloth, **1s. 6d.**

MOLESWORTH (MRS.), NOVELS BY.
HATHERCOURT RECTORY. Post 8vo, illustrated boards, **2s.**
THAT GIRL IN BLACK. Crown 8vo, cloth, **1s. 6d.**

MOORE (THOMAS), WORKS BY.
THE EPICUREAN; and ALCIPHRON. Post 8vo, half-bound, **2s.**
PROSE AND VERSE, Humorous, Satirical, and Sentimental, by THOMAS MOORE;
with Suppressed Passages from the MEMOIRS of LORD BYRON. Edited by R.
HERNE SHEPHERD. With Portrait. Crown 8vo, cloth extra, **7s. 6d.**

MUDDOCK (J. E.), STORIES BY.
STORIES WEIRD AND WONDERFUL. Post 8vo, illust. boards, **2s.**; cloth, **2s. 6d.**
THE DEAD MAN'S SECRET; or, The Valley of Gold. With Frontispiece by
F. BARNARD. Crown 8vo, cloth extra, **5s.**; post 8vo, illustrated boards, **2s.**
FROM THE BOSOM OF THE DEEP. Post 8vo, illustrated boards, **2s.**
MAID MARIAN AND ROBIN HOOD: A Romance of Old Sherwood Forest. With
12 Illustrations by STANLEY L. WOOD. Crown 8vo, cloth extra, **5s.**

MURRAY (D. CHRISTIE), NOVELS BY.
Crown 8vo, cloth extra, **3s. 6d.** each ; post 8vo, illustrated boards, **2s.** each.

A LIFE'S ATONEMENT.	HEARTS.	BY THE GATE OF THE SEA.
JOSEPH'S COAT.	WAY OF THE WORLD	A BIT OF HUMAN NATURE.
COALS OF FIRE.	A MODEL FATHER.	FIRST PERSON SINGULAR.
VAL STRANGE.	OLD BLAZER'S HERO.	CYNIC FORTUNE.

BOB MARTIN'S LITTLE GIRL. Crown 8vo, cloth extra, **3s. 6d.**
TIME'S REVENGES. Three Vols , crown 8vo.

MURRAY (D. CHRISTIE) & HENRY HERMAN, WORKS BY.
ONE TRAVELLER RETURNS. Cr. 8vo, cl. extra, **6s.**; post 8vo, illust. bds., **2s.**
Crown 8vo, cloth extra, **3s. 6d.** each ; post 8vo, illustrated boards, **2s.** each.
PAUL JONES'S ALIAS. With 13 Illustrations. | THE BISHOPS' BIBLE.

MURRAY (HENRY), NOVELS BY.
A GAME OF BLUFF. Post 8vo, illustrated boards, **2s.**; cloth, **2s. 6d.**
A SONG OF SIXPENCE. Post 8vo, cloth extra, **2s. 6d.**

NEWBOLT.—TAKEN FROM THE ENEMY. By HENRY NEWBOLT.
Fcap. 8vo, cloth boards, **1s. 6d.**

NISBET (HUME), BOOKS BY.
"BAIL UP!" Crown 8vo, cloth extra, **3s. 6d.**; post 8vo, illustrated boards, **2s.**
DR. BERNARD ST. VINCENT. Post 8vo, illustrated boards, **2s.**
LESSONS IN ART. With 21 Illustrations. Crown 8vo, cloth extra, **2s. 6d.**
WHERE ART BEGINS. With 27 Illusts. Square 8vo, cloth extra, **7s. 6d.**

NOVELISTS.—HALF-HOURS WITH THE BEST NOVELISTS OF
THE CENTURY. Edit. by H. T. MACKENZIE BELL. Cr. 8vo, cl., **3s. 6d.** [*Preparing.*

O'HANLON (ALICE), NOVELS BY. Post 8vo, illustrated boards, **2s.** each.
THE UNFORESEEN. | CHANCE? OR FATE?

OHNET (GEORGES), NOVELS BY.
DOCTOR RAMEAU. 9 Illusts. by E. BAYARD. Cr. 8vo, cl., **6s.**; post 8vo, bds., **2s.**
A LAST LOVE. Crown 8vo, cloth, **5s.**; post 8vo, boards, **2s.**
A WEIRD GIFT. Crown 8vo, cloth, **3s. 6d.**; post 8vo, boards, **2s.**

OLIPHANT (MRS.), NOVELS BY. Post 8vo, illustrated boards, **2s.** each.
THE PRIMROSE PATH. | THE GREATEST HEIRESS IN ENGLAND
WHITELADIES. With Illustrations by ARTHUR HOPKINS and HENRY WOODS,
A.R.A. Crown 8vo, cloth extra, **3s. 6d.**; post 8vo, illustrated boards, **2s.**

O'REILLY (HARRINGTON).—FIFTY YEARS ON THE TRAIL: Adventures of JOHN Y. NELSON. 100 Illusts. by P. FRENZENY. Crown 8vo, **3s. 6d.**

O'REILLY (MRS.).—PHŒBE'S FORTUNES. Post 8vo, illust. bds., 2s.

O'SHAUGHNESSY (ARTHUR), POEMS BY.
LAYS OF FRANCE. Crown 8vo, cloth extra, **10s. 6d.**

OUIDA, NOVELS BY. Cr. 8vo, cl., 3s. 6d. each; post 8vo, llust. bds., 2s. eac

HELD IN BONDAGE.	FOLLE-FARINE.	MOTHS.
TRICOTRIN.	A DOG OF FLANDERS.	PIPISTRELLO.
STRATHMORE.	PASCAREL.	A VILLAGE COMMUNE
CHANDOS.	TWO LITTLE WOODEN	IN MAREMMA.
CECIL CASTLEMAINE'S	SHOES.	BIMBI. | SYRLIN
GAGE.	SIGNA.	WANDA.
IDALIA.	IN A WINTER CITY.	FRESCOES. | OTHMAR
UNDER TWO FLAGS.	ARIADNE.	PRINCESS NAPRAXINE
PUCK.	FRIENDSHIP.	GUILDEROY. | RUFFIN

BIMBI. Presentation Edition, with Nine Illustrations by EDMUND H. GARRET Square 8vo, cloth, 5s.

SANTA BARBARA, &c. Square 8vo, cloth, 6s.; crown 8vo, cloth, 3s. 6d.

WISDOM, WIT, AND PATHOS, selected from the Works of OUIDA by F. SYDN MORRIS. Post 8vo, cloth extra, 5s. CHEAP EDITION, illustrated boards, 2s.

PAGE (H. A.), WORKS BY.
THOREAU: His Life and Aims. With Portrait. Post 8vo, cloth limp, 2s. 6d.

ANIMAL ANECDOTES. Arranged on a New Principle. Crown 8vo, cloth extra, 5

PARLIAMENTARY ELECTIONS AND ELECTIONEERING, A HI
TORY OF, from the Stuarts to Queen Victoria. By JOSEPH GREGO. A New Editio with 93 Illustrations. Demy 8vo, cloth extra, 7s. 6d.

PASCAL'S PROVINCIAL LETTERS. A New Translation, with H
torical Introduction and Notes by T. M'CRIE, D.D. Post 8vo, cloth limp, 2s.

PAUL.—GENTLE AND SIMPLE. By MARGARET A. PA
piece by HELEN PATERSON. Crown 8vo, cloth, 3s. 6d.; post

PAYN (JAMES), NOVELS BY.
Crown 8vo, cloth extra, 3s. 6d. each; post 8vo, illustrated boards, 2s. each.

LOST SIR MASSINGBERD.	A GRAPE FROM A THORN.
WALTER'S WORD.	FROM EXILE.
LESS BLACK THAN WE'RE	THE CANON'S WARD.
PAINTED.	THE TALK OF THE TOWN.
BY PROXY.	HOLIDAY TASKS.
HIGH SPIRITS.	GLOW-WORM TALES.
UNDER ONE ROOF.	THE MYSTERY OF MIRBRIDGE.
A CONFIDENTIAL AGENT.	THE WORD AND THE WILL.

Post 8vo, illustrated boards, 2s. each.

HUMOROUS STORIES.	FOUND DEAD.
THE FOSTER BROTHERS.	GWENDOLINE'S HARVEST.
THE FAMILY SCAPEGRACE.	A MARINE RESIDENCE.
MARRIED BENEATH HIM.	MIRK ABBEY.|SOME PRIVATE VIEW
BENTINCK'S TUTOR.	NOT WOOED, BUT WON.
A PERFECT TREASURE.	TWO HUNDRED POUNDS REWARD
A COUNTY FAMILY.	THE BEST OF HUSBANDS.
LIKE FATHER, LIKE SON.	HALVES. | THE BURNT MILLIO
A WOMAN'S VENGEANCE.	FALLEN FORTUNES.
CARLYON'S YEAR.|CECIL'S TRYST.	WHAT HE COST HER.
MURPHY'S MASTER.	KIT: A MEMORY. | FOR CASH ONL
AT HER MERCY.	A PRINCE OF THE BLOOD.
THE CLYFFARDS OF CLYFFE.	SUNNY STORIES.

IN PERIL AND PRIVATION: Stories of MARINE ADVENTURE. With 17 Illi trations. Crown 8vo, cloth extra, 3s. 6d.

NOTES FROM THE "NEWS." Crown 8vo, portrait cover, 1s.; cloth, 1s. 6d.

PENNELL (H. CHOLMONDELEY), WORKS BY. Post 8vo, cl., 2s. 6d. eac
PUCK ON PEGASUS. With Illustrations.

PEGASUS RE-SADDLED. With Ten full-page Illustrations by G. DU MAURIER.

THE MUSES OF MAYFAIR. Vers de Société, Selected by H. C. PENNELL.

PHELPS (E. STUART), WORKS BY. Post 8vo, 1s. each; cloth, 1s. 6d.

BEYOND THE GATES. By the Author	AN OLD MAID'S PARADISE.
of "The Gates Ajar."	BURGLARS IN PARADISE.

JACK THE FISHERMAN. Illustrated by C. W. REED. Cr. 8vo, 1s.; cloth, 1s. 6

PIRKIS (C. L.), NOVELS BY.
TROOPING WITH CROWS. Fcap. 8vo, picture cover, 1s.

PLANCHE (J. R.), WORKS BY.
THE PURSUIVANT OF ARMS. With Six Plates, and 209 Illusts. Cr. 8vo, cl. 7s. 6d.
SONGS AND POEMS, 1819-1879. Introduction by Mrs. MACKARNESS. Cr. 8vo, cl., 6s.

PLUTARCH'S LIVES OF ILLUSTRIOUS MEN. Translated from the
Greek, with Notes Critical and Historical, and a Life of Plutarch, by JOHN and
WILLIAM LANGHORNE. With Portraits. Two Vols., demy 8vo, half-bound, 10s. 6d.

POE'S (EDGAR ALLAN) CHOICE WORKS, in Prose and Poetry. Introduction by CHAS. BAUDELAIRE, Portrait, and Facsimiles. Cr. 8vo, cloth, 7s. 6d.
THE MYSTERY OF MARIE ROGET, &c. Post 8vo. illustrated boards, 2s.

POPE'S POETICAL WORKS. Post 8vo, cloth limp, 2s.

PRAED (MRS. CAMPBELL), NOVELS BY. Post 8vo, illust. bds.. 2s. ea.
THE ROMANCE OF A STATION. | THE SOUL OF COUNTESS ADRIAN.
"THE RIGHT HONOURABLE." By Mrs. CAMPBELL PRAED and JUSTIN McCARTHY,
M.P. Crown 8vo, cloth extra, 6s.

PRICE (E. C.), NOVELS BY.
Crown 8vo, cloth extra, 3s. 6d. each; post 8vo, illustrated boards. 2s. each.
VALENTINA. | THE FOREIGNERS. | MRS. LANCASTER'S RIVAL.
GERALD. Post 8vo, illustrated boards. 2s.

PRINCESS OLGA.—RADNA; or, The Great Conspiracy of 1881. By
the Princess OLGA. Crown 8vo. cloth extra, 6s.

PROCTOR (RICHARD A., B.A.), WORKS BY.
FLOWERS OF THE SKY. With 55 Illusts. Small crown 8vo, cloth extra, 3s. 6d.
EASY STAR LESSONS. With Star Maps for Every Night in the Year. Cr. 8vo, 6s.
FAMILIAR SCIENCE STUDIES. Crown 8vo, cloth extra, 6s.
SATURN AND ITS SYSTEM. With 13 Steel Plates. Demy 8vo, cloth ex., 10s. 6d.
MYSTERIES OF TIME AND SPACE. With Illustrations. Cr. 8vo, cloth extra, 6s.
THE UNIVERSE OF SUNS. With numerous Illustrations. Cr. 8vo, cloth ex., 6s.
WAGES AND WANTS OF SCIENCE WORKERS. Crown 8vo, 1s. 6d.

PRYCE.—MISS MAXWELL'S AFFECTIONS. By RICHARD PRYCE.
Frontispiece by HAL LUDLOW. Cr. 8vo, cl., 3s. 6d.; post 8vo, illust boards, 2s.

RAMBOSSON.—POPULAR ASTRONOMY. By J. RAMBOSSON, Laureate
of the Institute of France. With numerous Illusts. Crown 8vo, cloth extra, 7s. 6d.

RANDOLPH.—AUNT ABIGAIL DYKES: A Novel. By Lt.-Colonel
GEORGE RANDOLPH, U.S.A. Crown 8vo, cloth extra, 7s. 6d.

READE (CHARLES), NOVELS BY.
Crown 8vo, cloth extra, illustrated, 3s. 6d. each; post 8vo, illust. bds., 2s. each.
PEG WOFFINGTON. Illustrated by S. L. FILDES, R.A.—Also a POCKET EDITION,
set in New Type, in Elzevir style, fcap. 8vo, half-leather, 2s. 6d.
CHRISTIE JOHNSTONE. Illustrated by WILLIAM SMALL.—Also a POCKET EDITION,
set in New Type, in Elzevir style, fcap. 8vo, half-leather, 2s. 6d.
IT IS NEVER TOO LATE TO MEND. Illustrated by G. J. PINWELL.
COURSE OF TRUE LOVE NEVER DID RUN SMOOTH. Illust HELEN PATERSON.
THE AUTOBIOGRAPHY OF A THIEF, &c. Illustrated by MATT STRETCH.
LOVE ME LITTLE, LOVE ME LONG. Illustrated by M. ELLEN EDWARDS.
THE DOUBLE MARRIAGE. Illusts. by Sir JOHN GILBERT, R.A., and C. KEENE.
THE CLOISTER AND THE HEARTH. Illustrated by CHARLES KEENE.
HARD CASH. Illustrated by F. W. LAWSON.
GRIFFITH GAUNT. Illustrated by S. L. FILDES, R.A., and WILLIAM SMALL.
FOUL PLAY. Illustrated by GEORGE DU MAURIER.
PUT YOURSELF IN HIS PLACE. Illustrated by ROBERT BARNES.
A TERRIBLE TEMPTATION. Illustrated by EDWARD HUGHES and A. W. COOPER.
A SIMPLETON. Illustrated by KATE CRAUFURD.
THE WANDERING HEIR. Illust. by H. PATERSON, S. L. FILDES, C. GREEN, &c.
A WOMAN-HATER. Illustrated by THOMAS COULDERY.
SINGLEHEART AND DOUBLEFACE. Illustrated by P. MACNAB.
GOOD STORIES OF MEN AND OTHER ANIMALS. Illust. by E. A. ABBEY, &c.
THE JILT, and other Stories. Illustrated by JOSEPH NASH.
A PERILOUS SECRET. Illustrated by FRED. BARNARD.
READIANA. With a Steel-plate Portrait of CHARLES READE.
BIBLE CHARACTERS: Studies of David, Paul, &c. Fcap. 8vo, leatherette, 1s.
THE CLOISTER AND THE HEARTH. With an Introduction by WALTER BESANT.

RIDDELL (MRS. J. H.), NOVELS BY.
Crown 8vo, cloth extra, **3s. 6d.** each; post 8vo, illustrated boards, **2s.** each.
THE PRINCE OF WALES'S GARDEN PARTY. | WEIRD STORIES.
Post 8vo, illustrated boards, **2s.** each.
THE UNINHABITED HOUSE.   HER MOTHER'S DARLING.
MYSTERY IN PALACE GARDENS.   THE NUN'S CURSE.
FAIRY WATER.   IDLE TALES.

RIMMER (ALFRED), WORKS BY.   Square 8vo, cloth gilt, **7s. 6d.** eac
OUR OLD COUNTRY TOWNS. With 55 Illustrations.
RAMBLES ROUND ETON AND HARROW. With 50 Illustrations.
ABOUT ENGLAND WITH DICKENS. With 58 Illusts. by C. A. VANDERHOOF,

RIVES (Amélie).—BARBARA DERING. By AMÉLIE RIVES, Au
of "The Quick or the Dead?" Crown 8vo, cloth extra, **3s. 6d.**

ROBINSON CRUSOE. By DANIEL DEFOE. (MAJOR'S
37 Illustrations by GEORGE CRUIKSHANK. Post 8vo, half-bound,

ROBINSON (F. W.), NOVELS BY.
WOMEN ARE STRANGE. Post 8vo, illustrated boards, **2s.**
THE HANDS OF JUSTICE. Cr. 8vo, cloth ex., **3s. 6d.**; post 8vo, illust. bd

ROBINSON (PHIL), WORKS BY. Crown 8vo, cloth extra, **6s.** each.
THE POETS' BIRDS. | THE POETS' BEASTS.
THE POETS AND NATURE: REPTILES, FISHES, AND INSECTS.

ROCHEFOUCAULD'S MAXIMS AND MORAL REFLECTIONS.
Notes, and an Introductory Essay by SAINTE-BEUVE. Post 8vo, cloth limp, **2**

ROLL OF BATTLE ABBEY, THE : A List of the Principal Warri
who came from Normandy with William the Conqueror, and Settled in this Coun
A.D. 1066-7. With Arms emblazoned in Gold and Colours. Handsomely printed.

ROWLEY (HON. HUGH), WORKS BY. Post 8vo, cloth, **2s. 6d.** each
PUNIANA: RIDDLES AND JOKES. With numerous Illustrations.
MORE PUNIANA. Profusely Illustrated.

RUNCIMAN (JAMES), STORIES BY.
SKIPPERS AND SHELLBACKS. | GR
SCHOOLS AND SCHOLARS.

RUSSELL (W. CLARK), BOOKS AND NOVELS BY:
Cr. 8vo, cloth extra, **6s.** each; post 8vo, illust. boards, **2s.** each; cloth limp, **2s. 6d**
ROUND THE GALLEY-FIRE.   A BOOK FOR THE HAMMOCK.
IN THE MIDDLE WATCH.   MYSTERY OF THE "OCEAN STAR
A VOYAGE TO THE CAPE.   THE ROMANCE OF JENNY HARLO

Cr. 8vo, cl extra, **3s. 6d.** ea.; post 8vo, illust. boards, **2s.** ea.; cloth limp, **2s. 6d.**
AN OCEAN TRAGEDY. | MY SHIPMATE LOUISE.
ALONE ON A WIDE WIDE SEA.
ON THE FO'K'SLE HEAD. Post 8vo, illust. boards, **2s.**; cloth limp, **2s. 6d.**

SAINT AUBYN (ALAN), NOVELS BY.
Crown 8vo, cloth extra, **3s. 6d.** each; post 8vo, illust. boards, **2s.** each.
A FELLOW OF TRINITY. Note by OLIVER WENDELL HOLMES and Frontispiec
THE JUNIOR DEAN.
Fcap. 8vo, cloth boards, **1s. 6d.** each.
THE OLD MAID'S SWEETHEART. | MODEST LITTLE SARA.
THE MASTER OF ST. BENEDICT'S. Two Vols., crown 8vo.

SALA (G. A.).—GASLIGHT AND DAYLIGHT. Post 8vo, b

SANSON.—SEVEN GENERATIONS OF EXECUTIONERS
of the Sanson Family (1688 to 1847). Crown 8vo, cloth extra. **3s. 6d.**

SAUNDERS (JOHN), NOVELS BY.
Crown 8vo, cloth extra, **3s. 6d.** each; post 8vo, il
GUY WATERMAN. | THE LION IN THE PAT
BOUND TO THE WHEEL. Crown 8vo, cloth extr

SAUNDERS (KATHARINE), NOVELS BY.
Crown 8vo, cloth extra. **3s. 6d.** each; post 8vo, illustrated boards, **2s.** each.
MARGARET AND ELIZABETH. | HEART SALVAGE.
THE HIGH MILLS. | SEBASTIAN.

SCIENCE-GOSSIP. Edited by Dr. J. E. TAYLOR, F.L S., &c. Devoted to Geology, Botany, Physiology, Chemistry, Zoology, Microscopy, Telescopy, Physiography, &c. **4d.** Monthly. Pts. 1 to 300, **8d.** each; Pts. 301 to date, **4d.** each. Vols. I. to XIX, **7s. 6d.** each; Vols. XX. to date, **5s.** each. Cases for Binding, **1s. 6d.**

SCOTLAND YARD: Experiences of 37 Years. By Chief-Inspector CAVANAGH. Post 8vo, illustrated boards. **2s.**; cloth, **2s. 6d.**

SECRET OUT, THE: One Thousand Tricks with Cards; with Entertaining Experiments in Drawing-room or "White Magic." By W. H. CREMER. With 300 Illustrations. Crown 8vo, cloth extra, **4s. 6d.**

SEGUIN (L. G.), WORKS BY.
THE COUNTRY OF THE PASSION PLAY (OBERAMMERGAU) and the Highlands of Bavaria. With Map and 37 Illustrations. Crown 8vo, cloth extra, **3s. 6d.**
WALKS IN ALGIERS. With 2 Maps and 16 Illusts. Crown 8vo. cloth extra. **6s.**

SENIOR (WM.).—BY STREAM AND SEA. Post 8vo, cloth, **2s. 6d.**

SHAKESPEARE FOR CHILDREN: LAMB'S TALES FROM SHAKE-SPEARE. With Illustrations, coloured and plain, by J. MOYR SMITH. Cr. 4to, **6s.**

SHARP.—CHILDREN OF TO-MORROW: A Novel. By WILLIAM SHARP. Crown 8vo, cloth extra, **6s.**

SHARP, LUKE (ROBERT BARR), STORIES BY.
IN A STEAMER CHAIR. With 2 Illustrations. Crown 8vo, cloth extra, **3s. 6d.**
FROM WHOSE BOURNE? &c. With Fifty Illustrations. [Shortl .

SHELLEY.—THE COMPLETE WORKS IN VERSE AND PROSE OFPERCY BYSSHE SHELLEY. Edited, Prefaced, and Annotated by R. HERNE SHEPHERD. Five Vols., crown 8vo, cloth boards, **3s. 6d.** each.
POETICAL WORKS, in Three Vols.:
Vol. I Introduction by the Editor; Posthumous Fragments of Margaret Nicholson; Shelley's Correspondence with Stockdale; The Wandering Jew; Queen Mab, with the Notes, Alastor, and other Poems; Rosalind and Helen: Prometheus Unbound; Adonais, &c.
Vol II. Laon and Cythna; The Cenci; Julian and Maddalo; Swellfoot the Tyrant, The Witch of Atlas; Epipsychidion· Hellas.
Vol III Posthumous Poems; The Masque of Anarchy; and other Pieces.
PROSE WORKS, in Two Vols.:
Vol. I. The Two Romances of Zastrozzi and St Irvyne; the Dublin and Marlow Pamphlets; A Refutation of Deism, Letters to Leigh Hunt, and some Minor Writings and Fragments.
Vol. II. The Essays; Letters from Abroad; Translations and Fragments, Edited by Mrs. SHELLEY. With a Bibliography of Shelley, and an Index of the Prose Works.

SHERARD (R. H.).—ROGUES: A Novel. Crown 8vo, **1s.**; cloth, **1s. 6d.**

SHERIDAN (GENERAL). — PERSONAL MEMOIRS OF GENERALP. H. SHERIDAN. With Portraits and Facsimiles. Two Vols., demy 8vo, cloth, **24s.**

SHERIDAN'S (RICHARD BRINSLEY) COMPLETE WORKS. With Life and Anecdotes. Including his Dramatic Writings, his Works in Prose and Poetry, Translations, Speeches and Jokes. 10 Illusts. Cr. 8vo, hf.-bound, **7s. 6d.**
THE RIVALS, THE SCHOOL FOR SCANDAL, and other Plays. Post 8vo, printed on laid paper and half-bound. **2s.**
SHERIDAN'S COMEDIES: THE RIVALS and THE SCHOOL FOR SCANDAL. Edited, with an Introduction and Notes to each Play, and a Biographical Sketch, by BRANDER MATTHEWS. With Illustrations. Demy 8vo. half-parchment, **12s. 6d.**

SIDNEY'S (SIR PHILIP) COMPLETE POETICAL WORKS, including all those in "Arcadia." With Portrait, Memorial-Introduction, Notes, &c. by the Rev. A.B. GROSART, D.D. Three Vols., crown 8vo, cloth boards, **18s.**

SIGNBOARDS: Their History. With Anecdotes of Famous Taverns and Remarkable Characters. By JACOB LARWOOD and JOHN CAMDEN HOTTEN. With Coloured Frontispiece and 94 Illustrations. Crown 8vo, cloth extra, **7s. 6d.**

SIMS (GEORGE R.), WORKS BY.
Post 8vo, illustrated boards, **2s.** each; cloth limp, **2s. 6d.** each.

ROGUES AND VAGABONDS.	MARY JANE MARRIED.
THE RING O' BELLS.	TALES OF TO-DAY.
MARY JANE'S MEMOIRS.	DRAMAS OF LIFE. With 60 Illustrations.

TINKLETOP'S CRIME. With a Frontispiece by MAURICE GREIFFENHAGEN.
ZEPH: A Circus Story, &c.

Crown 8vo, picture cover, **1s.** each; cloth, **1s. 6d.** each.
HOW THE POOR LIVE; and HORRIBLE LONDON.

SISTER DORA: A Biography. By MARGARET LONSDALE. With Fo
Illustrations   Demy 8vo, picture cover, **4d.**; cloth, **6d.**

SKETCHLEY.—A MATCH IN THE DARK. By ARTHU
Post 8vo, illustrated boards, **2s.**

SLANG DICTIONARY (THE): Etymological, Historical, and A
dotal.   Crown 8vo, cloth extra, **6s. 6d.**

SMITH (J. MOYR), WORKS BY.
THE PRINCE OF ARGOLIS. With 130 Illusts. Post 8vo, cloth extra, **3s. 6d**
TALES OF OLD THULE. With numerous Illustrations. Crown 8vo, cloth gilt
THE WOOING OF THE WATER WITCH. Illustrated. Post 8vo, cloth, **6s**

SOCIETY IN LONDON. By A FOREIGN RESIDENT.   Crown
1s.; cloth, **1s. 6d.**

SOCIETY IN PARIS: The Upper Ten Thous:
from Count PAUL VASILI to a Young French Diplomat.

SOMERSET. — SONGS OF ADIEU. By L
Small 4to, Japanese vellum, **6s.**

SPALDING.—ELIZABETHAN DEMONOLOGY : An Essay on the Be
in the Existence of Devils. By T. A. SPALDING, LL.B. Crown 8vo, cloth extra,

SPEIGHT (T. W.), NOVELS BY.
Post 8vo, illustrated boards, **2s.** each.

THE MYSTERIES OF HERON DYKE. | HOODWINKED; and THE SAN
BY DEVIOUS WAYS, &c. | CROFT MYSTERY.
THE GOLDEN HOOP. | BACK TO LIFE.

Post 8vo, cloth limp, **1s. 6d.** each.
A BARREN TITLE. | WIFE OR NO WIFE?
THE SANDYCROFT MYSTERY. Crown 8vo, picture cover, **1s.**

SPENSER FOR CHILDREN. By M. H. TOWRY.   With Ill
by WALTER J. MORGAN. Crown 4to, cloth gilt, **6s.**

STARRY HEAVENS (THE): A POETICAL BIRTHDAY BOOK
16mo, cloth extra, **2s. 6d.**

STAUNTON.—THE LAWS AND PRACTICE OF CHESS.
Analysis of the Openings. By HOWARD STAUNTON. Edited by ROBERT B
Crown 8vo, cloth extra, **5s.**

STEDMAN (E. C.), WORKS BY.
VICTORIAN POETS. Thirteenth Edition. Crown 8vo. cloth
THE POETS OF AMERICA. Crown 8vo, cloth extra, **9s.**

STERNDALE. — THE AFGHAN KNIFE: A Novel
ARMITAGE STERNDALE. Cr. 8vo, cloth extra **3s. 6d.**; post 8vo,

STEVENSON (R. LOUIS), WORKS BY.   Post 8vo, cl. limp, **2s. 6d.** ea
TRAVELS WITH A DONKEY. Seventh Edit. With a Frontis. by WALTER CRA
AN INLAND VOYAGE. Fourth Edition. With a Frontispiece by WALTER CRAI

Crown 8vo, buckram, gilt top, **6s.** each.
FAMILIAR STUDIES OF MEN AND BOOKS. Sixth Edition.
THE SILVERADO SQUATTERS. With a Frontispiece. Third Edition.
THE MERRY MEN. Third Edition. | UNDERWOODS: Poems. Fifth Editi
MEMORIES AND PORTRAITS. Third Edition.
VIRGINIBUS PUERISQUE, and other Papers. Seventh Edition. | BALLAD
ACROSS THE PLAINS, with other Memories and Essays.

NEW ARABIAN NIGHTS. Eleventh Edition. Crown 8vo, buckram, gilt top, **6**
post 8vo, illustrated boards, **2s.**
THE SUICIDE CLUB; and THE RAJAH'S DIAMOND. (From NEW ARAB
NIGHTS.) With Six Illustrations by J. BERNARD PARTRIDGE. Crown 8vo, cl
extra, **5s.**
PRINCE OTTO. Sixth Edition. Post 8vo, illustrated boards, **2s.**
FATHER DAMIEN: An Open Letter to the Rev. Dr. Hyde. Second Editi
Crown 8vo, hand-made and brown paper, **1s.**

STODDARD. — SUMMER C
C. WARREN STODDARD. Illustr

STORIES FROM FOREIGN

STRANGE MANUSCRIPT (A) FOUND IN A COPPER CYLINDER. With 19 Illustrations by GILBERT GAUL. Third Edition. Crown 8vo, cloth extra, **5s.**

STRANGE SECRETS. Told by CONAN DOYLE, PERCY FITZGERALD, FLORENCE MARRYAT, &c. Cr. 8vo, cl. ex., Eight Illusts., **6s.**; post 8vo, illust. bds, **2s.**

STRUTT'S SPORTS AND PASTIMES OF THE PEOPLE OF ENGLAND; including the Rural and Domestic Recreations, May Games, Mummeries, Shows, &c., from the Earliest Period to the Present Time. Edited by WILLIAM HONE. With 140 Illustrations. Crown 8vo, cloth extra, **7s. 6d.**

SUBURBAN HOMES (THE) OF LONDON : A Residential Guide. With a Map, and Notes on Rental, Rates, and Accommodation. Crown 8vo, cloth, **7s. 6d.**

SWIFT'S (DEAN) CHOICE WORKS, in Prose and Verse. With Memoir, Portrait, and Facsimiles of the Maps in "Gulliver's Travels." Cr. 8vo, cl., **7s. 6d.**
GULLIVER'S TRAVELS, and **A TALE OF A TUB.** Post 8vo, half-bound, **2s.**
A MONOGRAPH ON SWIFT. By J. CHURTON COLLINS. Cr. 8vo, cloth, **8s.** [Shortly.

SWINBURNE (ALGERNON C.), WORKS BY.

SELECTIONS FROM POETICAL WORKS OF A. C. SWINBURNE. Fcap. 8vo, **6s.**
ATALANTA IN CALYDON. Crown 8vo, **6s.**
CHASTELARD: A Tragedy. Cr. 8vo, **7s.**
POEMS AND BALLADS. FIRST SERIES. Crown 8vo or fcap 8vo, **9s.**
POEMS AND BALLADS. SECOND SERIES. Crown 8vo or fcap 8vo, **9s.**
POEMS AND BALLADS. THIRD SERIES. Crown 8vo, **7s.**
SONGS BEFORE SUNRISE. Crown 8vo, **10s. 6d.**
BOTHWELL: A Tragedy. Crown 8vo, **12s. 6d.**
SONGS OF TWO NATIONS. Cr. 8vo, **6s.**
GEORGE CHAPMAN. (See Vol. II. of G. CHAPMAN'S Works.) Crown 8vo, **6s.**

ESSAYS AND STUDIES. Cr. 8vo, **12s.**
ERECHTHEUS: A Tragedy. Cr. 8vo, **6s.**
SONGS OF THE SPRINGTIDES. Crown 8vo, **6s.**
STUDIES IN SONG. Crown 8vo, **7s.**
MARY STUART: A Tragedy. Cr. 8vo, **8s.**
TRISTRAM OF LYONESSE. Cr. 8vo, **9s.**
A CENTURY OF ROUNDELS. Sm. 4to, **8s.**
A MIDSUMMER HOLIDAY. Cr. 8vo, **7s.**
MARINO FALIERO: A Tragedy. Crown 8vo. **6s.**
A STUDY OF VICTOR HUGO. Cr. 8vo, **6s.**
MISCELLANIES. Crown 8vo, **12s.**
LOCRINE: A Tragedy. Cr. 8vo, **6s.**
A STUDY OF BEN JONSON. Cr. 8vo, **7s.**
THE SISTERS: A Tragedy. Cr. 8vo, **6s.**

SYMONDS.—WINE, WOMEN, AND SONG : Mediæval Latin Students' Songs. With Essay and Trans. by J. ADDINGTON SYMONDS. Fcap. 8vo, parchment, **6s.**

SYNTAX'S (DR.) THREE TOURS : In Search of the Picturesque, in Search of Consolation, and in Search of a Wife. With ROWLANDSON'S Coloured Illustrations, and Life of the Author by J. C. HOTTEN. Crown 8vo, cloth extra, **7s. 6d.**

TAINE'S HISTORY OF ENGLISH LITERATURE. Translated by HENRY VAN LAUN. Four Vols., small demy 8vo, cl. bds., **30s.**—POPULAR EDITION, Two Vols., large crown 8vo, cloth extra, **15s.**

TAYLOR'S (BAYARD) DIVERSIONS OF THE ECHO CLUB : Burlesques of Modern Writers. Post 8vo, cloth limp, **2s.**

TAYLOR (DR. J. E., F.L.S.), WORKS BY. Cr. 8vo, cl. ex., **7s. 6d.** each.
THE SAGACITY AND MORALITY OF PLANTS : A Sketch of the Life and Conduct of the Vegetable Kingdom. With a Coloured Frontispiece and 100 Illustrations
OUR COMMON BRITISH FOSSILS, and Where to Find Them. 331 Illustrations.
THE PLAYTIME NATURALIST. With 360 Illustrations. Crown 8vo, cloth, **5s.**

TAYLOR'S (TOM) HISTORICAL DRAMAS. Containing "Clancarty," "Jeanne Darc," "'Twixt Axe and Crown," "The Fool's Revenge," "Arkwright's Wife," "Anne Boleyn," "Plot and Passion." Crown 8vo, cloth extra, **7s. 6d.**
₊ The Plays may also be had separately, at **1s.** each.

TENNYSON (LORD) : A Biographical Sketch. By H. J. JENNINGS. With a Photograph-Portrait. Crown 8vo, cloth extra, **6s.**—Cheap Edition, post 8vo, portrait cover, **1s.**; cloth, **1s. 6d.**

THACKERAYANA : Notes and Anecdotes. Illustrated by Hundreds of Sketches by WILLIAM MAKEPEACE THACKERAY. Crown 8vo, cloth extra, **7s. 6d.**

THAMES.—A NEW PICTORIAL HISTORY OF THE THAMES. By A. S. KRAUSSE. With 340 Illustrations Post 8vo, **1s.**; cloth, **1s. 6d.**

THOMAS (BERTHA), NOVELS BY. Cr. 8vo, cl., **3s. 6d.** ea.; post 8vo, **2s.** ea.

THOMSON'S SEASONS, and CASTLE OF INDOLENCE. With I1 duction by Allan Cunningham, and 48 Illustrations. Post 8vo, half-bound, **2s**

THORNBURY (WALTER), WORKS BY. Cr. 8vo, cl. extra, **7s. 6d.** eac
THE LIFE AND CORRESPONDENCE OF J. M. W. TURNER. Founded u Letters and Papers furnished by his Friends. With Illustrations in Colours.
HAUNTED LONDON. Edit. by E. Walford, M.A. Illusts. by F. W. Fairholt, F.

Post 8vo, illustrated boards, **2s**. each.
OLD STORIES RE-TOLD. | TALES FOR THE MARINES.

TIMBS (JOHN), WORKS BY. Crown 8vo, cloth extra, **7s. 6d.** each.
THE HISTORY OF CLUBS AND CLUB LIFE IN LONDON: Anecdotes of Famous Coffee-houses, Hostelries, and Taverns. With 42 Illustrations.
ENGLISH ECCENTRICS AND ECCENTRICITIES: Stories of Delusions, Imp tures, Sporting Scenes, Eccentric Artists, Theatrical Folk, &c. 48 Illustratic

TROLLOPE (ANTHONY), NOVELS BY.
Crown 8vo, cloth extra, **3s. 6d.** each; post 8vo, illustrated boards, **2s**. each.
THE WAY WE LIVE NOW. | MARION FAY.
KEPT IN THE DARK. | MR. SCARBOROUGH'S FAMILY.
FRAU FROHMANN. | THE LAND-LEAGUERS.

Post 8vo, illustrated boards, **2s**. each.
GOLDEN LION OF GRANPERE. | JOHN CALDIGATE. | AMERICAN SENAT

TROLLOPE (FRANCES E.), NOVELS BY.
Crown 8vo, cloth extra, **3s. 6d.** each; post 8vo, illustr
LIKE SHIPS UPON THE SEA. | MABEL'S PROGR

TROLLOPE (T. A.).—DIAMOND CUT DIAMOND. P

TROWBRIDGE.—FARNELL'S FOLLY: A Novel.
BRIDGE. Post 8vo, illustrated boards, **2s**.

TYTLER (C. C. FRASER-).—MISTRESS JUDITH: A Novel.
C. C. Fraser-Tytler. Crown 8vo, cloth extra, **3s. 6d.**; post 8vo, illust. boar

TYTLER (SARAH), NOVELS BY.
Crown 8vo, cloth extra, **3s. 6d.** each; post 8vo, illustrated boards, **2s**. each.
THE BRIDE'S PASS. | BURIED DIAMONDS.
LADY BELL. | THE BLACKHALL GHOSTS.

Post 8vo, illustrated boards, **2s**. each.
WHAT SHE CAME THROUGH. | BEAUTY AND THE BEAST.
CITOYENNE JACQUELINE. | DISAPPEARED.
SAINT MUNGO'S CITY. | THE HUGUENOT FAMILY.
NOBLESSE OBLIGE.

VILLARI.—A DOUBLE BOND. By Linda Villari. Fcap. 8vo, pict cover, **1s**.

WALT WHITMAN, POEMS BY. Edited, with Introduction,
William M. Rossetti. With Portrait. Cr. 8vo, hand-made paper and buckram,

WALTON AND COTTON'S COMPLETE ANGLER; or, The C templative Man's Recreation, by Izaak Walton; and Instructions how to Angle f Trout or Grayling in a clear Stream, by Charles Cotton. With Memoirs and N by Sir Harris Nicolas, and 61 Illustrations. Crown 8vo, cloth antique, **7s. 6d**

WARD (HERBERT), WORKS BY.
FIVE YEARS WITH THE CONGO CANNIBALS. With 92 Illustrations by Author, Victor Perard, and W. B. Davis. Third ed. Roy. 8vo, cloth ex., **1**
MY LIFE WITH STANLEY'S REAR GUARD. With a Map by F. S. Wel F.R.G.S. Post 8vo, **1s**.; cloth, **1s. 6d**

WARNER.—A ROUNDABOUT JOURNEY. By Charles Dud Warner. Crown 8vo, cloth extra, **6s**.

WARRANT TO EXECUTE CHARLES I. A Facsimile, with the Signatures and Seals Printed on paper 22 in. by 14 in. **2s**.
WARRANT TO EXECUTE MARY QUEEN OF SCOTS. A Facsimile, includ Queen Elizabeth's Signature and the Great Seal. **2s**.

WASSERMANN (LILLIAS), NOVELS BY.
THE DAFFODILS. Crown 8vo. **1s**.; cloth. **1s. 6d**.

WALFORD (EDWARD, M.A.), WORKS BY.

WALFORD'S COUNTY FAMILIES OF THE UNITED KINGDOM (1893). Containing the Descent, Birth, Marriage, Education, &c., of 12,000 Heads of Families, their Heirs, Offices, Addresses, Clubs, &c. Royal 8vo. cloth gilt. **50s.**

WALFORD'S WINDSOR PEERAGE, BARONETAGE, AND KNIGHTAGE (1893). Crown 8vo, cloth extra, **12s. 6d.**

WALFORD'S SHILLING PEERAGE (1893). Containing a List of the House of Lords, Scotch and Irish Peers, &c. 32mo. cloth, **1s.**

WALFORD'S SHILLING BARONETAGE (1893). Containing a List of the Baronets of the United Kingdom, Biographical Notices, Addresses, &c. 32mo, cloth, **1s.**

WALFORD'S SHILLING KNIGHTAGE (1893). Containing a List of the Knights of the United Kingdom, Biographical Notices, Addresses, &c. 32mo, cloth, **1s.**

WALFORD'S SHILLING HOUSE OF COMMONS (1893). Containing a List of all Members of the New Parliament, their Addresses, Clubs, &c. 32mo, cloth, **1s.**

WALFORD'S COMPLETE PEERAGE, BARONETAGE, KNIGHTAGE, AND HOUSE OF COMMONS (1893). Royal 32mo, cloth extra, gilt edges, **5s.**

TALES OF OUR GREAT FAMILIES. Crown 8vo, cloth extra, **3s. 6d.**

WEATHER, HOW TO FORETELL THE, WITH POCKET SPECTROSCOPE. By F. W. CORY. With 10 Illustrations. Cr. 8vo, **1s.**; cloth, **1s. 6d.**

WESTALL (William).—TRUST-MONEY. Three Vols., crown 8vo.

WHIST.—HOW TO PLAY SOLO WHIST. By ABRAHAM S. WILKS and CHARLES F. PARDON. New Edition. Post 8vo, cloth limp. **2s.**

WHITE.—THE NATURAL HISTORY OF SELBORNE. By GILBERT WHITE, M.A. Post 8vo, printed on laid paper and half-bound, **2s.**

WILLIAMS (W. MATTIEU, F.R.A.S.), WORKS BY.

SCIENCE IN SHORT CHAPTERS. Crown 8vo, cloth extra, **7s. 6d.**

A SIMPLE TREATISE ON HEAT. With Illusts. Cr. 8vo, cloth limp, **2s. 6d.**

THE CHEMISTRY OF COOKERY. Crown 8vo, cloth extra, **6s.**

THE CHEMISTRY OF IRON AND STEEL MAKING. Crown 8vo, cloth extra, **9s.**

WILLIAMSON (MRS. F. H.).—A CHILD WIDOW. Post 8vo, bds., 2s.

WILSON (DR. ANDREW, F.R.S.E.), WORKS BY.

CHAPTERS ON EVOLUTION. With 259 Illustrations. Cr. 8vo, cloth extra, **7s. 6d.**

LEAVES FROM A NATURALIST'S NOTE-BOOK. Post 8vo, cloth limp, **2s. 6d.**

LEISURE-TIME STUDIES. With Illustrations. Crown 8vo, cloth extra, **6s.**

STUDIES IN LIFE AND SENSE. With numerous Illusts. Cr. 8vo, cl. ex., **6s.**

COMMON ACCIDENTS: HOW TO TREAT THEM. Illusts. Cr. 8vo, **1s.**; cl., **1s. 6d.**

GLIMPSES OF NATURE. With 35 Illustrations. Crown 8vo, cloth extra, **3s. 6d.**

WINTER (J. S.), STORIES BY. Post 8vo, illustrated boards, 2s. each; cloth limp, 2s. 6d. each.

CAVALRY LIFE. | **REGIMENTAL LEGENDS.**

A SOLDIER'S CHILDREN. With 34 Illustrations by E. G. THOMSON and E. STUART HARDY. Crown 8vo, cloth extra, **3s. 6d.**

WISSMANN.—MY SECOND JOURNEY THROUGH EQUATORIAL AFRICA. By HERMANN VON WISSMANN. With 92 Illusts. Demy 8vo, **16s.**

WOOD.—SABINA: A Novel. By Lady WOOD. Post 8vo, boards, 2s.

WOOD (H. F.), DETECTIVE STORIES BY. Cr. 8vo, 6s. ea.; post 8vo, bds. 2s.

PASSENGER FROM SCOTLAND YARD. | **ENGLISHMAN OF THE RUE CAIN.**

WOOLLEY.—RACHEL ARMSTRONG; or, Love and Theology. By CELIA PARKER WOOLLEY. Post 8vo, illustrated boards, **2s.**; cloth, **2s. 6d.**

WRIGHT (THOMAS), WORKS BY. Crown 8vo, cloth extra, 7s. 6d. each.

CARICATURE HISTORY OF THE GEORGES. With 400 Caricatures, Squibs, &c.

HISTORY OF CARICATURE AND OF THE GROTESQUE IN ART, LITERATURE, SCULPTURE, AND PAINTING. Illustrated by F. W. FAIRHOLT, F.S.A.

WYNMAN.—MY FLIRTATIONS. By MARGARET WYNMAN. With 13 Illustrations by J. BERNARD PARTRIDGE. Crown 8vo, cloth extra, **3s. 6d.**

YATES (EDMUND), NOVELS BY. Post 8vo, illustrated boards, 2s. each.

LAND AT LAST. | **THE FORLORN HOPE.** | **CASTAWAY.**

NOVELS BY. Crown 8vo, cloth extra, 3s. 6d. each.

LISTS OF BOOKS CLASSIFIED IN SERIES.

₊ *For fuller cataloguing, see alphabetical arrangement, pp. 1–25.*

THE MAYFAIR LIBRARY. Post 8vo, cloth limp, 2s. 6d. per Volume.

A Journey Round My Room. By XAVIER DE MAISTRE.
Quips and Quiddities. By W. D. ADAMS.
The Agony Column of "The Times."
Melancholy Anatomised: Abridgment of "Burton's Anatomy of Melancholy."
The Speeches of Charles Dickens.
Poetical Ingenuities. By W. T. DOBSON.
The Cupboard Papers. By FIN-BEC.
W. S. Gilbert's Plays. FIRST SERIES.
W. S. Gilbert's Plays. SECOND SERIES.
Songs of Irish Wit and Humour.
Animals and Masters. By Sir A. HELPS.
Social Pressure. By Sir A. HELPS.
Curiosities of Criticism. H. J. JENNINGS.
Holmes's Autocrat of Breakfast-Table.
Pencil and Palette. By R. KEMPT.
Little Essays: from LAMB's Letters.

Forensic Anecdotes. By JACOB LARWOO
Theatrical Anecdotes. JACOB LARWOO
Jeux d'Esprit. Edited by HENRY S. LEIG
Witch Stories. By E. LYNN LINTON.
Ourselves. By E. LYNN LINTON.
Pastimes & Players. By R. MACGREGO
New Paul and Virginia. W.H.MALLOC
New Republic. By W. H. MALLOCK.
Puck on Pegasus. By H. C. PENNELL.
Pegasus Re-Saddled. By H.C. PENNEL
Muses of Mayfair. Ed. H. C. PENNEL
Thoreau: His Life & Aims. By H. A. PAG
Puniana. By Hon. HUGH ROWLEY.
More Puniana. By Hon. HUGH ROWLE
The Philosophy of Handwriting.
By Stream and Sea. By WM. SENIOR
Leaves from a Naturalist's Note-Boo
By Dr. ANDREW WILSON.

THE GOLDEN LIBRARY. Post 8vo, cloth limp, 2s. per Volume.

Bayard Taylor's Diversions of the Echo Club.
Bennett's Ballad History of England.
Bennett's Songs for Sailors.
Godwin's Lives of the Necromancers.
Pope's Poetical Works.
Holmes's Autocrat of Breakfast Table.

Jesse's Scenes of Country Life.
Leigh Hunt's Tale for a Chimn Corner.
Mallory's Mort d'Arthur: Selections.
Pascal's Provincial Letters.
Rochefoucauld's Maxims & Reflection

THE WANDERER'S LIBRARY. Crown 8vo, cloth extra, 3s. 6d. each.

Wanderings in Patagonia. By JULIUS BEERBOHM. Illustrated.
Camp Notes. By FREDERICK BOYLE.
Savage Life. By FREDERICK BOYLE.
Merrie England in the Olden Time. By G. DANIEL. Illustrated by CRUIKSHANK.
Circus Life. By THOMAS FROST.
Lives of the Conjurers. THOMAS FROST.
The Old Showmen and the Old London Fairs. By THOMAS FROST.
Low-Life Deeps. By JAMES GREENWOOD.

Wilds of London. JAMES GREENWOO
Tunis. Chev. HESSE-WARTEGG. 22 Illus
Life and Adventures of a Cheap Jac
World Behind the Scenes. P.FITZGERAL
Tavern Anecdotes and Sayings.
The Genial Showman. By E.P. HINGSTO
Story of London Parks. JACOB LARWOO
London Characters. By HENRY MAYHE
Seven Generations of Executioners.
Summer Cruising in the South Sea
By C. WARREN STODDARD. Illustrate

POPULAR SHILLING BOOKS.

Harry Fludyer at Cambridge.
Jeff Briggs's Love Story. BRET HARTE.
Twins of Table Mountain. BRET HARTE.
Snow-bound at Eagle's. By BRET HARTE.
A Day's Tour. By PERCY FITZGERALD.
Esther's Glove. By R. E. FRANCILLON.
Sentenced! By SOMERVILLE GIBNEY.
The Professor's Wife. By L. GRAHAM.
Mrs. Gainsborough's Diamonds. By JULIAN HAWTHORNE.
Niagara Spray. By J. HOLLINGSHEAD.
A Romance of the Queen's Hounds. By CHARLES JAMES.
Garden that Paid Rent. TOM JERROLD.
Cut by the Mess. By ARTHUR KEYSER.
Teresa Itasca. By A. MACALPINE.
Our Sensation Novel. J. H. MCCARTHY.
Doom! By JUSTIN H. MCCARTHY.
Dolly. By JUSTIN H. MCCARTHY.

Lily Lass. JUSTIN H. MCCARTHY.
Was She Good or Bad? By W. MINTC
Notes from the "News." By JAS. PAY
Beyond the Gates. By E. S. PHELPS.
Old Maid's Paradise. By E. S. PHELP
Burglars in Paradise. By E. S. PHELP
Jack the Fisherman. By E. S. PHELP
Trooping with Crows. By C. L. PIRKI
Bible Characters. By CHARLES READ
Rogues. By R. H. SHERARD.
The Dagonet Reciter. By G. R. SIMS.
How the Poor Live. By G. R. SIMS.
Case of George Candlemas. G. R. SIM
Sandycroft Mystery. T. W. SPEIGHT
Hoodwinked. By T. W. SPEIGHT.
Father Damien. By R. L. STEVENSON.
A Double Bond. By LINDA VILLARI.
My Life with Stanley's Rear Guard. HERBERT WARD.

HANDY NOVELS. Fcap. 8vo, cloth boards, 1s. 6d. each.

The Old Maid's Sweetheart. A.ST.AUBYN
Modest Little Sara. ALAN ST. AUBYN

Taken from the Enemy. H. NEWBOLT
A Lost Soul. By W. L. ALDEN.

The Seven Sleepers of Ephesus. By M. E. COLERIDGE.

MY LIBRARY.

Choice Works, printed on laid paper, bound half-Roxburghe, **2s. 6d.** each.

Four Frenchwomen. By AUSTIN DOBSON.
Citation and Examination of William Shakspeare. By W. S. LANDOR.
The Journal of Maurice de Guerin.

Christie Johnstone. By CHARLES READ
With a Photogravure Frontispiece.
Peg Woffington. By CHARLES READE.
The Dramatic Essays of Charles Lam

THE POCKET LIBRARY.　Post 8vo, printed on laid paper and hf.-bd., **2s.** each

The Essays of Elia. By CHARLES LAMB.
Robinson Crusoe. Edited by JOHN MAJOR.
With 37 Illusts. by GEORGE CRUIKSHANK.
Whims and Oddities. By THOMAS HOOD.
With 85 Illustrations.
The Barber's Chair, and The Hedgehog Letters. By DOUGLAS JERROLD.
Gastronomy. By BRILLAT-SAVARIN.
The Epicurean, &c. By THOMAS MOORE.
Leigh Hunt's Essays. Ed E. OLLIER.

White's Natural History of Selborne
Gulliver's Travels, and The Tale of Tub. By Dean SWIFT.
The Rivals, School for Scandal, and oth
Plays by RICHARD BRINSLEY SHERIDA.
Anecdotes of the Clergy. J. LARWOOD
Thomson's Seasons. Illustrated.
The Autocrat of the Breakfast-Tabl
and **The Professor at the Breakfas**
Table. By OLIVER WENDELL HOLME

THE PICCADILLY NOVELS.

LIBRARY EDITIONS OF NOVELS, many Illustrated, crown 8vo, cloth extra, **3s. 6d.** each

By F. M. ALLEN.
Green as Grass.

By GRANT ALLEN.
Philistia.
Babylon
Strange Stories.
Beckoning Hand.
In all Shades.
Dumaresq's Daughter.
The Duchess of Powysland.
The Tents of Shem.
For Maimie's Sake.
The Devil's Die.
This Mortal Coil.
The Great Taboo.
Blood Royal.

By EDWIN L. ARNOLD.
Phra the Phœnician.

By ALAN ST. AUBYN.
A Fellow of Trinity.

By Rev. S. BARING GOULD.
Red Spider. | Eve.

By W. BESANT & J. RICE.
My Little Girl.
Case of Mr. Lucraft.
This Son of Vulcan.
Golden Butterfly.
Ready-Money Mortiboy.
With Harp and Crown.
'Twas in Trafalgar's Bay.
The Chaplain of the Fleet.
By Celia's Arbour.
Monks of Thelema.
The Seamy Side.
Ten Years' Tenant.

By WALTER BESANT.
All Sorts and Conditions of Men.
The Captains' Room. | Herr Paulus.
All in a Garden Fair
The World Went Very Well Then.
For Faith and Freedom.
Dorothy Forster.
Uncle Jack.
Children of Gibeon.
Bell of St. Paul's.
To Call Her Mine.
The Holy Rose.
Armorel of Lyonesse.
St. Katherine's by the Tower.

By ROBERT BUCHANAN.
The Shadow of the Sword. | Matt.
A Child of Nature. | Heir of Linne.
The Martyrdom of Madeline.
God and the Man.
Love Me for Ever.
Annan Water.
The New Abelard.
Foxglove Manor.
Master of the Mine.

MORT. & FRANCES COLLIN
Transmigration.
From Midnight to Midnight.
Blacksmith and Scholar.
Village Comedy. | You Play Me Fals

By WILKIE COLLINS.
Armadale.
After Dark.
No Name.
Antonina. | Basil.
Hide and Seek.
The Dead Secret.
Queen of Hearts.
My Miscellanies.
Woman in White.
The Moonstone.
Man and Wife.
Poor Miss Finch.
Miss or Mrs?
New Magdalen.
The Frozen Deep
The Two Destinie
Law and the Lad
Haunted Hotel.
The Fallen Leave
Jezebel's Daughte
The Black Robe.
Heart and Scienc
"I Say No."
Little Novels.
The Evil Genius.
The Legacy of Ca
A Rogue's Life.
Blind Love.

By DUTTON COOK.
Paul Foster's Daughter.

By MATT CRIM.
Adventures of a Fair Rebel.

By B. M. CROKER.
Diana Barrington. | Pretty Miss Nevill
Proper Pride. | A Bird of Passag

By WILLIAM CYPLES.
Hearts of Gold.

By ALPHONSE DAUDET.
The Evangelist; or, Port Salvation.

By ERASMUS DAWSON.
The Fountain of Youth.

By JAMES DE MILLE.
A Castle in Spain.

By J. LEITH DERWENT.
Our Lady of Tears. | Circe's Lovers

By DICK DONOVAN.
Tracked to Doom.

By Mrs. ANNIE EDWARDE
Archie Lovell.

By G. MANVILLE FENN.
The New Mistress.

By PERCY FITZGERALD
Fatal Zero.

By R. E. FRANCILLON.
Queen Cophetua.　A Real Queen.

THE PICCADILLY (3/6) NOVELS—continued.

By EDWARD GARRETT.
The Capel Girls.

By CHARLES GIBBON.
Robin Gray. | The Golden Shaft.
Loving a Dream. | Of High Degree.
The Flower of the Forest.

By E. GLANVILLE.
The Lost Heiress. | The Fossicker.

By CECIL GRIFFITH.
Corinthia Marazion.

By THOMAS HARDY.
Under the Greenwood Tree.

By BRET HARTE.
A Waif of the Plains.
A Ward of the Golden Gate.
A Sappho of Green Springs.
Colonel Starbottle's Client.
Susy. | Sally Dows.

By JULIAN HAWTHORNE.
Garth. | Dust.
Ellice Quentin. | Fortune's Fool.
Sebastian Strome. | Beatrix Randolph.
David Poindexter's Disappearance.
The Spectre of the Camera.

By Sir A. HELPS.
Ivan de Biron.

By ISAAC HENDERSON.
Agatha Page.

By Mrs. ALFRED HUNT.
The Leaden Casket. | Self-Condemned.
That other Person.

By R. ASHE KING.
A Drawn Game.
"The Wearing of the Green."

By E. LYNN LINTON.
Patricia Kemball. | Ione.
Under which Lord? | Paston Carew.
"My Love!" | Sowing the Wind.
The Atonement of Leam Dundas.
The World Well Lost.

By HENRY W. LUCY.
Gideon Fleyce.

By JUSTIN McCARTHY.
A Fair Saxon. | Donna Quixote.
Linley Rochford. | Maid of Athens.
Miss Misanthrope. | Camiola.
The Waterdale Neighbours.
My Enemy's Daughter.
Dear Lady Disdain.
The Comet of a Season.

By AGNES MACDONELL.
Quaker Cousins.

By D. CHRISTIE MURRAY.
Life's Atonement. | Val Strange.
Joseph's Coat. | Hearts.
Coals of Fire. | A Model Father.
Old Blazer's Hero.
By the Gate of the Sea.
A Bit of Human Nature.
First Person Singular. | Cynic Fortune.
The Way of the World.

By MURRAY & HERMAN.
The Bishops' Bible.
Paul Jones's Alias.

By HUME NISBET.
"Bail Up!"

By GEORGES OHNET.

THE PICCADILLY (3/6) NOVELS—contin

By OUIDA.
Held in Bondage. | Two Little Woo
Strathmore. | Shoes.
Chandos. | In a Winter Ci
Under Two Flags. | Ariadne.
Idalia. | Friendship.
CecilCastlemaine's | Moths. | Ruff
Gage. | Pipistrello.
Tricotrin. | Puck. | A Village Comm
Folle Farine. | Bimbi. | Wan
A Dog of Flanders. | Frescoes. | Othm
Pascarel. | Signa. | In Maremma.
Princess Naprax- | Syrlin. | Guilder
ine. | Santa Barbara.

By MARGARET A. PAUL
Gentle and Simple.

By JAMES PAYN.
Lost Sir Massingberd.
Less Black than We're Painted.
A Confidential Agent.
A Grape from a Thorn.
In Peril and Privation.
The Mystery of Mirbridge.
The Canon's Ward.
Walter's Word. | Talk of the Tow
By Proxy. | Holiday Tasks.
High Spirits. | The Burnt Milli
Under One Roof. | The Word and
From Exile. | Will.
Glow-worm Tales. | Sunny Stories.

By E. C. PRICE.
Valentina. | The Foreigners
Mrs. Lancaster's Rival.

By RICHARD PRYCE.
Miss Maxwell's Affections.

By CHARLES READE.
It is Never Too Late to Mend.
The Double Marriage.
Love Me Little, Love Me Long.
The Cloister and the Hearth.
The Course of True Love.
The Autobiography of a Thief.
Put Yourself in his Place.
A Terrible Temptation.
Singleheart and Doubleface.
Good Stories of Men and other Anim
Hard Cash. | Wandering He
Peg Woffington. | A Woman-Hat
ChristieJohnstone. | A Simpleton.
Griffith Gaunt. | Readiana.
Foul Play. | The Jilt.
A Perilous Secret.

By Mrs. J. H. RIDDELL.
The Prince of Wales's Garden Part
Weird Stories.

By F. W. ROBINSON.
Women are Strange.
The Hands of Justice.

By W. CLARK RUSSELL
An Ocean Tragedy.
My Shipmate Louise.
Alone on a Wide Wide Sea.

By JOHN SAUNDERS.
Guy Waterman. | Two Dreamers.
Bound to the Wheel.
The Lion in the Path.

By KATHARINE SAUNDE

By R. ASHE KING.

A Drawn Game. | Passion's Slave.
"The Wearing of the Green."
Bell Barry.

By JOHN LEYS.

The Lindsays.

By E. LYNN LINTON.

Patricia Kemball. | Paston Carew.
World Well Lost. | "My Love!"
Under which Lord? | Ione.
The Atonement of Leam Dundas.
With a Silken Thread.
The Rebel of the Family.
Sowing the Wind.

By HENRY W. LUCY.

Gideon Fleyce.

By JUSTIN McCARTHY.

A Fair Saxon. | Donna Quixote.
Linley Rochford. | Maid of Athens.
Miss Misanthrope. | Camiola.
Dear Lady Disdain.
The Waterdale Neighbours.
My Enemy's Daughter.
The Comet of a Season.

By HUGH MACCOLL.

Mr. Stranger's Sealed Packet.

By AGNES MACDONELL.

Quaker Cousins.

KATHARINE S. MACQUOID.

The Evil Eye. | Lost Rose.

By W. H. MALLOCK.

The New Republic.

By FLORENCE MARRYAT.

Open! Sesame! | Fighting the Air.
A Harvest of Wild Oats.
Written in Fire.

By J. MASTERMAN.

Half-a-dozen Daughters.

By BRANDER MATTHEWS.

A Secret of the Sea.

By LEONARD MERRICK.

The Man who was Good.

By JEAN MIDDLEMASS.

Touch and Go. | Mr. Dorillion.

By Mrs. MOLESWORTH.

Hathercourt Rectory.

By J. E. MUDDOCK.

Stories Weird and Wonderful.
The Dead Man's Secret.
From the Bosom of the Deep.

By D. CHRISTIE MURRAY.

A Model Father. | Old Blazer's Hero.
Joseph's Coat. | Hearts.
Coals of Fire. | Way of the World.
Val Strange. | Cynic Fortune.
A Life's Atonement.
By the Gate of the Sea.
A Bit of Human Nature.
First Person Singular.

By MURRAY and HERMAN.

One Traveller Returns.
Paul Jones's Alias.
The Bishops' Bible.

By HENRY MURRAY.

A Game of Bluff.

By HUME NISBET.

"Bail Up!"
Dr. Bernard St. Vincent.

By ALICE O'HANLON.

By GEORGES OHNET.

Doctor Rameau. | A Last Love.
A Weird Gift.

By Mrs. OLIPHANT.

Whiteladies. | The Primrose Pa
The Greatest Heiress in England.

By Mrs. ROBERT O'REILL

Phœbe's Fortunes.

By OUIDA.

Held in Bondage. | Two Little Wood
Strathmore. | Shoes.
Chandos. | Friendship.
Under Two Flags. | Moths.
Idalia. | Pipistrello.
Cecil Castlemaine's | A Village Co
Gage. | mune.
Tricotrin. | Bimbi.
Puck. | Wanda.
Folle Farine. | Frescoes.
A Dog of Flanders. | In Maremma.
Pascarel. | Othmar.
Signa. | Guilderoy.
Princess Naprax- | Ruffino.
ine. | Syrlin.
In a Winter City. | Ouida's Wisdo
Ariadne. | Wit, and Path

MARGARET AGNES PAUl

Gentle and Simple.

By JAMES PAYN.

Bentinck's Tutor. | £200 Reward.
Murphy's Master. | Marine Residen
A County Family. | Mirk Abbey.
At Her Mercy. | By Proxy.
Cecil's Tryst. | Under One Roo
Clyffards of Clyffe. | High Spirits.
Foster Brothers. | Carlyon's Year.
Found Dead. | From Exile.
Best of Husbands. | For Cash Only.
Walter's Word. | Kit.
Halves. | The Canon's Wa
Fallen Fortunes. | Talk of the Tow
Humorous Stories. | Holiday Tasks.
Lost Sir Massingberd.
A Perfect Treasure.
A Woman's Vengeance.
The Family Scapegrace.
What He Cost Her.
Gwendoline's Harvest.
Like Father, Like Son.
Married Beneath Him.
Not Wooed, but Won.
Less Black than We're Painted.
A Confidential Agent.
Some Private Views.
A Grape from a Thorn.
Glow-worm Tales.
The Mystery of Mirbridge.
The Burnt Million.
The Word and the Will.
A Prince of the Blood.
Sunny Stories.

By C. L. PIRKIS.

Lady Lovelace.

By EDGAR A. POE.

The Mystery of Marie Roget.

By Mrs. CAMPBELL PRAE

The Romance of a Station.
The Soul of Countess Adrian.

By E. C. PRICE.

Valentina. | The Foreigners

Miss Maxwell's Affections.

By CHARLES READE.

It is Never Too Late to Mend.
Christie Johnstone.
Put Yourself in His Place.
The Double Marriage.
Love Me Little, Love Me Long.
The Cloister and the Hearth.
The Course of True Love.
Autobiography of a Thief.
A Terrible Temptation.
The Wandering Heir.
Singleheart and Doubleface.
Good Stories of Men and other Animals.

Hard Cash.	A Simpleton.
Peg Woffington.	Readiana.
Griffith Gaunt.	A Woman-Hater.
Foul Play.	The Jilt.

A Perilous Secret.

By Mrs. J. H. RIDDELL.

Weird Stories.	Fairy Water.

Her Mother's Darling.
Prince of Wales's Garden Party.
The Uninhabited House.
The Mystery in Palace Gardens.

The Nun's Curse.	Idle Tales.

By F. W. ROBINSON.

Women are Strange.
The Hands of Justice.

By JAMES RUNCIMAN.

Skippers and Shellbacks.
Grace Balmaign's Sweetheart.
Schools and Scholars.

By W. CLARK RUSSELL.

Round the Galley Fire.
On the Fo'k'sle Head.
In the Middle Watch.
A Voyage to the Cape.
A Book for the Hammock.
The Mystery of the "Ocean Star."
The Romance of Jenny Harlowe.
An Ocean Tragedy.
My Shipmate Louise.
Alone on a Wide Wide Sea.

GEORGE AUGUSTUS SALA.

Gaslight and Daylight.

By JOHN SAUNDERS.

Guy Waterman.	Two Dreamers.

The Lion in the Path.

By KATHARINE SAUNDERS.

Joan Merryweather.	Heart Salvage.
The High Mills.	Sebastian.

Margaret and Elizabeth.

By GEORGE R. SIMS.

Rogues and Vagabonds.
The Ring o' Bells.
Mary Jane's Memoirs.
Mary Jane Married.

Tales of To-day.	Dramas of Life.

Tinkletop's Crime.
Zeph: A Circus Story.

By ARTHUR SKETCHLEY.

A Match in the Dark.

By HAWLEY SMART.

Without Love or Licence.

By T. W. SPEIGHT.

The Mysteries of Heron Dyke.

The Golden Hoop.	By Devious Ways.
Hoodwinked, &c.	Back to Life.

By R. A. STERNDALE.

The Afghan Knife.

By R. LOUIS STEVENSON

New Arabian Nights.	Prince Otto.

BY BERTHA THOMAS.

Cressida.	Proud Maisie.

The Violin-player.

By WALTER THORNBUR

Tales for the Marines.
Old Stories Re-told.

T. ADOLPHUS TROLLOP

Diamond Cut Diamond.

By F. ELEANOR TROLLOP

Like Ships upon the Sea.

Anne Furness.	Mabel's Progres

By ANTHONY TROLLOP

Frau Frohmann.	Kept in the Da
Marion Fay.	John Caldigate.

The Way We Live Now.
The American Senator.
Mr. Scarborough's Family.
The Land-Leaguers.
The Golden Lion of Granpere.

By J. T. TROWBRIDGE.

Farnell's Folly.

By IVAN TURGENIEFF, &

Stories from Foreign Novelists.

By MARK TWAIN.

A Pleasure Trip on the Continent.
The Gilded Age.
Mark Twain's Sketches.

Tom Sawyer.	A Tramp Abroa

The Stolen White Elephant.
Huckleberry Finn.
Life on the Mississippi.
The Prince and the Pauper.
A Yankee at the Court of King Arth

By C. C. FRASER-TYTLEI

Mistress Judith.

By SARAH TYTLER.

The Bride's Pass.	Noblesse Oblige
Buried Diamonds.	Disappeared.
Saint Mungo's City.	Huguenot Fami
Lady Bell.	Blackhall Ghos

What She Came Through.
Beauty and the Beast.
Citoyenne Jaqueline.

By Mrs. F. H. WILLIAMSOI

A Child Widow.

By J. S. WINTER.

Cavalry Life.	Regimental Legen

By H. F. WOOD.

The Passenger from Scotland Yard.
The Englishman of the Rue Cain.

By Lady WOOD.

Sabina.

CELIA PARKER WOOLLE

Rachel Armstrong; or, Love & Theolo

By EDMUND YATES.

The Forlorn Hope. | Land at Last.
Castaway.

OGDEN, SMALE AND CO. LIMITED, PRINTERS, GREAT SAFFRON HILL, E.C.

CPSIA information can be obtained
at www.ICGtesting.com
Printed in the USA
BVHW081115211118

533723BV00012B/677/P